"*Deadly Faux* is a fast, fun read with plo⸺⸺⸺⸺⸺ d a satisfying ending." —**Phillip Margolin, N**⸺⸺⸺⸺⸺ **of** *Sleight of Hand*

"Nearly a decade may have passed since Wolfgang's first appearance, but the affable rogue remains as charming as ever, in part because his air of cynical self-interest is clearly a patina over a far more sympathetic character. Brooks is clearly an advocate of tossing his characters into the deepest, most shark-infested waters; the result is a quick-moving, engaging comic escapade." —*Publishers Weekly* **on** *Deadly Faux*

"An absolute must read, *Deadly Faux* is guaranteed entertainment. In Wolfgang Schmitt, Larry Brooks has created a wisecracking protagonist who is witty, resourceful, intelligent, and, most surprisingly, vulnerable. Brooks plunges Wolf into a seemingly unwinnable caldron involving Las Vegas casinos, the mob, and femme fatales, then turns the heat up high. . . . Step aside Nelson DeMille and Stuart Woods—Schmitt happens!" —**Robert Dugoni,** *New York Times* **bestselling author of** *The Jury Master*

"Crime novelist Raymond Chandler was widely acknowledged in his day as the Poet Laureate of The Dark Side (he looked about as inconspicuous as a tarantula on a slice of angel food cake). . . . After half a century of being on the lookout for a crime fiction writer with a voice that rivals Chandler's, one has finally appeared, quietly chugging his way up the bestseller lists with *Darkness Bound, Whisper of the Seventh Thunder, Serpent's Dance,* and *Bait and Switch.* His name is Larry Brooks. The guy has a slick tone and a crackling, cynical wit with lots of vivid descriptions (of both interior and exterior landscapes), and the sparkling figures of speech dance off the page and explode in your inner ear. Though as modern as an iPad 5S, he is truly and remarkably Chandleresque. He's dazzling. Check out his new one, *Deadly Faux*—it's sexy, complex, intelligent; a truly delightful novel with more plot twists than a plate of linguine swimming in olive oil." —**James N. Frey, author of** *How to Write a Damn Good Novel*

"This intoxicating and intelligent tale of corporate corruption feels as authentic as a true crime chronicle, but Schmitt's first-person narration ensures that it is much more entertaining." —*Publishers Weekly* **on** *Bait and Switch*

"Full of surprises, *Darkness Bound* is one sneaky read." —**Leslie Glass,** *New York Times* **bestselling author of** *Stealing Time* **(for** *Darkness Bound***)**

The Seventh Thunder

The Seventh Thunder

A NOVEL

LARRY BROOKS

TURNER

Turner Publishing Company
424 Church Street • Suite 2240 Nashville, TN 37219
445 Park Avenue • 9th Floor New York, NY 10022

www.turnerpublishing.com

The Seventh Thunder

Previously published as *Whisper of the Seventh Thunder*

Cover Design: Susan Olinsky
Book Design: Kym Whitley

Library of Congress Control Number: 2014956033

ISBN: 978-1-62045-492-3 (paperback), 978-1-63026-750-6 (hardcover), 978-1-62045-493-0 (e-book)

Printed in the United States of America
15 16 17 18 0 9 8 7 6 5 4 3 2 1

For Laura

Children, it is the last hour;
and just as you heard that
Antichrist is coming,
even now many antichrists
have appeared;
from this we know that
it is the last hour.
—1 John 2:18

Prologue

Technion-Israel
Institute of Technology
Haifa, Israel

IT WOULD BE, quite literally, the beginning of the end.

The young man hadn't come here to solve the mysteries of the universe. Or of the Torah, for that matter, as his parents believed. Mordecai Rosen simply wanted to master the art of software, to graduate and make obscene money at a high-tech outfit with a good dental plan. His country had the highest concentration of startups outside the Silicon Valley in California, a place he had read about as a child with the same wide-eyed fascination others reserved for Disneyland. Call him a geek—most did—but he was happiest when bathing in the glow of a high-resolution liquid crystal display.

The great physicists had been here before him—Newton, Einstein, Oppenheimer, even Gary Zukov—committed pragmatists who by definition were the most cynical of atheists. Yet when they pried apart the atom and glimpsed the symmetry of the most basic elements in the universe, what they beheld was the imprint of Omnipotence. They saw *design,* the ultimate contradiction of randomness. The atom had been *created.* And so, according to the discipline of their profession, they were forced to acknowledge the unthinkable: the existence of a *Creator.*

But Mordecai Rosen hadn't found God hiding inside the realm of the nuclear particle. He had found him among the words of men. And tonight he would hear what Omnipotence had to *say.*

He sat before an oversized plasma monitor, wearing a black Metallica t-shirt, a can of Red Bull within reach. The room was dark, his face bathed in a warm glow. He had assisted Professor Gerson in the design and assembly of what was, for lack of a better term, a supercomputer. Based on a parallel processing theory as radical as it was massive, then programmed in Hebrew with a contextual Canaanite filter, they had optimized the architecture for a single, focused purpose that justified its military funding: de-encryption. Mordecai's fingers commanded the most powerful code-breaking technology the world had ever known.

Though only twenty-one and three years ahead of his peers in the graduate program, Mordecai felt his first pangs of fatherhood. Because tonight his baby would take its first steps. The phenomenon of a Bible code—hidden messages found in the original texts of the first five books in the Old Testament, also known as The Torah—was old news, and his three-dimensional software had found and deciphered each and every known code in record time. That little test had been child's play.

Tonight, without Professor Gerson's knowledge, and certainly without his consent, and after downloading an ancient-Greek-language filter during a few lunch breaks, Mordecai would scan the original text of the New Testament Book of Revelation. No code had been discovered outside of the original Torah, ever, much to the professor's smug pleasure. But Mordecai wasn't much for following directions, just as he didn't share his mentor's orthodox sensibilities. Whether his father—dead two years from a Jerusalem bus bombing—or Professor Gerson would admit it, Revelation promised too much to be restricted to the two dimensions of human comprehension.

He inserted a disk into the drive and downloaded the bitmap of the original first-century Greek text, with St. John's letters to the seven churches and the apocalyptic visions that had confounded Bible scholars for the last two thousand years. The program would then commence a sequential execution on all possible matrixes—digital gaps between letter sequences, known as an ELS, or equidistant letter sequencing—beginning with one-digit gaps, up to an arbitrarily chosen parameter of one hundred spaces. If finding a spec of salt on a sheet of typing paper was an apt metaphor for previous Bible code searches, this was like searching for a grain of sand suspended in the Mediterranean Sea, a task until now all but impossible for lesser computers.

Mordecai was certain he could do it in under a minute.

His stomach churned, sensing the moment at hand. If a message were found, it could come from only one source: the author of the document itself.

Not John the Divine, the political prisoner on the island of Patmos who many scholars believed transcribed those words, but the very spirit of the angelic narrator who had instilled them into John's consciousness.

Mordecai closed his eyes as he pressed the Enter key.

He didn't breathe. His eyes remained tightly closed as he listened to the turning of hard drives and the muted whirring of fans deep inside the belly of the beast.

And then, just that fast, a sound. A tiny electronic chime he had programmed to signal a hit. He opened his eyes to see a text message: *1 result detected.*

He clicked the link. A word materialized on the screen.

He stared. Moments later his body convulsed, reminding him to breathe. He was looking at a message written two thousand years ago, a communication that could not possibly have been written by human hands, yet was expressed here in very human terms.

Only now, two millennia later, with several thousand advanced microprocessors listening in parallel, could the digital key be turned, the divine circle made complete.

The word stared back at Mordecai Rosen, digitally converted into English:

WELCOME

The Seventh Thunder

Book One

And when the first thunder sounded,
I saw a demon cloud arise from the sea,
melting the sand from which it came
and killing all things in the waters and in the air
and on the ground.
And then it fell as if from heaven,
killing seven score and ten times a thousand,
and from it a plague upon the flesh
and a curse upon the land,
and a promise to devour the world.
And with the Great War thusly stilled,
the demon cloud returned to the sea from whence it came,
and all the world wondered after it,
trembling.

"WHISPER OF THE SEVENTH THUNDER"
by Gabriel Stone

Auburn, California

ON THE FIRST day of the rest of his life, Gabriel Stone wept.

Mourners milled about his lakeside home with paper plates bearing meatballs and potato salad, exchanging reverent comments about the beauty of the memorial service and the astounding depth of character of the woman it honored. Gabriel remained outside on the cedar deck, staring vacantly at the shimmering water his wife had loved. Fall would soon arrive, Lauren's favorite season, when gentle hues of burnt orange would imbue the surrounding trees, the water darkening under a muted sky.

Sitting here, visualizing her standing alone on the dock with a morning cup of coffee, Gabriel summoned yet one more strained smile for a queue of largely right-leaning neighbors and coworkers asking if there was anything they could do.

He marveled at the question. And he forgave them all, if not for their politics, then for their sense of propriety.

His grief masked a painful secret, one that he would take to his grave. Six years into their marriage they had conceived a carefully planned child, only to lose the fetus at eight weeks. Soon thereafter a misguided attempt to adopt a Cambodian orphan was squashed by the US State Department for reasons that were never fully explained. And now, following six years of healing from the pain of both, Lauren was again with child. She had been carrying an eleven-week fetus—despite not knowing the gender, they had already named it Andy, after her father—when her airplane cartwheeled-

into a Chicago suburb while attempting an emergency landing.

He and God would be having a little chat about that.

On the second day he took Lauren's clothes to the Goodwill. The smell was cruel, her perfume and her soap and the musk of her morning warmth still fresh in the fabric. Those who claimed to know said it was too soon to empty her closet, but, as it had always been, Gabriel Stone didn't listen. No one would tell him how to mourn.

On the third day he made a list of things he should have said, pecks on the cheek that should have been tender kisses, cards that should have been poems, of the times he should have listened and comforted with a silent embrace. At the bottom of the list he wrote the words *Forgive Me,* then lit the paper on fire and set it afloat on the lake. He watched the dark water until dawn, staying warm beneath Lauren's favorite quilt, under which they used to cuddle while watching television. Upon which they had made love on the night she conceived their child.

On the fourth day he resigned his job as an ad exec who wished he was still a copywriter. This, too, was against all conventional wisdom, but he was clear on what he must do next. That evening he wrote thank-you notes on Lauren's stationery to everyone who had sent flowers and brought food. She had taught him this and so much more, and it made him smile.

On the fifth day he attended to the business of ending one life and launching another. Calls to Lauren's company regarding her 401K and insurance, to their insurance agent, calls to shut down her credit cards and wholesale her Audi. There would be more than enough money to carry him through what he had planned.

After that he didn't care.

That night, drowning in memories, Gabriel thought his heart might stop. His body had curled into a fetal position on Lauren's side of the bed, the scent of her wafting from the pillow, and he was quite certain he heard her voice summoning from the depths of the lake, where he had deposited her ashes the morning of the service. He wasn't sure which he preferred—a sudden cardiac death, or this sweet, reminiscent madness.

It was then, lying there in a cold sweat, that Gabriel had his little chat with God. He railed, he raised his arms and cursed a Creator that would allow such sorrow. He demanded understanding and the peace it would bestow, but like all of his efforts at prayer over the years, no answer came.

Just the lapping of water against the shore, echoing in a house now cold as mausoleum marble. When he was done he drifted off to sleep with a strange, unexpected lightness in his heart, as if he'd unburdened himself of an unpaid debt using stolen money.

If there were no answers, then perhaps the questions were moot. Maybe it was the randomness of it all that demanded acceptance. The pure, unmitigated shitty luck of life.

On the night of the sixth day, his enraged spirit fortified, he emptied Lauren's library. She had been quietly religious, and her shelves bore the weight of her devotion, which, despite his strict Catholic upbringing—indeed, *because* of it—Gabriel did not share. He waited until after dark—the local lake patrol officers with their double-digit IQs would give no quarter with his means of mourning—to take the boxes of books out to the deepest water and finish it. He dumped them in precisely the same place he'd poured the ashes. Perhaps, in the cosmic complexity of it all, there might be some small comfort in that reunion.

But comfort was not waiting in the middle of the lake. In the quiet of the night, the water turbulent beneath him, his faith cast to the depths with her remains, Gabriel realized he just might be confusing lightness with emptiness. Either way, he rationalized, he was now very much alone.

On the seventh day, he rested.

He would begin his new life first thing in the morning.

He would begin writing the book that had haunted him for years. He would write it for Lauren, to honor her memory, any consequences of the blasphemy she feared for him be damned.

IN HIS FORTIETH year, after nine obsessed weeks of wandering the netherworld of his imagination, Gabriel Stone finished the novel his wife had encouraged him to write. He'd never tried his hand at fiction before, preferring the proximity of money to his copywriting talents, but this story would not let him go. Long ago both a priest and a well-meaning psychic had pleaded with him not to do it, and while he never mentioned this to Lauren, he always understood their reticence.

One should not tinker with The Word of God.

Lauren, however, saw things differently. If his heart was pure, she assured him, the book would be pleasing to God. Her faith promised this. She believed that as long as he kept the story on an apocalyptic course according to scripture, his efforts would, in fact, be blessed. God had drawn a celestial line in the sands of time, and it was not to be crossed.

But Gabriel viewed this through a different contextual lens. Lines were for crossing, especially in apocalyptic fiction. Writing the book would be cathartic, a head-on collision between the guilt of his childhood Catholicism and the temptation of a liberal new age filled with sinning right-wing legislators and gunslinging whack jobs.

Now, widowed and alone, and with the greatest respect for them all, Gabriel was certain he had nothing left to lose.

The story had poured from him like blood from a severed artery, an orgy of angst and elation. Certifiable type-O-negative art, extracted from his very soul, the fate of which, he had been assured, was at risk. He liked the analogy, his sins gushing crimson onto the pages, the splattering of his essence among the words, nourishing the seeds of his fiction to bear fruit upon a landscape of his dreams.

Or some such metaphoric babble.

He had to admit, he loved the pure unmitigated suffering of it all. The sad widower possessed of some demon. The disillusioned altar boy crafting a bittersweet revenge. The hack copywriter gone utterly mad. He had a dogmatic ax to grind, one he had sharpened with a vengeance.

If God had a problem with that, let Him show Himself.

He had slaved at a laptop on a cluttered dining room table. He saved, he backed up, he double-zipped the zip files. There were moments of great insecurity; a sense of being lost that sometimes consumed an entire day, forcing rewrites, extracting screams. Sometimes a wave of loneliness knocked him to his knees. Often he hated the blinking cursor that seemed to mock him, and other times he ran his fingertips over the keys with a lover's touch.

As fall began to wrap a crisp embrace around the lake, Gabriel finally finished his manuscript.

Now he sensed he must turn to a darker aspect of artistic pursuit. He searched out a list of literary agents on the Internet who, according to the asterisk next to their names, would consider accepting new clients.

He queried sixteen of them.

Five didn't respond. Six sent form letters no longer than twenty chilly words, which was almost worse. And four sent personal letters praising his idea but cited challenges in the business that made it impossible for them to offer hope.

One agent, however, told him his story sounded interesting and asked him to send the completed manuscript at his earliest convenience. The precise words were boilerplate, but he was nonetheless elated.

The agent's address was 666 Fifth Avenue in New York. Despite the genre of his story, Gabriel assigned the number no particular significance.

- 3 -

Washington, D.C.

THE WORKING MAN'S gym was crowded, but the mark was easy to spot. Sheared-off sweats, unlaced Converse high-tops, baggy top ripped under the arms to make room for lats the size of holiday hams, baseball cap pulled low and cockeyed, a cheap gold hoop in one ear. And a chin only an anthropologist could love and a tire iron could break.

A lean, middle-aged man watched as the young meatball did sloppy dead lifts in excess of six hundred pounds, screaming like a wounded beast with each repetition. The smaller man waited until the barbell dropped to the wood platform. He stepped closer and, with a cheerful tone, said, "Kiss my lily-white ass."

The meatball looked up in disbelief. The little man looking at him had sparse hair and wire-rimmed glasses, more runner than lifter, the kind of guy who, if he knew his ass from second base, only came in here to deliver sandwiches. The kind of face you couldn't remember, even if you had to.

"Say *what?*" He had already assumed an imposing offensive stance.

"Your arm. It says *kiss my lily-white ass.*"

The kid quickly glanced down at the elaborate tattoo that encircled his significant left biceps. The Chinese lettering had faded slightly, and with the frequent use of dianabol over the years had stretched as the underlying tissue expanded to the size of a rugby ball. He looked back with hard eyes.

"Dude, you dissin' me?"

"Do I *look* stupid? I'm just sayin', ink like that . . . takes some balls."

"Dude who did me said it meant *one with God*."

"Get a refund. It says *kiss my lily-white ass,* I shit you not."

Hard eyes again. "So what if it does?"

"You bench, what, three eighty-five? Four hundred?"

"Four fifty-five. You writin' a book, or what?"

The man straightened his glasses, standing his ground with a confident smile and unwavering eye contact.

"Not today. Today I'm hiring."

GETTING PAST THE sleepy gate guard at the downtown construction site was easy. At one in the morning all it took was a pint of Jäger and a sad story about someone forgetting to call in the delivery. A favor for a favor, two asses saved.

Moments later the lean man with no name and the muscular assistant named Craig stood in a wire-cage elevator, descending into the dark bowels of the nearly completed Columbia Center Hotel and Conference Center. As he followed his employer through a dusty void of shadows, pushing a three-hundred-pound case on a handcart, Craig realized he'd read about this place, which was four months from completion and quite the political football.

He had no idea what was inside the case. When asked, the older guy said if he answered he'd have to kill him, then apologized for the cliché. Hadn't smiled, either. "It's a matter of national security. Are we clear? You can never mention this to a soul. You do good, I have more work for you."

Hell, for five hundred bucks a night he wouldn't even admit it to himself.

THEY ARRIVED AT a service door beneath a concrete staircase. Craig pushed the package inside a small darkened chamber.

"Wait here. I'll call you."

Before disappearing into the space, the man tossed Craig a can of beer from his briefcase.

Forty-five minutes later Craig heard his name whispered. He stepped inside. One of the air ducts had been opened, with wires protruding from a newly exposed conduit pipe. The case he'd schlepped down here rested next to the door, now open. Also nearby was the man's briefcase, revealing a laptop computer, the screen filling the space with a warm glow.

The man saw Craig staring at the device. "Your big moment," he said.

"You lift it out, you place it right here. That simple. You drop it, we're both dead. Also that simple."

Craig swallowed hard. No wonder he'd been hired for this; the thing weighed more than he did. As he bent for it he noticed that what appeared to be brackets had already been installed along the back panel inside the open duct. Seems his new boss knew his way around a toolbox.

So far it seemed the guy knew just about everything.

TEN HOURS LATER at the gym where they'd met, on his third repetition on the bench at three sixty-five, Craig's aorta would pop like a brittle garden hose, killing him instantly. An autopsy would lead the medical examiner to conclude that he'd died of a severe coronary artery spasm caused by an overdose of illegal substances, including ephedra, exacerbated by the presence of gingkoba in the blood, which promotes internal bleeding.

The chemicals causing the rupture had been ingested with the celebratory beer he'd consumed the night before, the fact of which would be both irrelevant and invisible to the rookie coroner conducting the autopsy.

In another drawer in that same morgue, the body of a grave-shift security officer awaited vivisection later that afternoon. The man had been found dead in the guard hut at a downtown construction site, having succumbed to a simple but massive myocardial infarction exacerbated by the presence of alcohol in his system.

A bad day for fragile hearts in greater Washington. But nothing all that odd, certainly nothing that would draw the attention of an otherwise overburdened district attorney's office. No one on the ME crew cared or even noticed that the cause of the security guard's death had been almost exactly the same as that of the weight lifter.

Construction at the Columbia Center site would proceed as usual, as no one on the day crew knew the graveyard gate guy anyhow. Besides, it wasn't the first fatality on the site.

The place, some said, had a palpably dark vibe to it.

- 4 -

Auburn, California

When the seven peals of thunder had spoken, I was about to write; and I heard a voice from heaven saying, "Seal up the things which the seven peals of thunder have spoken, and do not write them."

—REVELATION 10:4

GABRIEL STONE DREADED the night. Not because he was alone—solitude had never been a problem in his life—but because the ghost of Lauren still lingered on the neighboring pillow. During the day he could lose himself in his writing and the very real minutiae of life, but darkness brought the twin inevitabilities of pain and clarity. Images from his past mounted a relentless assault, immune to alcohol or Ambien or even the effects of self-induced fatigue. He indulged this cerebral scrapbook like the guilty pleasure it was, despite the fact that the sweetest memories were the most troubling.

On this night, as he had done many times in recent weeks, he drifted back thirteen years to a time when his search for meaning had no hewn path, to a tiny Greek island on the eastern borderline of the Aegean Sea, 158 nautical miles off the coast of Turkey. His first glimpse of the sunbaked, horseshoe-shaped archipelago had been from a small boat ferrying him from a cruise ship to the port of Skala, and, perhaps because of the sacred mythology of the place, the mental snapshot had not faded over the years. Low barren hills were cut with tiny plateaus, and a jagged coastline had been torn from the sea to create hundreds of rocky coves and cays. Atop it all, the magnificent Monastery of St. John the Theologian held court over two millennia of compelling religious and political legend.

One of the greatest mysteries of all time had been written here.

The island was called Patmos. And, in the circle that was Gabriel Stone's life, it was where it all began.

A VISCERAL PRESENCE permeated the cave. It spoke through a textured silence, something gentle and—depending on one's frame of mind—holy. Maybe it was the warm shade of purple that imbued the walls with a surreal embrace, or the facsimile artifacts on display to channel the ambiance of the age. This place, known as *The Sacred Grotto of the Revelation,* was believed to be where St. John the Divine had been graced with apocalyptic visions while in political exile some two thousand years before, and where in a state of eschatological passion he rendered them into what would later become the holy Book of the Apocalypse, or as it would be translated and forever known, Revelation.

Gabriel Stone, still very much a man-in-training at twenty-seven, had stood to the side as the monk leading their tour channeled the past with a carefully rehearsed reverie: the indentation where John had rested his head, a flat pulpit of rock upon which he wrote the prophecy, the three fissures from which a holy voice had narrated the forthcoming end of days. Gabriel had studied Revelation years ago, part of a sociology assignment, finding it more metaphoric than fascinating. Yet he couldn't shake the image of John trembling before the rocks as the visions overwhelmed him, and through the years he'd cultivated an intellectual curiosity that he steadfastly refused to acknowledge as spiritual.

But St. John would not let him go. And so, when the opportunity arose, Gabriel came here to find him.

The small crowd had obediently moved into the adjoining Chapel of St. Anne, built in 1088 as a sort of foyer to the cave, leaving Gabriel alone with what he realized was perhaps the first truly religious experience of his life. An inexplicable and quite unexpected emotion had washed over him, rendering him humble and full of awe, and he was hesitant to leave until he understood why.

Later, looking back on this moment, he believed he knew.

A soft voice suddenly pierced his awareness, echoing off the rocks, sending a shiver up his spine.

"He was a virgin, you know. Until the day he died."

Gabriel turned to see a woman standing at the opposite wall. She was near his age, her eyes scanning their surroundings as if she'd said nothing at all. He'd noticed her around the ship and, more recently, that morning as the small entourage departed for Patmos. It wasn't her significant beauty that attracted him—stylish dark hair with ebony highlights framing ice blue eyes, classic full lips below finely etched cheekbones—but rather, a latent intensity that underpinned her every action. The graceful way she moved, the delicate manner with which she held a glass, the way her gaze penetrated those to whom she spoke . . . he had noticed it all from across a dozen floating rooms.

An awkward moment of calculated quiet preceded his answer.

"I didn't know that."

But he did know that, and much more. Prior to this trip Gabriel had studied John's life at length, and despite his altar-boy past had never truly understood the great apostle's role in the discipleship of Jesus. John was the only one of The Twelve who hadn't denied or deserted Christ at the cross. At Jesus' request he had cared for Mary after the passion and the ensuing resurrection, to which John had been the first witness. And later, as an old man fated to martyrdom for his devotion, legend held that he had emerged unscathed from a cauldron of oil at the behest of the Roman emperor Dometian as punishment for his devotion to Christ. That defiant miracle had been the reason for his banishment to Patmos, to live out his days in pious suffering, pitched to the masses as an act of mercy.

"Jesus called him a *Son of Thunder*," the woman said, not sure he was tracking. "He and James, John's older brother. The Sons of Thunder."

Gabriel smiled. "Interesting nickname for a virgin, don't you think?"

A smile lit up her face. "Would you like to hear something else they don't put in the brochures?"

"Will it ruin the moment? Because I think I'm about to find God in here."

Her smile had a mischievous warmth, her eyes vivid amid the strange purple glow of the grotto. Gabriel hoped it meant she wanted to crack the ice between them as much as he did.

"The Islamics," she continued, "believe that white folks were created here on Patmos by an evil scientist."

"No kidding? Whatever you do, don't tell the folks at Augusta National."

She giggled. "Swear to God."

"Theirs or ours?"

She was smiling as she moved to the opposite wall, placing her hand on the flat stone upon which John had written his letters to the seven great churches of the Asia-Minor kingdom. The smile faded, displaced by a reverent contemplation.

"You don't believe?"

"Working on it." He stepped closer and extended his hand. "My name is Gabriel."

Her smile blossomed again as they shook, her eyes locked onto where their hands touched.

"I've seen you around the ship," he added, every nerve in his body firing. "You're sorta hard to miss."

"Thank you," she said, looking deeply into him. "I've seen you, too. I'm Lauren."

There was a pause, the moment two people silently acknowledge a connection. The moment when, as Elton John once sang, the hammer hits.

Her eyes drifted to the ceiling, perhaps out of shyness. "There's an energy in here. Can you feel it?"

His eyes remained fixed on hers as he said "Absolutely" a little too quickly.

She shot him a look that suddenly flushed his cheeks. He tried to hold her amused stare—perhaps this was a woman who enjoyed toying with men—but then looked away, the intensity too much, her beauty too imposing. He realized he still had a firm grip on her hand, which he quickly relinquished.

When he looked back, he saw that her smile was warm rather than victorious.

"They sent me back for you," she said, cocking her head toward the door through which the others had departed, en route to the next chapel as the group worked its way up the road toward the Monastery, their final destination of the day. "Actually, I volunteered."

He turned his palms up and said, "I'm all yours."

Another moment, another quiet acknowledgment.

"We have to go."

Lauren led him out of the cave, stepping through the stone archway into what would prove to be an altered reality for them both.

LYING THERE IN the dark of his lakeside bedroom, Gabriel didn't realize he was smiling. Or that there were tracks of tears lining his face.

But other memories lurked, awaiting their moment. This was how it worked, the yin and the yang of the past.

Twelve years of marriage, and the only thing they'd argued about was the book he was writing. Gabriel wanted a fresh and edgy take on the biblical apocalypse, something riskier than the overtly Christian propaganda that had soared to the top of the bestseller lists. He had been fascinated by one verse from Revelation in particular—chapter ten, verse four—in which John, sequestered in that purple cave on Patmos, had been shown certain visions by the angel of the seven thunders, but was in no uncertain terms forbidden to write down.

Gabriel asked himself the Big Question, one that had haunted countless millions across two millennia: what might those visions have been? As had others before him, Gabriel took it a step further: what if the thunders were foreshadowed warnings of current events that pegged the apocalyptic time with a degree of absolute certainty?

. . . if anyone adds to these things, God will add to him the plagues that are written in this book . . .

On the night Lauren died, Gabriel had given her an outline of his story. He'd asked her to read it on the airplane, and to call him with her thoughts when she landed in Chicago.

He assured her that the outline would prove his intentions to write the story her way. Which was, she assured him in return, God's way.

. . . and if anyone takes away from the words of the book of this prophecy, God shall take away his part from the Book of Life . . .

He remembered Lauren's face as she took the pages from his hands, that of a woman receiving a great gift.

He had to remember it. It was the last time he would see his wife alive.

In what some might consider a sign, the outline had been lost two weeks after the crash, when a power surge fried the hard drive on Gabriel's computer. Witnesses reported a bolt of lightning striking Gabriel's house during a rare summer storm. At the time Gabriel had been out on the lake, dumping his wife's ashes into the blackness.

He attached no cosmic significance to it at the time.

The only existing hard copy of the outline had burned in the wreckage that took Lauren's life. The story, or at least the one Gabriel had promised Lauren he would write, was gone.

Now, a little over two months later, its resurrection had been his salvation. But, just as Christ himself had emerged from the grave a transformed being, it had come back to him as something different, laden with darkness and danger.

He had written *Whisper of the Seventh Thunder* his way.

What if, the voices now whispered, Lauren been right?

THE TELEPHONE RANG just before seven. Gabriel bolted upright in his bed, pulse racing. After a few calming breaths he consulted the digital clock and checked it against the light filtering through the blinds.

"Am I speaking to Gabriel Stone?"

A woman's voice, more than a tinge of *New Yawk*.

Gabriel cleared his throat and managed to exhale an affirmative response.

"I woke you," said the woman, rather proud of the fact.

"Yeah," he said, cautiously sitting up. Lauren had cousins and friends he'd never heard of, some of whom still called to remind him how wonderful she had been.

"This is Kathryn Kline, calling from New York."

Gabriel thought about this for a moment.

"Hello?" she checked in. "You sent me your book? My God, it *is* early, isn't it."

Then it clicked. The agent. The lone respondent to his query. He had imagined her in his mind—she looked like Diane Sawyer—but the Fran Dresher voice shattered the image. It had been weeks since he'd received her letter.

"I'm sorry. You definitely have my attention now."

"Don't be sorry. Listen, I read your novel."

"I hope that's a good thing."

"It's a very, very good thing."

He rubbed the sleep from his eyes, stifling a yawn.

"You're with Worldwide Artists."

"I am, at least for now. I thought I made that clear in my letter."

There had been no letter.

"Right," he said, resigned to having missed something that should have been obvious. "It *is* early."

"Excellent. First question—you haven't signed with anyone else, have you? Tell me now so I can go shoot myself."

"No." He carried the cordless phone with him into the bathroom and splashed cold water into his eyes and mouth. The man who stared back from the mirror had aged, grief having carved lines around what used to be dangerously dark eyes, his lips drawn thin, once dark brown hair now laced with silver. He'd lost over twenty pounds, a fragile shadow of the handsome poster boy for athletic self-confidence he had once been. He badly needed a shave and a good haircut.

"That's good. Next question—are you sitting down?"

"Am I *what?*"

"Is your butt connected to some sort of supportive structure, such as a chair or a bed? The floor will do."

Gabriel laughed silently. "I'm sitting," he lied.

"I've sold your novel."

He froze for a moment. Then he said, "That's . . . wow. I didn't even know you were representing it."

"Old parlor trick. You make a few calls, see if you get lucky before signing anything. Day after I read it I gave it to a friend, guy I knew was looking for this type of material. He said you write like an old soul."

"Is that a compliment?"

A brief moment of silence ensued, one he would remember.

"He's offering a five-hundred-thousand-dollar advance."

Gabriel closed his eyes, absorbing the moment. The sensation was physical, beginning in his rumbling stomach and radiating to all points of his body, an embrace of hope.

He floated back to his bed and sat very still, basking in the moment, etching every microsecond into his memory.

"Still with me there, Gabriel?"

His voice was soft as he said, "I don't know what to say."

"It gets better. It's a two-book deal—trade paperback for this one, hardcover and mass market for the next. We retain key subsidiary rights, which includes audio, foreign, movie, and dramatic."

"I was hoping for a hardcover."

"Don't we all. Listen, this project is very special. The publisher wants it on the street before the election, given the conceit of your story. That's only a few months out. Normally it's a year or more in the pipeline, but they're putting you in front of everything else and fast-tracking it. Guerilla publishing 101. A trade paperback is the only way it can happen."

A moment passed. *"Guerilla* sounds sort of, I dunno, second string."

"Hardly. Listen, this is a home-fucking-run, Gabriel. It means they're throwing everything at this, it'll be huge. As I said, the second book will be in hardcover, then we come out in mass-market paperback within a year. Given the name equity you'll score on the first book, that one will be even bigger. Same terms on the second project. Half now, remainder on acceptance."

"Acceptance?"

"Of the manuscript. They don't like what you turn in, you rewrite until they're happy. Basically you just sold your soul."

Gabriel tried not to dwell on that ironic thought as he slid off the bed onto the floor. Kathryn seemed to sense that he needed a few seconds.

"Feels nice, doesn't it."

"Nice doesn't quite say it."

"It's all less my agency fee of fifteen percent, of course. Just to be on the record. I know we haven't signed an agreement."

"I'll sign it in blood if you want."

"Then I guess this means the terms are satisfactory, that you don't want me to go back in, squeeze their balls for more."

"You think you left money on the table?"

"The *only* thing on the table is blood, Gabriel, and I assure you it's theirs."

"Then I'm good."

He heard rustling on her end, as if she had covered the phone to whisper something to someone nearby.

"There's more," she finally said.

"I'm lying down now."

"We're going out to auction on the movie rights in a day or two. I'll be working with my old agency on that, they have the contacts and the expertise. We're splitting the deal."

"Which means?"

"I'm guessing a million, million-two." With a smile in her voice she added, "I'm assuming you're okay with that."

The confusion he had been feeling was quickly giving way to a sudden need to scream, to laugh out loud, to burst through the sliding doors and take a header into the lake.

All he could do was mumble a soft "Wow."

"Wow, indeed. I want you in New York tomorrow. We meet with the publisher day after next."

Gabriel felt a cold wave of dread wash over him. He hadn't flown since Lauren's accident. In fact, he had vowed never to fly again. Like other promises, it now meant nothing.

"Tight jeans and a blazer. City people love that California shit. Publicists love edgy. They're shooting your back cover and promo photo, so get a haircut."

They attended to the business of travel logistics, Gabriel taking notes. She would put him on an American flight out of San Francisco that afternoon, with a nice room at a very hip Central Park hotel. She'd try to meet him for dinner, but could make no promises.

Kathryn Kline ended the call with an abruptness that told him this was, for her, all in a day's work.

"Send me a digital file of the manuscript. Your paper submission was a little old school."

"I can do that."

Her final words were "I'm gonna make you a big star, Gabriel Stone. Nothing about your life will ever be the same."

GABRIEL STARED AT the phone for several minutes, waiting for his pulse to subside. Finally he picked up the receiver and punched in a number, followed by a four-digit code.

Voice mail. He closed his eyes as he listened. The voice of Lauren, calling from a borrowed iPhone on the airplane moments before the end.

"Honey, listen, there's a problem with the plane, so we're stopping in Chicago. I don't want you to worry, so I'll call you from there. But I wanted to tell you now . . . I read your pages. They're special, everything you said they would be. I mean that. I am so proud of you."

A pause. Then, with a voice that betrayed a trace of fear, Lauren uttered her final words.

> "*Write your book, Gabriel. Promise me. I will always be with you. And I will always love you.*"

The line went dead. Forever.

Gabriel hit the Save button. As he always did after he'd listened to this message.

Which happened daily.

After a moment of complete silence, conscious of his own pulse in every extremity, he got to do as his new agent had instructed. Two clicks and an email address and the digital manuscript of *Whisper of the Seventh Thunder* had been delivered.

- 6 -

New York City

THE PUBLISHING OFFICES at 666 Fifth Avenue were almost always deserted by eight. A young woman worked alone in the copier room, as generic and unremarkable as her job description, surrounded by shadows.

No one would ever peg her for a spy.

The woman focused on the screen, where a downloaded Trojan algorithm was scanning the database of all new projects entered within the prior week. When she saw the title she was looking for, she slipped a USB thumb drive into the slot and waited for the file to transfer. When she was certain no one was nearby, she opened her purse and withdrew what appeared to be a standard iPhone connected to a remote USB plug, into which she inserted the thumb drive.

As it downloaded she scanned the project data sheet still on the screen. She recognized the name of the agent on the cover sheet. A flaming bitch, that one. The Trojan algorithm had scanned the firm's manuscript database and had detected certain keywords in this particular manuscript that would be of particular interest to the people who were funding her children's college. People with titles and ranks and Washington D.C. addresses.

She checked the USB connection to the phone, then hit a few keys to transmit it to a Point B that would defy even the Pentagon's most astute IT forensic nerds. From that end the manuscript would be subjected to further analysis by trained specialists sitting in cubicles seven hundred miles to the south.

Interesting. She had never seen this many hits in her six months on the job. She had no idea what the dangerous words were or what they meant, only that this book met the criteria for download. What happened from there was none of her concern.

Once the transmission had been successfully completed, she deleted the Trojan from the PC she'd borrowed for this task and put the thumb drive, USB extension, and her phone back into her purse file. The book would remain on the publisher's server, available to editors and copy designers and public relations types whose job it was to ready it for market. The only trace of this intervention that anyone would ever be able to find was a text from her to her boyfriend, commenting on his annoying habit of leaving his pornography up on her laptop.

Beyond thinking that the title of the manuscript she'd just stolen had a certain compelling, apocalyptic *je ne se quai* to it, the young woman gave it no further thought. Because there would be another book tomorrow, just as there had been dozens since her stealth Federal employer had successfully gotten her hired on.

- 7 -

Technion-Israel
Institute of Technology
Haifa, Israel

PROFESSOR URIAH GERSON stared at the screen. The lab was quiet, laced with shadow in the basement of an otherwise dark Science and Technology building. Gerson had been none too pleased when Mordecai called just after midnight to confess the running of a program he considered a waste of perfectly good electricity.

They had bigger fish to fry, more urgent messages to unearth, a world to save from unthinkable evil.

Nonetheless, staring at Mordecai's screen, where the word WELCOME blinked up at him, he felt the old excitement return, a humble chill in the presence of the Holy.

Gerson had been an enthusiastic cynic where the so-called Bible Code was concerned. The first known code deciphered—the word "Torah," found at the beginning of each of the first five books of the Old Testament, with an identical fifty-letter gap between each character—was discovered by Rabbi Michoel Dov Weissmandel in the late 1930s. The research bore no further fruit until 1985, when an Israeli professor named Eliyahu Rips applied a computer to the task for the first time, searching for the names of history's most beloved rabbis. Cynics became believers when nearly every name was found in the code, with the correct date of their death in close proximity.

This could not be coincidence. This, claimed Rips, was nothing less than the Word of God.

Not everyone was convinced. Gerson was among those who believed Rips's so-called Bible code was a parlor trick, a statistical anomaly. A researcher in Australia had run a similar program on a copy of *Moby Dick* and had come up with several loosely interpreted messages about the Kennedy assassination. But when an associate of Rips called Gerson in 1994 and invited him to visit the Institute of Mathematics at Hebrew University in Jerusalem, Gerson's eyes were truly opened. Words and phrases relating to all eras of history were hidden in the text—Napoleon, Shakespeare, the American Revolution, Edison, the Wright Brothers, the Russian Revolution of 1917, the 1929 stock market crash, the Apollo 11 moon landing, Hitler and the Holocaust, the atomic bomb and the name of the airplane that had delivered it, both Kennedy assassinations, Oswald's death and the man who shot him—all were there in the code.

The statistical odds against this happening randomly were staggering. It was virtually impossible—unless someone, or something, had put them there.

But Gerson hadn't been summoned simply to review the evidence. He was there to discuss what was perhaps the first *predictive* code ever found: the assassination of Israeli Prime Minister Yitzhak Rabin. Near Rabin's name were the coded words, "assassin who will assassinate." Gerson was known to be an acquaintance of the Prime Minister's—over the years they had crossed paths at several university functions—and the associate pleaded with him to help warn Rabin.

Impressed as he was, Gerson was hesitant to reverse what had been a very public stand against the code. To approach the Prime Minister with such a mystical prediction would risk his credibility, and by association that of the university. Gerson promised to do what he could, but soon forgot about it.

Four months later, on November 4, 1995, Yitzhak Rabin was shot and killed by a Jewish law student named Yigal Amir. Soon thereafter the name "Amir" was discovered coded in close proximity to the warning about the impending assassination. Already distraught about the consequences of his choice, Gerson had a change of heart, one he felt was not entirely without a celestial shove.

It was then that a concept began to formulate in Uriah Gerson's mind. He was already researching an ancient scroll thought to be written by the disciple John, the same author who had transcribed his visions into the Book of Revelation, and it contained its own set of angelically dictated prophecies.

This scroll had been passed to Gerson by his father, a devout rabbi, who had labored over it his entire life after it was handed down to him by a fabled rabbi. Since then, like his father, Uriah had pored over the scrolls in quest of meaning, unearthing the names that John and the angel had meant for them to find.

When a name was found, an efficient death followed quickly. What if, Gerson speculated, there were codes embedded in the original Hebrew lettering of *that* scroll, as well? What if the one for whom they had been waiting for two millennia was waiting for them there?

Gerson knew that to engineer a three-dimensional matrix search on the vast text of the secret scrolls, one covering every possible variable, was far beyond the reach of the computers at his disposal. The solution was obvious—he would build a computer that could do the job. And he would get the military to fund it by giving it a security application they could not resist—encryption. Or *de-encryption*, in this case.

AND NOW, ON the very first attempt at a three dimensional scan, Mordecai had found a chilling message: the word WELCOME.

God, it seemed, was a cordial deity.

But the message hadn't come from a decoding of the secret scrolls of John, as Uriah had hoped. It had come from a decoding of the original Hebrew text of the New Testament Book of Revelation, a document Uriah had always discounted as Christian fantasy. In fact, Mordecai would find no coded messages whatsoever in the secret scrolls of John, while the Book of Revelation would prove to be a treasure chest of God's intentions.

Though humbled, Uriah was nonetheless hopeful.

After ordering Mordecai to go home and get some rest—the boy lived with his still-grieving mother—Gerson dialed a Washington D.C. telephone number. He was excited to tell his counterpart, the man who actually implemented the deadly commands extracted from the secret scrolls, that the moment of their long-awaited redemption just might be at hand.

After two thousand years, God willing, the killing might at last be over.

- 8 -

TWO MEN STROLLED along the Capital Mall reflecting pool on an early-fall day, both wearing colorless London Fogs that made them indistinguishable from scores of federal drones doing the same. Coats that matched the pallor of their skin. The older man, Brother Simon, stood significantly shorter, his thin hair helpless in the wind. The younger, Brother Daniel, appeared to be shy of fifty, broad of shoulder with the gait of an athlete and gelled black hair that didn't move. He had dark, nervous eyes that saw everything, a bird sensing danger, while Brother Simon seemed content to stare at his feet as they walked.

In a world of digital convenience, this was how they worked. They spoke cryptically of their business—today they were talking about computers and hidden codes and what it all might mean—the years having spawned an efficient shorthand that would seem innocent if not innocuous to anyone listening in.

Occasionally, within days after they parted, someone would die. Someone whose name was written two thousand years earlier. And with each death, the world would be safer than before.

Brother Daniel suddenly stopped in his tracks, squinting into the distance. Then, his gaze fixed, he put a finger to his lips.

His older companion cast a quick look around, silently mouthing the word *What?*

Brother Daniel covered his mouth with his hand as he answered, his voice barely audible. "To the right. White van. It was parked down the block from the mansion yesterday."

"You're sure? You've been paranoid before."

"It belongs to someone on staff."

They resumed walking, their body language stiffer now. A minute passed without words.

"This is not the time for a complication," Brother Simon finally said, covering his mouth as Brother Daniel had done.

Daniel Larsen stopped, again staring forward, not at the van but into an undefined distance. After a moment he produced a small notebook from his vest pocket, opened it and wrote something down, which he showed to Brother Simon.

Potential directional microphone.

He saw worry etch itself into the lines of the old man's face. Then he wrote something else.

Leave it to me.

Brother Simon nodded, his expression strained. He was tired of this game that disguised itself as destiny.

The men separated, Simon walking slowly to the south, Daniel Larsen with a much livelier pace to the north, heading directly toward the van in question. When he had gone fifty yards it suddenly pulled out into traffic and sped away, long before he got close enough to read a plate.

But that didn't matter. The entire Capital Mall was under constant video surveillance. And Brother Daniel Larsen knew exactly where and how to get at the encrypted digital video files.

It was, after all, his business to be *both* paranoid and sure.

- 9 -

New York City

AFTER THANKING THE gods of McDonnell Douglas for a safe touch-down, Gabriel took a taxi from Kennedy into midtown, where he checked into the Sherry Netherland Hotel. A message from Kathryn was waiting at the desk, with her regrets that dinner would be impossible and instructions on where to meet her for breakfast.

After an hour of relaxing in his room he decided on a stroll down Fifth Avenue. He found the building where his meeting would be the next morning, then he stopped to appreciate the Steuben window displays before heading farther down Fifth, pausing to glare at the doors to St. Patrick's Cathedral before crossing the street to shop at Saks.

As he was standing on the steps of St. Patrick's, his eyes met those of a woman who caused his heart to skip a beat. She looked startlingly like Lauren, and unlike other women he'd passed here in this city of strangers, held his stare before moving on.

THE WOMAN THOUGHT it was strange that the man she was following didn't stop to eat dinner. After a half hour at Saks he returned to his hotel, presumably for room service and an early lights out.

Interesting. An attractive single man in New York, and he rarely met the gaze of anyone on the street. A man with an entire evening to himself, and he had no interest in a cold beer and a steak. A man who glared at the face of the most famous church in the land as if it were his nemesis. This, the woman knew, was a man in pain.

He had nice eyes, she thought. Hazel, an essence of vulnerability.

His pain, she knew, was at once a strength and a weakness. It drove him, fortified him with courage. But it could also make a man who believes he has nothing to lose a bit reckless. A suffering man could easily be led into temptation, especially by a woman offering a bite of the right apple.

It would be difficult to deliver such a man from evil.

Reston Hospital
Tysons Corner, Virginia

SOMEHOW THE YOUNG patient the nursing staff secretly referred to as Archie knew that the stranger in the room with him was Death. At first he thought it might be a dream, but he soon understood it was all too real. He would die tonight because of what he knew. His own guilt made him certain of this.

The young man on the bed worked as a waiter at the mansion where the men gathered. That was not his real purpose, just as Archie was not his real name—it wasn't the first time his red hair and freckles had inspired comparison to Archie from the old comic strip—but he had pulled it off for three weeks now, long enough to find most of what he came for. He had seen their faces, knew most of their names and the pedigrees. They looked through him, and though they had prayed together, arm in arm in a circle of brotherly love, they had higher matters on their minds than the help.

He had listened when they thought they were alone.

And now they had tried to kill him. A hit-and-run driver hadn't completed the job, so here he was, waiting in a dim hospital ward, with no one to call for help.

The intruder stood next to the bed, staring down at his victim with vacant eyes, which were framed behind wire-rimmed glasses, round lenses with a retro design that made him look more academic than threatening. His face was featureless, like an animator's rendition in a digitally created movie.

He was not one of them, one of the Brothers. Or if he was, he had not appeared at the mansion during the past three weeks.

The young man could not move, even slightly. An attempt to raise his head brought a stabbing pain to his neck. He tried to speak, to yell out, but his jaw would not budge and his vocal cords were suddenly useless. Fully awake now, he could hear the sound of his own breathing. Cold night air wafting in through the open window caressed his face. He felt the touch of sheets on his flesh.

When the stranger placed a hand on his chest, he felt that, too. He was wearing blue latex medical gloves as he held up a syringe, facing toward the open hallway door.

In the dim light Archie suddenly thought he recognized his visitor.

"Who are you?"

"My name is McQuarrie," he said, his attention suddenly focused on the syringe his other hand had been cradling.

Archie's eyes went to the needle, then back to the man.

"It was you. Today, driving that car."

The man held the syringe to the light, pressing an arc of clear fluid into the air.

"Yes."

He turned to look the younger man in the eye.

"There's nothing on you. No AFIS match, which in itself is telling. Why is that? Everyone has a fingerprint match. No one knows you, no one seems to remember who hired you. One day you were there, praising the Lord and in need of work and a shower, and nobody asks why. You drive a white van with stolen plates traced to a car in upstate New York listed as having been destroyed, which is also telling."

The man leaned close, as if inspecting his victim's eyes. Archie could see his reflection in the wire-rimmed glasses.

"There was a cheap directional listening device in your van. Guy at a spy shop in Silver Spring remembered your picture. That's amateur hour, son. But disturbing nonetheless."

He positioned the syringe in front of the waiter's face.

"I like to think of what I do as art. The body is an instrument, and it can be played. Crescendo, allegro, fortissimo, it's all possible. Think of me as a sort of forensic Rachmaninov, only you get to play Name That Tune."

The man named McQuarrie grasped the waiter's jaw and held it open. With his other hand he pushed the needle under the tongue and pressed the plunger. White-hot agony immediately engulfed Archie's mouth.

He leaned closer, spoke softer.

"In ninety seconds your aorta will rupture like a melon dropped from the Washington Monument. It's congenital, you see, no one will wonder why. Pete Maravich went out that way, though you're probably too young to remember him. Changed the entire game of basketball, that guy. I have another needle, and I can change this game. I'm only going to ask you once. Who are you, who do you work for, and what are you after? Tell me, and you'll simply go to sleep, wake up, and remember nothing."

He waited a moment, allowing the words to penetrate the narcotic fog. Then he added, "A bona fide win-win, which I urge you to consider seriously."

He assumed the same vacant expression he'd held earlier.

"You were in a white van today, listening to two men as they walked through the Mall. I need to know why."

Archie felt his body turning inside out, as if every cell wanted to scream but was gagged. The pain was building by the second, including a deafening hissing in his ears. He tried to speak, his lips quivering with effort.

McQuarrie bent closer.

"Your larynx is dysfunctional," he said. "Breathe through your mouth, use the air to form words. Talk to me, son, please. Let's not end ugly."

Seeing that the waiter was trying to save himself, the intruder placed his ear close to the young man's lips. And heard him speak.

"Father . . . forgive them . . ."

McQuarrie stood upright. A tiny smile fractured the void of his expression as he finished Archie's sentence.

"For he knows *precisely* what he does."

He placed a gentle hand on the young man's chest. The smile had been one of admiration. Not many of his clients held to their beliefs in this final, irrevocable moment.

"I so rarely get to hear the sound of my own music."

The tiny smile vanished, replaced by a cold fascination.

Arlington, Virginia

DAWN WAS ANNOUNCING itself when the telephone rang.

Daniel Larsen, active in the group known as The Brethren, by day a professional in the art of lies, lay in his bed next to his second wife in a five-thousand-square-foot suburban home designed to emulate a Tuscan villa, their view of the city unparalleled. She hadn't stirred at the sound. After two decades of strange calls from men who had no names, she knew better than to ask for anything other than his money.

He picked up the phone, said nothing.

"It's done," said an even voice. Then the line disconnected.

Larsen stared into the predawn darkness as he replaced the receiver. Another potential complication checked off the list. With all that was at stake, they could take no chances. Anything that surfaced on the radar of their paranoia would be dealt with conclusively.

Larsen prayed, literally, that nothing else would come up. His work for Brother Simon was, after all, conducted in the name of Jesus Christ. Or so Brother Simon had been led to believe.

Then again, times had changed. Much to the surprise of his peers, one never knew which ticket God was voting these days. The smart money covered its ass either way.

Technion-Israel
Institute of Technology
Haifa, Israel

MORDECAI ROSEN WAS almost asleep when the computer began to sing. He had gone home for dinner with his mother, watched a George Clooney DVD before putting her to bed, then returned to the lab to run some experiments on the ELS parameters of the search program. That was the key to unlocking the mysteries of the Bible code in the third dimension, the constant expansion of one's field of vision.

At the sound of the alarm his body jolted, his elbow knocking over the can of Red Bull he'd believed would help him remain awake. As he stared at the screen another alarm sounded, and then another, all three then repeating like a cascade of electronic bells.

His heart pounded as he stared at the screen.

There were three new hits. All as a result of expanding the three-dimensional spacing parameters. The previous night he'd downloaded the entire text of the *Oxford English Dictionary* as a database reference, and whenever the computer found an array of Hebrew characters that, translated into English, seemed to form a known word in English, the alarm went off. Other than a few meaningless and unavoidable hits—single words such as "cat" and "spit" that were as coincidental as they were meaningless—the program had come up dry. He was on his fourth expansion of spacing parameters when this latest flurry of activity lit up the screen.

Mordecai grabbed a pad and began scribbling. In prior two-dimensional tests he had discovered that often the words made no sense without context.

If you were looking for a specific word, as he was in those experiments, it was easy enough to find. This, prior scholars believed, was why the code could not be used to predict the future, since those words were by definition unknown. But Mordecai believed he had found a solution, and there was nothing remotely high tech about it. Only the human mind understood the social context required to converse with the dead, or perhaps even the angelic. By simply analyzing a given word, then using human intuition to search for other nearby words that might logically link to it, he could unearth entire phrases.

His theory would be tested tonight.

URIAH GERSON GRUNTED a response to the ringing telephone. It was nearly three in the morning, and it was the second such nocturnal call within the past week.

"Professor, I apologize for the hour. But you said to call if I found something."

Professor Gerson eyed the clock, then he looked to see if Evelyn, his wife of fifty-four years, had been disturbed. She hadn't. Then again, she'd slept through more than one local terrorist bombing when they lived in Jerusalem and Lebanon, where he had taught history at the University of Beirut.

"Please" was all he said. He sat up, fighting off the dizziness that always assaulted him at this hour.

"Three hits. All with context. One is what I believe to be a Bible verse."

"Which?"

"Exodus, twenty-eight, sixteen. Found with a one hundred eleven ELS."

"The breastplate of Aaron," shot back the Professor, already confused by the presence of Old Testament scripture in a very New Testament Book of Revelation, code or no code.

"Any idea what it could mean?" asked Mordecai.

Gerson paused at this. He knew what he *wanted* it to mean, but the fact that the codes appeared in Revelation was troubling. He would have much preferred to have unearthed codes in the secret scrolls, which were the purpose of his life.

"None," he said at last. "What else?"

"A phrase—*thy will be done*. I found the word *done*, then manually interpolated the rest. Sort of a lucky guess, but when I ran the whole phrase, it was there."

"This is promising, Mordecai."

"I think so, too."

"What else?"

"This one is strange. I'm not completely sure, but I think it's a name."

There was a pause. Gerson felt an explosion of adrenaline detonating deep within him. A name was what they had been searching for since the beginning.

Mordecai pressed forward. "The word *stone* appears in very close proximity to the phrase. When I ran it again, I saw what I believe is a name appearing right next to it, with no break between them."

"What was the name?"

"Gabriel."

"The archangel," the old professor mumbled. "Gabriel Stone."

"At first it didn't strike me as a name," continued Mordecai, unsure about the angel reference. "Then I got lucky again. I scanned a database of names, some encrypted stuff we're not supposed to have. God must be on our side after all."

"Or he wants us to hear him."

Indeed. Since the secret scrolls and the revelation to John were authored by the same divine source, perhaps there was no difference after all. An open mind might just be his salvation here.

"This name appears right after *thy will be done.*"

"So who is this Gabriel Stone?"

"I checked," said Mordecai. "His name appears on a CIA watchlist. That's all I know."

It could not be the name of the one foretold ages ago. That name would be synonymous with power and agenda. But within the apocalyptic maze, it may very well be a clue.

After a moment Gerson said, "There is someone I can call."

"I thought that might be the case," said Mordecai. "Whether this Gabriel Stone knows it or not, he's involved in something God put into writing over two thousand years ago."

Book Two

The second thunder sounded, and behold,
the children of Israel were gathered
according to prophecy in the land promised them,
which is the land of their fathers,
in a time three years hence of the Great War.
And thus the foretold days of the Lamb have come,
though none will understand for many years hence,
and many will prophesize falsely,
for none may know the mystery of God.

"WHISPER OF THE SEVENTH THUNDER"
by Gabriel Stone

-12-

New York City

KATHRYN KLINE WAS speaking much too loudly into her Bluetooth headset as she made a grand entrance into the dining room at Michael's off Fifth Avenue, armed with a thousand-dollar bag, a two-thousand-dollar briefcase, and an attitude. This was, Gabriel assumed, *the* place for a literary power breakfast, and Kathryn Kline was definitely a player. She smiled when her eyes found him sitting at a corner table with a five-dollar cup of coffee, checking his watch. She was fifteen minutes late, which he had no way of knowing was, in her world, right on time. She continued to chat away as she sat, touching his arm with French-manicured talons after dropping her bag to the floor, a strong presence of perfume preceding her. She silently lip-synched the words "You are *hot!*" as she settled in, her eyes bright and quick.

From her telephone voice, he'd pictured her as ethnically dark and vainly overdone, the kind of *don't-mess-with-me* big-city woman who regularly kibitzed with Donna Karan over high tea. But Kathryn Kline was young for a self-professed ballbuster, early thirties tops, wearing a severe business suit that showed off her health club figure. Her hair was California gold, too obviously dyed and worn straight, her eyes brimming with mischief, a smoldering hazel that lit up the space around her with possibilities.

She concluded her call in the same abrupt manner she had terminated their conversation of the previous day, immediately extending her hand toward Gabriel.

"I knew you'd be gorgeous. I told Wyatt—he's your publisher—I bet he's a goddamn babe magnet."

Gabriel looked away, uncomfortable with the compliment.

"I'm Kathryn Kline, and I'm here to change your life."

Gabriel took her hand in his, the skin shockingly warm. He had always been a bit tentative with the cross-gender handshake, unsure of how much testosterone to put into it.

"I'm Gabriel," he said, suddenly feeling awkward.

"Yes you are indeed."

Gabriel pulled his hand away. Her eyes remained riveted, as if she were comparing his features to her expectations.

The waiter rescued them from a moment of awkwardness. She ordered cappuccino and a fruit tart, grinning slightly when Gabriel ordered a cinnamon bun and a refill.

"We have a lot to discuss," she said, pivoting in her seat as if he were the most important person on the planet.

"I'm all yours," he said, making sure his grin was as sheepish as it could possibly be. Behind the grin was a memory of the time he'd spoken these same words to Lauren in an island cave, but that was the past, dead and gone. He was half a dozen years older than this woman, yet he felt like a child trying to keep up with an adult obliged to tolerate his company.

"I take it you're single?" Her eyes were innocent, another obvious contrivance.

"Widower."

"Ouch, my bad. How long?"

"Four months. You?"

She grinned. "Not widowed. Pity, too. We were married eight years, he left me for his tax accountant. A guy named Stan."

They shared a quick chuckle. Then her voice softened. "Mind if I ask how?"

Gabriel swallowed hard. He reviewed the chronology in hushed tones. What he didn't describe was the size of the charred, gaping hole in his life.

"Okay, let's move on," she said, summoning a fresh energy. "Life story, thirty seconds or less."

Her posture indicated that she was serious.

"Pretty standard stuff . . . grew up in rural Northern California, parents were honest working stiffs who checked out when my older brother died in a car accident when I was ten. I was the quiet but smart kid in high school, pretty good jock, then a journalism major and a second-string outfielder at Cal Berkeley, along with being a failed musician and a fraternity washout. Post grad I had a quick fling as a stockbroker before I sold out to a career in advertising, where the women were both hotter and easier. Then ... well, you know the rest."

She nodded as he spoke. "Religious upbringing?"

"You could say that."

"Your bitterness comes through in the writing."

He nodded slowly, impressed.

"How are you with scripture?" he asked, hoping to divert the conversation before she pinned him down to the real reasons for writing his book, which had everything to do with Lauren and his agenda with the Almighty.

Kathryn rocked back as if ducking a punch.

"That particular author and I are not exactly on speaking terms."

He smiled gently. "Check out Revelation, chapter twenty-two, eighteen and nineteen sometime."

"My copy's not all that handy. Why don't you tell me?"

"The short of it is, anyone who changes the words in the Bible is toast. Straight to hell, non-negotiable."

"Hot dogs on Friday were non-negotiable once."

"God changed his mind about that in nineteen sixty-five, I think. Fired off a memo to the Vatican, done deal."

They shared a grin as she asked, "You're Catholic, then?"

"Was. My altar boy license expired."

"Well, then I guess I'll see you in hell."

"I no longer believe in *that,* either."

Kathryn's expression suddenly turned thoughtful. It had worked—she suddenly seemed more interested in the banter than in him. He suspected that this perception, however, might be the intention of a very adept seductress.

She grew startlingly pensive as she spoke.

"Anyone who studies the history of the Bible knows that it was assembled, some believe *written,* as a political tool by the ancient church. Today we know that there were other lost gospels, books that were not selected as part of the holy canon for political reasons. The book is arbitrary, its divinity self-declared and arbitrated by the church. Arguably the greatest PR whitewash in the history of the world."

Gabriel nodded. "I guess that's why they call it faith."

The server arrived with their drinks. She raised her cappuccino to him in a mock toast and said, "The blinder the better."

He clinked his cup to hers. "To the sin of thinking for oneself," she added, her eyes alive with mischief. "And to an obscene level of success."

He raised his coffee cup, saying nothing.

Several moments passed, Gabriel feigning interest in the interior design. Kathryn closed her eyes and rocked her head back, as if savoring the subtle flavors of her drink.

"So. Do you have *any* idea how controversial this book of yours will be?"

He looked away, a man uncomfortable with compliments. "Some. Not really."

"Don't expect an invitation from the White House. In fact, I'd stay out of Washington completely if I were you."

He smiled, appreciating that she had grasped the political agenda of his book as well as the spiritual one.

"I'll remember that."

"So why'd you do it?" she finally asked.

"*Do* it?"

"Write the novel."

He stared out the window, pondering the question. There was something about the moment that would remain, a marker placed, a sense of crossing into shadow.

"That's a good question."

"I look forward to the answer."

"Truth be known," he paused, "I've been thinking about this story for a long time."

"The story? Or the allure of the mystery of the seven thunders themselves?"

He looked hard at his new agent, her smile suddenly a bit frightening. As if she already knew the answer. Hannibal Lecter had done that, asked Clarice about her childhood pain, more interested in her eyes than in her answer.

"I think," she said, "you fell in love with a killer hook. The mystery of what John might have seen, something so telling that he was instructed to seal it up for all time. I think part of you gets off on the disrespect. I mean, your story is hot, bombs planted in new buildings for later use as a means of political assassination . . . that's smokin' stuff. It could *happen*, and no one has thought of it."

Now she paused, her eyes suddenly smug.

"But that's not why you wrote it. It's not the religious take, and it's not the politics."

She looked at him with a disturbing confidence. His face was void of expression, but his skin was beginning to crawl.

"You're in this for the *money*, Gabriel. You're selling your soul for a boatload of gold, pure and simple." Her smile exploded with a dark, arrogant victory. "And I'm here to get it for you. You just sit there and look pretty."

Kathryn's lips pursed seductively, her eyes burning with delight as her hand landed on his. She leaned closer, in a way that posed an unspoken question he hadn't expected. She was playing him, and from the look of her she expected to win. The tone of her voice, a guttural purr, confirmed his suspicion.

"And you know what? It's perfectly okay. The pursuit of wealth, of *pleasure* . . . the flock labels it as sin, but the enlightened soul understands. Guilt has always been the great hammer of religion. I prefer logic—if it's not hurting anyone else, how can it be evil? An ambition, a vanity, an act of sexual creativity . . . I mean, come on, who does it really harm?"

Her hand tightened around his wrist.

He turned his eyes away and drew a deep breath, conscious of the sudden pace of his heart, of her lingering touch. He withdrew his hand, not ready to offend her, but needing to change the tone.

He wished he were back on his deck, staring at the water.

"I believe in a soul, too," she went on, "and in a God who doesn't suffer fools. I believe he wants you to have it all, Gabriel. Everything you deserve, all that you desire."

Gabriel Stone hadn't felt a sexual urge of any kind in the last four months, and he wasn't feeling one now. This woman would happily swing open the gates of damnation itself and usher him through, tempting him with the compelling, liberating logic of the new age.

There was a time it would have been a sweet poison.

The past may indeed be dead, but apparently it wasn't quite yet gone.

This was a choice, and he made it easily. She was not his type, and this was not the time. Kathryn Kline would not be the one who brought him back into the world.

Not until his dead wife let him go.

NEITHER ONE NOTICED a woman departing the restaurant right behind them. She, too, wore a tailored taupe business suit, but unlike Kathryn she carried no briefcase, which, along with the sunglasses perched atop her head on this overcast day, made her seem a bit out of place. A poorly cast actress, too pretty for the part.

The woman stayed twenty feet behind until they entered the building at 666 Fifth Avenue. She remained on the sidewalk staring up at the address, which was carved into the stone of the entry facade.

She was smiling, as if she knew something no one else could.

THE DYNAMICS OF the meeting with Gabriel's publisher were not
unlike those he'd come to expect from his advertising days—smug under-
lings arriving with notepads and fake smiles that faded as soon as someone
with *real* clout began to speak, bad pastry and designer coffee, and a pecking
order with no give.

Wyatt Veerman entered the lush twenty-ninth-floor conference room
with a Trump-like flourish. Gabriel's new editor, his assigned publicist, and
a handful of suits from the marketing department were already there, and it
was obvious this was not to be the high point of their day. Veerman seemed
more like a Vegas pit boss than a titan of media—the word *palooka* popped
into Gabriel's head when he saw the guy—the extra pounds rendering the
two-thousand-dollar suit more parody than fashion.

The meeting began with eloquent testimony to Veerman's enthusiasm
for Gabriel's book and his house's vision for it as a slam-dunk bestseller. The
world was waiting for this story, he assured all, the collective appetite for all
things holy having been whetted with the *Left Behind* series and *The Da Vinci
Code* phenomenon, and then, of course, the Mel Gibson movie juggernaut.
Even the Romney-Obama showdown had evoked a fringe element of prophecy buffs. And while it had all quieted down, that appetite had not dissipated
over the years—religion was still hot hot hot, and Gabriel had provided an
unexpected twist in the oeuvre of apocalyptic literature. He had filled in
the blanks of prophecy. They were putting it ahead of everything in their

pipeline, literally stopping the presses to get this book on the streets by the election.

Veerman did all the talking, and the only response he elicited came upon eye contact with an underling, who obliged with a worshipful nod that conveyed the weight and great wisdom of the boss's thinking. As the day progressed there would be other meetings with specific functionaries, but this introductory huddle was to assure Gabriel that he was their new cleanup hitter, that he had the resources and commitment of the entire organization behind him. Whether he knew it or not—as if an industry secret was being revealed to him—bestsellers were not simply written; they were *made,* and he had just been anointed.

During a pause in the twenty-ninth-floor monologue, Gabriel thought he saw a quick exchange of meaningful glances between Veerman and Barry Lincoln, his new editor, who absolutely refused to look directly at him.

"There *is* one thing," said Veerman. "We've decided the novel needs a stronger title."

A long, excruciating silence filled the room. Veerman and the editor exchanged another glance, this one telling.

"Excuse me?" Gabriel wasn't sure he'd heard it right.

Kathryn quickly leaned in, nodding her reassurance as she grasped his arm. "This happens all the time."

Veerman raised his eyebrows toward Barry Lincoln, who was obviously uncomfortable with this handoff.

"We're thinking edgier, more visceral," said Barry.

"*Whisper of the Seventh Thunder* is sort of, I dunno, *busy,*" chimed in the head marketing suit, a woman who too obviously hid her insecurities with effort. "Too Tolkien."

"Sounds Disney to me," added another assistant. "It's soft."

Everyone in the room stared at Gabriel expectantly. He remained motionless, his face frozen.

Veerman couldn't stand giving up the floor for this long. "We're going with *Kingdom Come.*"

With that, the marketing glamour girl turned over a comp of their cover design. The new title, *Kingdom Come,* was emblazoned over angry clouds over a rocky shoreline, both of which swirled with all the fury John the Divine might have witnessed that ancient day on Patmos. Gabriel's name was embossed just below, only slightly smaller than the title.

"It's sort of Spielberg," said the assistant.

"Literate, yet mysterious," added Lincoln with a sudden vigor. "We think it cuts across several demographics, from King to Grisham to Clancy. Fifty shades of Armageddon, if you will."

Polite laughter burned out quickly.

"That's the thing," said Veerman, sensing that Gabriel was confused. "Readers need to *get it*. You gotta hook 'em hard. There's no mistaking the genre here."

"I don't get to name my own book?" Gabriel steered the question toward Kathryn.

The editor intervened. "It's not often the publisher personally titles a book like this," said Barry. Across the table, Veerman tried and failed at a humble posture. "That says something about our commitment. We think it rocks."

Gabriel leaned toward Kathryn. "Is this negotiable?"

She barely moved her lips. "Not if you have brain one in that gorgeous head it isn't. Just go with this. Trust me."

She looked up and smiled. Everyone in the room understood what had just happened, much more so than the author.

"We're delighted with the new title," she said.

Wyatt Veerman slapped the tabletop with both palms. "Excellent," he said, rising to his feet, others eagerly following his lead. He extended a hand to Gabriel with a huge, campaign trail smile. "Barry will get you settled in. Welcome to our humble neighborhood. This is gonna be fun."

Gabriel watched as they started to leave. Then, in a quiet voice that almost went unnoticed, he said, "Excuse me. Please."

Everyone froze, heads pivoting. It was as if someone had told the king he was stark raving naked in court. Kathryn Kline's eyes were blazing, but she remained silent.

Gabriel averted her glare as he went on.

"I appreciate your enthusiasm," said Gabriel, his smile inexplicably calm. "I really do. But the title is *Whisper of the Seven Thunders*. Not *Kingdom Come*."

Veerman shot a glance at Kathryn Kline. Then he just nodded and continued his departure, leaving his staff staring at their new author with complex expressions on their faces, ranging from outrage to thinly veiled admiration.

"Could you give us a moment?" said Kathryn as she ushered the others through the door, then closing it when they had the room to themselves. She leaned against it, clamping her eyes closed as if struggling for control.

Finally she opened them and, in a voice more appropriate to someone ordering a salad, said, "Are you fucking insane?"

Gabriel shrugged. "I'm not changing the title."

"You are if I say you are."

He nodded thoughtfully. "Is that a line you just drew in the sand, Kathryn? Because if it is, I'm out of here."

"The hell you are. You can't do this."

"Really? I haven't signed anything."

"Do you have the slightest idea who you're dealing with? What's at stake? Christ, the ego of you writers!"

"It's not ego," he said softly.

"Then just what in the name of God is it?"

Gabriel smiled at her choice of words.

"You wouldn't understand."

She folded her arms and said, "Try me."

"It's my wife's title." He allowed her to process the depth of this revelation, hoping she had the heart to understand. "She thought of it. She loved it. She gave it to me." He paused again, then added, "I'm sorry. I'm not changing it."

Kathryn stared hard at her new client, her eyes reduced to a squint. Finally, with a softer voice than he'd heard from her thus far, she said, "You have to move on with your life, Gabriel."

He smiled. "I know. Are you with me on this, or not?"

"No one tells Wyatt Veerman *no*," she said.

Gabriel got to his feet, shaking his head sadly. "Then I guess I'm no one," he said as he gathered up his notepad and started walking toward the door.

"Where are you going?"

"Home," he said. "I'm sorry."

She watched him leave, saying nothing more.

- 14 -

The Cathedral of St. John the Divine
New York City

NO ONE PAID attention to the man in the blazer and jeans sitting alone in the middle of a pew near the back of the central nave. Motionless, head slightly bowed, he could have easily been deep in prayer. There was an eerie silence in the great space, the massive house organ having been damaged in the fire of 2001 and still, much like the star of this show, awaiting the next resurrection.

Gabriel Stone, however, was not engaged in prayer. He was thinking about where someone might plant a bomb.

After leaving his publisher's building he'd gone back to his hotel, where the message light on his phone was blinking. He knew who it was. Kathryn could wait, think about his determination not to change his title for a while. He called the airline, learning that the next flight to San Francisco was at five. But the room was prepaid for two nights, and despite his hasty departure from the conference room he wasn't nearly the bonehead they undoubtedly considered him. He would give them a chance to change their minds, then, if necessary, fly out the next day with his original title intact.

Or not. The bravado was evaporating by the hour. Let them stew on it, see who really had the hammer here.

Having decided he would remain in New York, he quickly realized he had somewhere he needed to go.

THE CATHEDRAL OF St. John the Divine was the largest in the world. Six hundred one feet long, two football fields plus the football. Still, after well over one hundred years since the cornerstone had been laid, it remained only two-thirds complete. Theoretically, though he hadn't seen it with his own eyes, this meant construction crews could come and go, and that the infrastructure of the building would be accessible to anyone with an agenda and the resources to avoid detection. He and Lauren had been here a few years before, and while she gawked at the stained glass and the nave ceiling and the then-active 8,035 pipes of the Great Organ—she slugged him at the suggestion he adopt this as a nickname for himself—he gazed about with equally religious awe, a dark fiction formulating in his mind.

What if terrorists planted a bomb deep in the bowels of this place? What if they then waited until a target, the president perhaps, came here to attend a service, using the opportunity to make their next big statement to the world?

In deference to Lauren's wishes, he had changed the site of the bombing from the Cathedral to a fictional hotel under construction in Washington. The idea had come to him in a dream, and who was he to argue with the creative participation of the Providence.

Sitting here in the pew at St. John's, reviewing the road that had brought him back to this place, he felt a sudden touch on his shoulder. He flinched, as if someone had nailed him with a Taser.

But the first jolt was quickly surpassed by another. When he spun around in his seat, he saw that it was a woman.

Lauren.

He felt his heart seize. He froze, barely breathing.

"I'm sorry," the woman said, "I didn't mean to startle you."

He couldn't move. Even when she added a smile.

But it wasn't Lauren, of course. A little younger, a little leaner, almost too thin. They had the same eyes, an eerie, transparent ice blue. Eyes that missed nothing.

"You look like you've just seen a ghost," she said with absolutely no trace of irony.

He continued to stare. Her nose was pixyish, her features sharp and defined. Her skin was a rich olive, her blond hair laced with darker highlights, long and tied back with a black ribbon. She wore a dark brown leather jacket with a red cashmere scarf. Earrings, makeup, straight from a magazine ad announcing a definite style with a well-developed sense of class.

She smiled slightly. Perhaps she was used to this reaction in the men she interrupted.

"You are Gabriel Stone?"

There was a question mark at the end of the question, but it was only a formality. She knew precisely who he was.

He nodded without expression.

She held her formal identification to eye level. The words jumped out at him as his eyes darted from the wallet card, which was accompanied by a silver badge on the facing flap, to her face, which waited patiently.

"National Security Agency," she said. "Special Agent Sarah Meyers."

He shook his head, drawing a deep breath, more out of necessity than relief. She could have been Lauren's sister.

"Enjoying your time here in New York, Mr. Stone?" she asked as she stashed the wallet. There was no accent, her tone and her smile were genuine, her eye contact intense.

"What is this?" he asked, trying to keep a semblance of civility in his voice. "How do you know me?"

"I've been following you for some time now," she said.

"That's impossible. I just flew in, late yesterday."

She smiled. "American flight twenty-eight, departed SFO at five fifteen. You parked in row K, space thirty-nine. Got worked over pretty good by security, but you're a good sport. Sat in three-A. You had the chicken somewhere over Utah."

She allowed this to sink in, then added, "I was in eight-C."

He squinted. Studied her until the smile dissolved.

"Room twelve-sixteen at the Sherry Netherland. Breakfast with a moderately attractive woman at Michael's, cinnamon roll and coffee, black, followed by a short meeting with a publisher on the twenty-ninth floor of the Tishman Building. Six sixty-six Fifth Avenue. Interesting address, don't you think?"

"What's going on?"

She opened a leather-bound notebook to withdraw a piece of white paper, which she held out to him.

"Did you write this?"

He leaned in to read without taking it from her. It was the first page of the manuscript he had sent to Kathryn Kline. The quality was poor, a copy of a copy that had been faxed.

He nodded, almost in spite of himself, staring at his words.

"How did you get this? *Why* did you get this?"

"Both answers are long, Mr. Stone."

She put the page back in the notebook. He noticed her hands, long delicate fingers, French-manicured nails. A little uptown for an NSA agent.

"Am I in some kind of trouble?" he asked. His nerves were suddenly participating, sending hate notes to his stomach.

Sarah Meyers cast a quick glance around the Cathedral. As did Gabriel. Federal agents usually hunted in pairs, at least if you believed in prime time television.

"Can we talk somewhere?" she asked.

Gabriel didn't answer. He was weighing his options, and he had several. But who she was and why she was here would go unanswered if he refused, and the unspoken implications of not cooperating with the NSA lay heavier than the sense of paranoia that suddenly enveloped him.

"No long black cars," she said, that little smile returning. "No dimly lit alleys. Public, your pick."

"Is this official government business?"

"You think I'm trying to pick you up?"

"A guy can hope."

This made her smile. "I have a few questions."

"About my book."

The smile changed, softened somewhat. "And about you."

"Do I have a choice?"

"You always do," she said. "That's why we're here today."

15

THEY WALKED IN silence across a busy street to a deli with several weathered tables on the sidewalk. Sarah went inside, returning minutes later with two coffees. The early-fall breeze was chilly, so they were quite alone with their business.

He didn't wait for her to sit before launching an offensive.

"Something's wrong with this picture. You flash an NSA badge, but you're alone, no partner, no backup. You say you've been following me, blowing your cover in the process, explaining neither. You flash a page from my unpublished manuscript, then ask me to coffee with the promise you won't throw me into the back of a car. I suggest you talk fast."

She seemed amused, sipping her coffee as she listened.

"Happy to. You've just written a book with a perfectly credible presidential assassination plot, in a time of unprecedented sensitivity toward acts of terrorism."

He was nodding before she finished. "Guess I should have known. Question is, how do *you* know?"

She smiled approvingly. "Suffice it to say that there's a bunker full of recent poli-sci grads somewhere in rural Virginia paid to read everything slated for publication."

They locked eyes a moment, acknowledging the joust.

"What does the NSA want from *me?*"

Sarah Meyers took a leisurely sip of coffee before answering. "We're reasonably sure you're not associated with any radical entities, foreign or otherwise, or that you're even all that politically motivated. Which bears the very pertinent question—why did you write this book?"

"Did you ask LaHaye and Jenkins the same question?"

"LaHaye and Jenkins didn't lay out a feasible blueprint for an assassination strategy that wasn't already in our database, one that has our strategists taking notes."

"And I did? I think I want my taxes back."

Sarah Meyers didn't find this amusing.

"We could be having this conversation in a windowless room downtown. We, or should I say the collective agencies, could be all over you . . . tax audits, surveillance, covert searches. Frankly, I believe you're one of the good guys, and I'd like to spare you all that."

"You must be way up there on the org chart."

He noticed a subtle tick, a tiny fracture in her confidence. He let it hang between them, leaning back patiently.

"So why'd you write it?" she asked.

Now he took his own slow sip, unwilling to blink first. Her resemblance to Lauren made it easy to stare.

"Sometimes an idea won't let go. I had things to say."

"That's an understatement," she said.

She withdrew a photograph from her notebook and placed it on the table. It was a mug shot of a young man, the kind that appears on a driver's license or private ID tag.

"Know him?"

"No."

"Final answer?"

He nodded.

Gabriel thought he saw a sudden darkness in her eyes as she pulled the photo back.

"Ever heard of an organization called The Brethren?"

"No."

She looked up at him now.

"The Fellowship of Leaders for Jesus Christ?"

"No.

"National Organization for Christian Leadership? Consortium for

Global Leadership in Christ?"

"That's a lot of rubber chickens."

"They're all the same address."

He shook his head. "What the *hell* is this about?"

"Ever heard the name Phillip Reilly? Michael Cobb? Daniel Hergert?"

Gabriel noted them for later use as he shook his head.

She shifted on the hard metal seat, choosing her words carefully.

"What would you say if I told you there are people who are more than casually interested in your work?"

"I'd say send 'em over. I just pissed off my publisher and I could use a break."

"Some people think you're dangerous."

"Hardly."

She held his stare, which was suddenly intense.

Gabriel continued. "Are you saying I'm in some kind of danger? Because of my book?"

"Are you a patriot, Gabriel Stone?"

The jarring nature of her question was precisely the point. Gabriel squirmed in his chair, unable to hold her gaze. After a moment, though, his eyes returned to hers.

"You mean, in a Republican elitist gun-toting whack-job sort of way?"

"They have polluted the word, haven't they."

He didn't return her wry grin.

"Are you on or off the clock with this?" he asked.

"Why do you ask?"

"I think you're off the books. Working your own agenda."

"Someone's paranoid."

"Think so?

Yeah, I'm a patriot. Old school. Definitely. You want someone to spend five minutes alone in a room with the next Al-Qaeda capture, I'm your guy. But right now, I don't know which team *you're* on. And until I do, or until you tell me what this is about, and as much as I enjoy looking at you, this conversation is over."

Sarah Meyers smiled again.

"You think that's funny?" he asked.

"I think you're afraid. That's what you do when you're scared, you puff your chest, talk all tough. You like being in control, but suddenly you're involved in something bigger than you."

"You get all that by following me around?"

"You'd be surprised how much you can tell about a person by watching them for a while."

He allowed a grin to emerge. "You know what I think? I think you're not what you say you are. There's an agenda here, and it's hidden."

"You'd make a good agent."

"Call me. I may need a job." When she didn't smile, he went on. "What is it you want from me?"

"A connection. Something, someone, may surface on your radar. When they do, I'd like to know."

He nodded slowly. "You want me to be the bait."

"I like to think of it as a covert partnership."

"Is this on or off the federal books?"

Her eyes held his. "I can't answer that."

"Can't? Or *won't?*"

"I need your help. You may need mine."

Gabriel took note of the first-person context. There wasn't a "we" in sight.

Sarah again opened up the notebook, taking out a business card this time. She placed it on the table in front of him.

There was no name, no federal seal. Just a telephone number.

She smiled as she drained her coffee cup, something just short of a wink. "Buy a girl another?"

He thought this was odd, but he bit. There were several reasons, some he didn't want to acknowledge. He went inside, found the pot on the counter next to the register. Refills were free.

When he returned to the table, NSA Agent Sarah Meyers was gone. But the card remained, tucked under an empty cup.

16

Auburn, California

GABRIEL'S FIRST IMPULSE after coffee with Special Agent Sarah Meyers was to catch the next flight west. He'd even gone back to his hotel to pack and check out—there were three messages from Kathryn waiting for him—but never quite got the suitcase closed. He was in New York, with abundant time on his hands and booked for another prepaid night.

More important, the business of his book remained unresolved.

He visited the Metropolitan Museum of Art and the Guggenheim. Walked Central Park and showed a kid in a wheelchair how they toss a Frisbee in California. Went back to Fifth Avenue, tried on sports coats at Saks, bought a new pair of loafers at Gucci, for no other reason than the fact that Lauren had always raved about the brand. Caught a train to the financial district and toured Ground Zero. Ate a hot dog from a street vendor in Times Square and gave two bucks to a beggar, followed by an ass-chewing from a cop who saw it happen. Then he walked around the block and gave the same guy a five.

Before dinner he spent an hour at a copy center on a rented PC. He wanted to see what the search engines had on The Brethren. There were over three million hits, and from what he could see most led to some variation of Christian fellowship. He tried *The National Organization for Christian Leadership,* and there it was. Right above a link to the *Promise Keepers,* whose souvenir golf shirt he had somewhere in his closet back home. The group was composed of powerful players from industry and politics, all devoted Christian men of means. They even had a headquarters, a mansion located in a middle-class Washington, D.C. neighborhood. They were self-declared warriors for Jesus, and had ruffled their share of feathers with forays into third world and even hostile countries to court the favor of dictators and warmongers. Their singular mission was to introduce Jesus Christ to the movers and shakers of the planet, and besides money their most powerful weapon was prayer.

They were Patriots, both old and new school.

And apparently, they were sworn to secrecy. Their only public forum, it seemed, was an annual prayer luncheon attended by kings and presidents, including our own.

Gabriel fought off the sudden urge to call Sarah Meyers and ask her what interest such an old boys' network might have in him. Then again, it was obvious: The Bible-thumping Brethren wouldn't condone letting the secret of the seven thunders out of the bag. Even if the writer was making it all up.

No, he'd play the Sarah card when he had something to trade. Until then, dinner sounded like the better idea.

GABRIEL'S IPHONE RANG over appetizers, his ringtone a Springsteen song about lost glory days. It was Kathryn, her tone promising no hint of reconciliation.

"What state are you in?" she asked.

"State of anxiety, I think."

"Tell me you didn't fly home."

"I didn't fly home, Kathryn."

"We need to talk. That wasn't smart. Twelve years in this business, I've never seen a writer pull a stunt like that.

What the hell are you thinking? You should be kissing Wyatt Veerman's fat ass all the way to the bank."

"I was thinking I don't want my title changed."

"The business doesn't work like that, Gabriel."

"I knew you'd call."

"Really." She snorted. "Jesus, who taught you to think like that? Some self-help book on being true to yourself?"

"My wife."

There was a long pause.

"Where are you?"

"Sitting in Applebee's eating chicken fingers."

"Tourist."

"It's happy hour."

"How appropriate. Know what a preemptive offer is?"

"If you're talking movie rights, no."

"I am. It means a potential buyer wants to short-circuit the auction by making an offer that requires immediate response."

"A bid, in other words."

"Not exactly. In a bid situation you go back and forth between buyers, jacking the ante. With a preemptive you either take it or you pass. If you do, the buyer forfeits the right to bid going forward. It's all or nothing."

"So they shoot for the moon."

"See, you *are* smart. And what do you suppose the moon is worth these days?"

"You said a million, million two."

"I said that?"

"Kathryn, you're killing me."

"Just grab on to something."

"I'm holding a french fry."

"A million nine, Gabriel."

He gasped slightly, loud enough for her to hear. "Say that again. Slowly."

"One million, nine hundred thousand frickin' dollars. Outright purchase, no option. They've already got a major star interested, and they think they know the perfect director."

"How major?"

She told him the name, prompting a low whistle of approval.

"Who's the buyer?"

She told him that name, which he did not recognize.

"Do I get to write the screenplay?"

"Not a ghost's chance in hell."

"Then it's no deal."

For the first time in this staccato exchange, silence dominated the line. There certainly was precedent for her alarm.

He waited the appropriate moment.

"I'm busting your balls, Kathryn. And may I say, you have the biggest pair I've ever seen."

"I take it you're pleased."

"Do I get to keep my title?"

"What are you, a pit bull? I owe Wyatt Veerman an obscene act in an elevator, but yes, you get to keep your title."

"Thank you."

"You know the Hyatt at Grand Central?"

"I'm a tourist, remember?"

"One hour, lobby bar. I have papers for you to sign."

The line went dead.

Gabriel decided he would finish his dinner, maybe have some dessert. If that made him late, then Kathryn Kline and her papers would just have to wait.

17

KATHRYN KLINE CLICKED off her iPhone and smiled at the portly man sitting across the table from her. "Lamb to the slaughter," she said, her smile both smug and dark.

"You are such an exquisite bitch," said Wyatt. He leaned in to kiss her, but she pushed him away with her forearm.

The dimly lit uptown bar where they sat was frequented almost exclusively by the publishing crowd. Deals happened here, seven-figure dreams sealed with handshakes. A candle in the center of each small circular table provided the only light, other than the back-lit display of liquor behind the bar.

"You should seduce this guy," said Veerman. "Consummate the deal with a little old-fashioned sin." His comb-over was failing him miserably tonight, his jowls betraying a body gone to seed. An elegant designer suit and a huge gold pinkie ring were all that separated Veerman from complete mediocrity.

Kathryn Kline, her suit every bit as fresh as it had been that morning, sipped the last of the evening's third lemon drop. She ran her finger around the rim to pick up some sugar, then held it to Veerman's lips as she whispered.

"You'd like that, wouldn't you, Wyatt."

"Yes," he said, breathless.

"To watch me take him. Slowly, by candlelight."

He closed his eyes, inhaling deeply, savoring the words. "You play dirty," he said, kissing the back of her hand.

She allowed him this brief pleasure, then pulled it away.

"I don't think our new author is in the market for recreational debauchery," she said. "He's still grieving his wife."

"You underestimate yourself."

"Not lately."

"Come up when you're finished with him," he said. "Have your wicked way with me. Celebrate our little transaction."

She smiled the way she knew he liked it. "My ways can be painful," she said.

"I'm counting on it," he whispered, leaning in again.

Her hand suddenly gripped his bottom jaw with startling force. "I assure you, the pleasure will be mine."

Then she released her grip, amused at the complex expression that remained on his face.

She reached behind for her coat. "He's expecting me at eight," she said.

"I'll drop you," said Wyatt Veerman.

18

THE NONDESCRIPT MAN with wire-rimmed glasses sat alone at the bar and stared at the mirror behind a four-tier rack of bottles. From this line of sight on Kathryn and her chubby co-conspirator he could easily read their lips, even as they sipped drinks and played a little tongue hockey during whispered exchanges. When he saw them shift into exit mode, he tossed a twenty onto the counter for his two Diet Cokes and slipped toward the door. The bartender, who had been unable to engage the wiry little man in conversation, pocketed the money with a swipe of a rag and a quick glance around the room.

McQuarrie emerged into a rainy New York evening, standing outside the double glass doors of the bar while he put on his overcoat. A few feet away waited a black Escalade, the driver behind the wheel. When McQuarrie nodded at him, the driver returned the gesture with a quick nod.

McQuarrie walked to the next doorway, the entrance to a fur salon that was closed and therefore in shadow. He leaned against the iron bars and pretended to hold a phone to his ear, watching the limo in the reflection of the glass in front of him.

KATHRYN KLINE AND Wyatt Veerman folded into the backseat of the Escalade, the door held by the club's doorman. Veerman's cigar filled the space with its rank aroma immediately.

"Evening, Mr. Veerman," said the driver, half turning.

The man squinted back. "Who the fuck are you?"

"Phillip, sir. Enrique had a family thing."

"You guys just change drivers and I don't even know?"

"We aim to please, sir."

Kathryn snuggled in under her companion's arm. She smiled at the driver as if she, at least, appreciated the situation.

"Where to, sir?"

"Grand Hyatt," he grunted, the car already pulling into traffic.

"By the way, Enrique is fine, sir. Sick kid, nothing serious. Thanks for asking."

Veerman gave no indication that he heard. In the rearview mirror, the driver—whose name was not Phillip—could see that Veerman's head was resting against the back of the seat, eyes shut, the cigar clamped between his teeth.

And that Kathryn Kline had disappeared from view.

MCQUARRIE HELD THE dead phone to his ear as he watched the SUV pull away into a sea of yellow taxis. Then he moved it in front of his face and punched in a number, for real this time. He waited a moment, until someone picked up without saying anything.

"Go," he said.

He then clicked off and walked down the street, shoulders hunched, eyes lowered.

19

ON THE TWENTY-NINTH floor of the Tishman Building, in the offices of the publishing company run by Wyatt Veerman, another man dressed as a janitor pocketed his own mobile device and looked around. The office was fully lit but empty, the last editorial assistant with no life having departed just minutes earlier.

He had to hurry. The real janitor would be here in half an hour.

He hit Wyatt Veerman's office first, assuming it would be the least likely to receive an unexpected visit. Using a master key provided by his contact and wearing latex gloves, he went through the desk and credenza, finding nothing. Using what appeared to be a smartphone, he hard-wired a USB connection to the man's PC and allowed a very proprietary software program originally developed by the CIA to bypass the password-protected firewall and enter the company data system. There was nothing in the desktop memory, but, using a search function, he found a copy of *Whisper of the Seventh Thunder* on the server. With several quick keystrokes he erased it, then erased all references, logs, caches, and temporary files that would indicate it had been there in the first place.

He had no idea it was the second time the database had been compromised in the past week.

He took the elevator down to the seventh floor and his next target. There were two copies of the book on this editor's PC, both of which ceased to exist with four untraceable keystrokes.

He then pushed his janitor's cart to the file storage room, where all of the files were left unlocked. There he found a freshly printed hard copy, as he'd been told he would. It would depart the premises with him minutes later, along with the lone index of the contents of these files, kept on a clipboard hanging next to the door.

It was as if the book had never existed.

He had one more task to perform, the most dangerous of all. He returned to the editor's desk, carefully inspecting his gloves to ensure that no rips had materialized. He withdrew a vial from his pocket, within which was a clear and odorless gel. He scooped some onto his index finger, then capped the vial and returned it to his pocket. Opening the lid to the metallic Starbucks coffee mug on Barry Lincoln's desk, he smeared the gel around the inner circumference until it was invisible to the naked eye. He replaced the mug in precisely the position he had found it, then pulled the glove off, wadding it into a ball in the opposite palm. He pulled that glove off so that it turned inside out, encasing the wadded-up glove completely. The ball of latex went into his pocket for disposal on the outside, miles away.

He walked briskly toward the elevator, stopping for the janitor's cart, which he'd leave in front of the supply room in the basement. He would be on the street in less than eight minutes from the time of McQuarrie's call, a package the size of a manuscript under one arm.

After dropping off the package, he had another stop to make. An apartment on Sutton Place, where the assignment would be very much the same as this one.

Only this time, there would be no risk of interruption, since the occupant would not be coming home tonight.

The driver who had introduced himself as Phillip drove south on Park to 42nd, then turned left toward the East River. His passengers were too preoccupied savoring the exchange of interpersonal fluids to notice that a car, an identical black SUV with tinted windows, now followed fifty yards behind them, headlights off. They did, however, notice when their car shot through the Lexington intersection without even slowing in front of the Grand Hyatt.

"Hey, Sparky, you just missed the goddamn stop!"

The driver didn't seem to hear. Instead he raised a window separating him from the passengers behind.

They picked up speed, then suddenly wheeled into a garage. The SUV that had been following did the same. They were in a deserted parking lot, the lights of which had been conveniently disconnected.

The driver hit the brakes, jammed the Escalade into Park, and threw open the door. Then he sprinted into the dark, leaving the door open.

The other SUV suddenly skidded to a halt abreast of them, freezing the two occupants with surprise. Two men leapt from it and rushed to either side, throwing open both rear doors. They said nothing, nor did they hesitate.

Both gunmen fired a single shot, one striking Kathryn in the forehead, the other entering Veerman's temple and exiting the opposite side of his skull with a baseball-sized globe of cerebrum in tow. Gloved hands stripped the still-convulsing bodies of jewels, watches—Veerman's was insured for fifty grand—wallets, and Kathryn's purse.

Then the SUV with the shooters was gone, streaking into an ocean of darkness.

Two hours later Veerman's Escalade would be discovered, engine running, the bodies in the backseat having stiffened, their shoes immersed in pools of blood already cooled to the temperature of the night.

AFTER AN HOUR'S wait in the lobby bar at the Grand Hyatt, Gabriel Stone was back in his hotel room.

He called Kathryn's mobile number on the hour, every hour. He called the publisher's office, but couldn't get past the chilly receptionist. He remained in his room, too nauseous to eat, too nervous to chance missing a call of explanation.

The call never came.

He had written his book his way, which Lauren would say was in defiance of divine command. Perhaps now he was paying a price for his arrogance. She had always claimed that everything happens for a reason. He wondered now what that reason might be.

He checked out early the next morning. Took a taxi to Kennedy and, after chipping in a hundred bucks for the change fee, got the last business-class seat on a red-eye to San Francisco.

It had been nothing but a dream, after all. And dreams, he had learned, had a way of dying before your eyes.

Palm Desert, California

THE ELITE INNER circle of Armand Brenner's staff often worked through lunch, gathered around a hotel conference room table blanketed with the latest polls and press clippings and the occasional fishing magazine. Today lunch consisted of the house panini, served with vegetables cut to resemble little farm animals, with a spicy hummus dip in which to drown them.

Without looking up from the *Wall Street Journal*, Armand Brenner said through a mouthful of sandwich, "Remind me to fire whoever ordered this shit."

His five top aides all laughed with appropriate restraint, including the one who had ordered the shit in question. The election was within sight, and any humor in the room belonged exclusively to the boss.

Armand Brenner always sat at the end of the table. As usual he wore a crisp white shirt, the sleeves rolled up for business, his tie and top button loosened to reveal a tuft of black chest hair, which no one on the planet knew was dyed with the same product he used to darken the thick mop on his head. Because he was big—six three, a solid two thirty, an ex-fullback at a Corn Belt school—he slouched when he read, sometimes planting his size thirteen loafer on the edge of the table. Everything about the man was huge, from his thick lips to his drooping ears, from his reported family fortune to the volume of his voice when he addressed Congress, where he had sat with visible ambition for the last fourteen years as the junior senator from California.

After a stellar turn at running the company his father had founded fifty-five years earlier, followed by a steep climb through the California political farm system and his marriage to a congresswoman who many believed had bigger balls than his, Armand Brenner was running for President of the United States.

These staff meetings, which happened daily following the candidate's morning jog and a session in the nearest gym, were actually run by Brenner's top lieutenant, Alex Goldman. Brenner liked to pretend apathy toward anything remotely political in favor of what he called "the real shit," while Alex sweated the details—the logistics of schedule, the interpretation of issues, the gonad-sniffing of fundraising. It was known that if you got on Alex's bad side, which was easy to do, your bag would precede you out the door, through which you would soon follow. Few knew that it had been Alex who handpicked Brenner's running mate based on a cunning demographic strategy—the man was young and of mixed ethnic heritage, a move designed to really piss off the old school—and had taken great pains to keep the two of them apart as much as possible. Brenner thought his future vice president was a mindless ass. At least he wasn't posing for pictures with dumbbells in a tank top and a backwards hat like the previous party VP candidate, who had the arms of a high school freshman golfer.

Alex held up a sheet of paper, a rare smirk visible. This was how the meetings concluded, a dramatic flourish given to the final agenda item, which was rarely amusing.

"And lastly, something for us from the extreme right."

Brenner raised an eyebrow. "What, the rifle boys throwing another beer bash? Tell the crackers in the NRA lobby I'm busy. Tell 'em that's Yiddish for *fuck off.*"

Again the polite tittering of well-paid sycophants. The NRA had screwed the pooch with their reaction to a variety of public shootings, suggesting they arm kindergarten teachers and bus drivers with automatic weapons and user manuals.

"Close," said Alex, the grin turning dark. "Invitation to the National Prayer Luncheon." The last words were spoken slowly and enunciated with staccato emphasis.

Brenner allowed the newspaper he'd been holding to fall to his lap.

"Say again?"

"I shit you not," replied Alex, biting his lip. "It's a sector we can't ignore. You've said so yourself."

"Bunch of born-again vigilantes. They're dangerous."

Brenner had been openly critical of The Brethren, the sponsoring entity behind the National Prayer Luncheon. Alex had warned him to back off, that The Brethren had more friends in high places than Jesus Christ himself. Because he felt he must to survive among the sharks of public service, and to make his wife happy, Brenner had forsaken his Jewish blood to adopt Roman Catholicism, though his liberal stance, at least for his party of choice, on abortion and right-to-life had distanced him from anyone wearing a robe. "Something to piss off everybody" had once been his motto among insiders, but his middle-of-the-road, foot-in-every-camp platform had worked. After the polarizing antics of his predecessors, anything he could do with his left hand was scoring him points.

As for the National Prayer Luncheon, his grandparents would spin in their Dachau graves if they knew he was breaking bread with a bunch of WASPs in pretentious suits.

"The President attends this thing, right?" offered one of the other staffers, the same aspiring strategist who had ordered panini for a man who liked his hamburgers rare and his beer ice cold.

"Every year," said Alex. "Even Clinton in his cigar period. The Lord loves a winner."

"Pious little circus," continued Brenner, his cheeks flushing. He had been critical of the last several administrations that had inserted their right-wing Protestant bias into public policy, but he had to make nice to stay in the game. "What in the *hell* do they want with *me?*"

At this they all smiled. The Brethren was largely invisible to the public but very much a factor in the political game plan of everyone who had designs on a Washington address. Part of him would love nothing more than to plant his ass in their midst and talk humbly about his destiny as the first person of Jewish descent to lead the nation. His advisors, however, had shown him the wisdom in approaching these particular demographics with tolerance and an enlightened smile. He had a piece of the Jewish vote by virtue of his heritage, he had the Catholic vote by virtue of the cross on his name tag—both groups cared more about the label than the content of the speeches—and now he had a chance to impress the noisy Christian right with his utterly enlightened and conservative yet compassionate worldview.

"You know we need to do this," said Alex.

"I need a goddamn colonoscopy, too. Tell 'em to call Gingrich, for chrissakes. I hear he's available."

"Maybe we should ask Charlotte?" offered Alex, his expression one of mock humility. Charlotte Brenner, who had given up her seat in Congress to help her husband run for the highest office in the land, was known among Brenner's insiders to have the final vote in matters of political expedience. Some said she would make an even better candidate than her husband— she was his intellectual superior, and everyone knew it—but this was never acknowledged among the staff on pain of immediate termination. Others had suggested that she be named his running mate, the notion of which had been dismissed out of hand, by her. Charlotte Brenner, daughter of a Lebanese cook who grew up on the mean streets of Chicago, champion of women's rights and minority opportunity, and lately the darling of a fourth estate that appreciated her witty candor, took a backseat to no one.

The country had never seen conservatives like this. And though cynics claimed post–Romney-Ryan 180 strategy was behind it all, the polls liked them. Charlotte was off on other business today, otherwise she'd have simply declared the National Prayer Luncheon a done deal.

"You let me handle my wife," said Brenner, his eyes burning with disapproval. He was sick to death of Charlotte's press, and delighted she spent most of her time on the road working on his behalf, where she could suck up with whomever she pleased.

He raised the paper back to his face. The others looked at Alex, who showed no reaction.

But they all knew. Armand Brenner would be going to the National Prayer Luncheon a month from now. Alex was nothing if not a master strategist, one who had Charlotte Brenner's ear—he had actually worked for her first—and the one to whom Brenner owed his current political platform, which was carefully crafted around medical and insurance reform, a radical new tax structure and zero tolerance for anyone who would do harm of any kind to an American citizen. Like most of Brenner's tirades, this had all been for show, the bluster of a man who knew the job was bigger than he was.

Washington, D.C.

THE DRIZZLE WAS made to order. That is, if a clandestine meeting was your reason for being here on the steps of the Lincoln Memorial. There was no higher technology than the common umbrella for masking one's identity without enlisting the participation of a scalpel.

Daniel Larsen waited next to the reflecting pool at the base of the lower staircase in front of the monument. He checked his watch. His contact was six minutes late, which was one of several reliable ways to piss Larsen off.

Despite the weather there was a small crowd this morning—wide-eyed retired couples, a tour group, a few stray tourists, including a young man with a backpack taking photographs.

A security guard whose eyes missed nothing lingered to the side. Larsen was surveying the tourists when he noticed the guard walking toward him.

"Brother Daniel," said the guard when he arrived next to him. "I suggest you lose the sunglasses. Just a fashion tip."

McQuarrie peered out through wire-rimmed glasses from beneath a baseball-style cap that matched the uniform.

"You should talk," replied an irritated Larsen. "You look like you just got off the bus from Mayberry."

"Hey, double-oh-seven, I'm not the one who likes to play secret agent in broad daylight. Last time I looked it wasn't your ass in the sling." He glanced down at his own costume. "I sorta like the epaulets, though, don't you?"

Their joust was not uncommon, both men considering themselves the superior of the other. Larsen frequently hired McQuarrie for wet work, assignments that never showed on paper and paid for with money that was never missed. Such as the murder of a certain publisher and a rogue literary agent on the streets of New York. And the ensuing cleanup of loose ends.

All but one. The writer had gotten away.

"How did this happen?" asked Larsen. He was covering his mouth, ever conscious of the possibility of surveillance.

McQuarrie grinned, delighting in Larsen's anxiety. "You said do the publisher first, I did him first. Got lucky, hit the agent with the same rock. You said make sure the manuscript is secure, that's what happened. When we got to the hotel to arrange a little cardiac event for our writer friend, the mark was gone. I have to assume he went back to California."

"This is a problem," said Larsen.

"This is your problem," said McQuarrie.

"You're going to California. To finish it."

"I may have a few days off before the next coup d'état."

"The risk factor has become exponential."

"I'll think of something. And it'll cost you."

Now it was McQuarrie who looked around, checking the perimeter more out of habit than need.

"Give me a number," said Larsen, wishing he'd eaten.

McQuarrie pursed his lips, his eyes scanning up toward the monument and the tourists that stood before it in apparent awe. Then, much to Larsen's frustration, McQuarrie smiled, his eyes fixed on the statue of Lincoln.

"What's so funny?"

"Someone's taking our picture."

Larsen was less than discreet as he turned and peered out from under his umbrella toward the monument. All he saw were people, hats and umbrellas and heads thrown back to read the inscription that encircled the roofline of the structure.

"Where?"

"See? You should leave this to us professionals."

"Where the hell is he?" Larsen's voice tense.

"She."

Larsen's head snapped sharply back toward McQuarrie. The smug smile was very much still in place.

"She's trying to look like a guy. Baseball cap, backpack, the whole Birkenstock thing. But it's a woman. Behind the column on the left."

Larsen saw nothing there, just the eastward-facing columns, twelve of thirty-six meant to represent the states of the union at the time of Lincoln's death.

McQuarrie moved closer. "Two million dollars."

When Larsen turned, all he saw was the back of a security guard's uniform, stolen and as yet unmissed from a vacationing employee's apartment. It would be returned to the closet from whence it came before dinner, no one the wiser.

Larsen would come up with the funds. Because he knew that if he did, the next time he saw McQuarrie, Gabriel Stone would be dead.

Which meant the Columbia Center project could proceed as planned.

Book Three

And when the third thunder sounded,
I saw a great king of the west fallen in a chariot of iron,
his bride attending him,
beheld by men of all nations and all times to come,
for there would be great debate.
Three years hence his brother would fall,
he who would be king in his brother's stead.
And threescore and six years on,
his only son,
cast down from the sky and swallowed by the sea.
And their names were stricken from the scrolls
by men of humble servitude,
who labor in the faith of the Lamb.

"WHISPER OF THE SEVENTH THUNDER"
by Gabriel Stone

Washington, D.C.

SIMON WINGER, PERHAPS the richest low-profile player in the world, couldn't remember the last time he'd slept through the night. Which was why he wasn't upset when his mobile phone rang just after one o'clock in the morning.

He answered on the first ring, a habit from years of sleeping with a woman who was less than patient with his business. His wife had been dead for fourteen years now, but still, long after he'd let the business go and given his life to God, she remained in his heart.

"You should be sleeping," said Uriah Gerson.

"I *was* sleeping. I dreamed the phone rang."

The two men went back over forty years. Together they had engineered the deaths of seventeen people, all at the behest of the secret scrolls of John the Divine. Uriah had been keeping Simon abreast of their progress in decoding the book of Revelation, which suddenly promised to change everything.

"Mordecai ran a new grid," said Uriah, his voice unusually animated. "One with greatly expanded spacing parameters. Revelation, it seems, is trying to tell us something."

"Praise God," said Simon, his stomach suddenly tight.

"There were three hits. Mordecai says they're the most complex patterns we've seen yet. The first appears to be a verse from the Old Testament, specifically the Torah."

Simon sat up on one elbow. He smiled to himself, realizing how this must rub Uriah the wrong way. Over the years Simon's unyielding Christianity had been at odds with Uriah's Jewish heritage. Cats and dogs playing together, they liked to call it.

"Old, new, it seems the lines are blurring. Exodus twenty-eight, verse sixteen. Do you know it?"

"I will in a moment."

Simon kept a copy of the New American Standard Bible on his nightstand, from which he read every night and again every morning upon rising. He had come to prefer the American take on the translation, the nuance of which allowed him to fill in his own blanks when necessary. It was signed by Billy Graham, a gift in gratitude for Simon's financial support and friendship. With the phone awkwardly wedged between his ear and his shoulder—he dearly missed the old days and their simpler tools, and was resentful of his peers who read their scripture from an iPad—Simon now flipped to the second book in the Old Testament.

He read the verse aloud: *"It shall be square and folded double; a span shall be the length thereof, a span in length and a span in width."*

"The breastplate of Aaron," said Uriah, who was a world-renowned Old Testament scholar. The verse offered instructions for the creation of an elaborate breastplate to be worn by Aaron, the brother of Moses and his chosen spokesperson, to memorialize the children of Israel as he bore witness before the Lord. At first blush there was no obvious connection to anything remotely apocalyptic, or to the dark work Simon and Uriah shared.

"Thoughts?" asked Simon.

"Very few. But Mordecai says the code's array with the grid is most interesting. It appears in simple linear form several times, the first four of which formed the shape of a perfect square."

"The *first* four?"

"When Mordecai ran the analysis again, he found the identical sequence appearing twelve times, all connected. A perfect cubical array."

Simon stared at the open Bible before him, as if it might speak the answer.

"What could it mean?" he asked.

"We have been given a key."

"Ah, but to what?"

A moment of silence ensued. As Simon listened to pages being turned from across an ocean, he visualized Uriah sitting before an open Bible with a perplexed expression.

It was Simon who broke the silence. "You said there were three hits."

"Indeed. The last two are remarkable for their proximity to the scripture beneath which they were coded. Revelation ten, verse four."

"The seven thunders." Both men knew Simon had one up on Uriah where the New Testament was concerned.

"There was a familiar phrase, and what we must assume is a name. The phrase was *thy will be done.*"

"A verifier," said Simon. "Telling us to pay attention."

"Then I suggest we do just that."

"And the name?"

"No one I've heard of. It seems, however, that he's on a CIA watchlist. We must be certain, Simon, that this is not an extension of the scrolls themselves. We must act with care."

Simon knew precisely what Uriah meant. They were in the business of extracting names from the ancient scrolls and discovering what those names meant in the grand scheme of global destiny.

And, when they were certain, doing what was necessary to make the name go away.

"Tell me who it is," said Simon. "I'll vet it from this end."

He again heard the rustling of paper, as if Uriah was checking his notes.

"The name is Gabriel Stone."

Simon was already writing it down. Within hours he would know everything about him.

"I'll get back to you."

"Mordecai is going deeper. I have faith there is much more to learn from the code. Until then, my friend."

"God be with you," said Simon, already formulating a plan.

"And with you," said Uriah.

The line went dead.

Washington, D.C.

THEY WERE SHOOTING hoops for Jesus. Rebounding for redemption, driving the lane for love.

The game was called Bump. But to the ten devotees gathered in the driveway court alongside the colonial mansion that housed The Brethren, it was not so much a game as a demonstration of will, the warrior heart to fight for Christ. This wasn't your classic game of H-O-R-S-E, this was a full-contact, no-whining metaphor for life. There were rules, and there weren't rules—one's willingness to bend them to achieve an objective was part of the metaphor. Like some bizarre Mark Burnett–produced reality series, the players were gradually eliminated as their shots were blocked by any means possible, one by one, sometimes with blood and profanity smeared across their lips, but always with grace and a contrived humility.

Brother Simon, as he was known here, watched from the safety of the back porch, a glass of iced tea in his hands, thankful the game wasn't around in his day. His age was enough to mask the athlete he once was, not to mention the handsome socialite he could have become had he chosen another road.

Or had that road not chosen him.

When it was over—Brother Daniel emerged victorious—the men huddled arm-over-arm in the driveway as they prayed in the rain, thanking Jesus for Bump and the lessons it imparted.

During the prayer Simon saw Larsen's head rise to look at him. He issued a subtle nod, meaning they had to talk.

Moments later they were alone on the street, walking.

"Very impressive," said Simon, looking at Larsen's soaked t-shirt, where a few drops of blood were visible. "You do enjoy pounding on the younger bucks."

"It shows?"

Simon's face suddenly changed. "I have a name."

This was nothing new. It was, in fact, how all these conversations started. Simon communicated with someone in Israel, yielding a name extracted from the secret scrolls. Invariably it was a name soon destined to headline an obituary somewhere.

This was the will of God. These men were God's sword in the war with darkness. When the one true name appeared, the foretold Beast of Armageddon, God would intervene to stop them.

Simon, at least, believed this with every fiber of his being.

"Context?" asked Larsen. This, too, was a standard question. Regardless of how vague or how familiar the name, Larsen had the means to find anyone on the planet, and quickly.

"This is different," said Simon.

Larsen waited. Winger was a man who measured his words.

"The name is not from the parchment. It was derived from a New Testament code."

"Explain."

A car passed. It was a Brother, perhaps a congressman, heading for the mansion at the end of the cul-de-sac behind them. They exchanged waves and brief smiles, then walked a few more steps.

"This man is not a target. At least not yet. He is not to be harmed. He is to be *understood*."

Simon produced a scrap of paper, which he held out. Larsen took it, looked down. The name written there gave him a chill.

Gabriel Stone.

Heat suddenly assaulted his cheeks, his pulse accelerating. He resumed walking, hoping Simon wouldn't notice.

Larsen knew the name. He had already found him. By his own order, Gabriel Stone would be dead by this time tomorrow.

THE MAN HIS peers knew only as McQuarrie stood next to his wife in the rain. They were in the parking lot of a small airport on the outskirts of Washington, a scene they had repeated many times over the past few years. Her name was Joan, and as usual, she didn't want him to leave.

For the six years of their marriage Joan McQuarrie believed her husband was a self-employed business consultant serving the upper crust of the pharmaceutical lobby. Over the years it had been easy for him to perpetuate his façade of legitimacy, occasionally cashing in favors to enlist shills and phony clients as required. He even took her on a business trip to Los Angeles, dropping her off for an afternoon of shopping on Rodeo Drive while he drove down to Long Beach to put two bullets into the back of the head of an enterprising lawyer who had been threatening to sue the wrong special interest group for the right reasons.

But that had been an emergency. Most of the time his contracts played like a theatrical performance, resulting in someone dropping dead of what appeared to be the most natural of causes.

McQuarrie never met a medical examiner he couldn't fool.

Now things were different. The people pulling the strings in this latest series of assignments had more on their minds than the cauterization of bleeding loose ends. They believed with the fervent passion of martyrs that they were, in fact, the very Sword of God itself. With the unexpected intrusion of this Gabriel Stone fellow into the script, McQuarrie sensed things were about to come apart.

He would disappear when this was over. It was time to retire. It was also time to tell his wife the truth.

Joan was twelve years younger, and at thirty she clung to the American dream that had eluded her immigrant parents. With Asian and Italian blood running in her veins, only two generations removed, she was a dark and lithe beauty whose confidence had always lagged behind her wholesome, Miss America looks. They had a nice house in Arlington, his and hers SUVs, they were well-liked at the Church of God, and for the past year she had been making noises about children.

McQuarrie had heard her, far more clearly than she knew.

"We need to talk," he said, speaking over the ambient roar of a leased Falcon 2000 that was already warming up on the ramp. The airfield was enveloped by a shroud of mist, illuminated by headlights and streetlamps. He took off his wire-rimmed glasses for a moment, looking at her with an alarming intensity.

Her face melted into an expression of concern. Very little that was good followed the words *we need to talk.*

"I want us to go off the pill."

McQuarrie sensed a sudden halt to his wife's breathing. Then her face exploded with joy as she threw her arms around him.

"Listen to me," he said, wiping a tear from her face as she backed away. "This is very important."

She nodded, once again a blank page of trust.

"I don't know how long I'll be gone this time."

The smile vanished. "You said a few days."

"I know what I said. But not everything I say is what it seems. I need you to trust me."

She just stared, the trust under test.

"I am very much the man you married. Except for one thing, everything you know about my past is true."

She knew he studied chemistry at Boston University, that he had gone to grad school in New York, and that he had worked in the research department of a major pharmaceutical firm in Pennsylvania. She knew he had been in the military for a while, and that he had worked for the government in various technical capacities before going solo as a consultant to various pharmaceutical lobbies.

And now he was telling her what she didn't know. That he had been a decorated Navy Seal after medical school, where he augmented his chemical acumen with an expertise in munitions and hand-to-hand confrontation that made him doubly effective in the field. His government experience had been as an operative with the CIA, where he had been involved with covert operations in places and in roles he knew she wouldn't fully understand, and to which the government would never own up.

He told her he still worked for them now, only as an independent contractor. He didn't elaborate.

"What I do is dangerous. What I do is *necessary.*"

She didn't nod this time. She just stared.

"This is the last one. I will come home to you, we will go away together and set up our lives away from the game. We will travel, have our child. And we will never have to work again.

"*If* you come home to me."

Now it was McQuarrie who nodded.

"A man may contact you," he said. "Name of Aimes. If that happens, do exactly as he says. Promise me."

After a moment she nodded warily.

"He may give you something."

She didn't move. Another tear appeared, which he wiped away gently.

"There are several accounts, all offshore. More than you know. There are things you'll have to do to protect yourself, and to access the money. Aimes will help you."

"I will do whatever is necessary," she said. Her husband, like many men of ambition and great success, had no idea of his wife's capacity to achieve a goal, however dark.

Monroe Aimes was McQuarrie's childhood friend and now his personal attorney. If McQuarrie didn't call in according to a prearranged schedule, Aimes was to assume he was dead. And a contingency plan would go into effect.

Joan suddenly buried her face in his shoulder. He held her for a moment, then continued.

"Listen to me. What you do from that point on is up to you. Take it to the FBI if you want, to the *New York Times,* the *Washington Post.* Hell, you can throw it away and move on. Your call. Revenge, justice, peace . . . you get to say."

She pulled away and looked at him. Revenge, too, was something of which she was more than capable.

"I have no idea what you're talking about," she said.

"You will."

She returned to his shoulder. "Don't go," she said. "Give the money back."

He smiled, then kissed the top of her head. Through it all she had remained his final hope, his connection to a world he had helped protect from evil.

"They don't accept refunds," he said quietly, wishing for the moment that things were different. "And neither do I."

She pulled back, a new strength in her eyes.

"The video I shot at the monument this morning," she said, "it has something to do with all this, doesn't it."

He had told her it was a practical joke on a coworker, which explained the ridiculous security guard uniform he had worn. It wasn't the first time he'd pulled an elaborate prank, and it wasn't the first time he'd had her secretly photograph his actions, so she didn't think to question his wishes.

And didn't think to credit her with an agenda of her own.

He smiled and touched her face. "That's my girl," he said, just before he kissed her good-bye.

- 25 -

Auburn, California

GABRIEL ARRIVED HOME to a house that seemed emptier than when he'd left. Before lunch he couldn't stand it anymore and placed a call to Kathryn, determined to express his disenchantment for the way it ended in New York. But there was no answer on her mobile, the only number he had.

Later, after summoning the courage to violate what he assumed to be industry decorum, he called the publisher's office. A chilly receptionist refused to forward him to anyone. She simply took his name while offering nothing in the way of explanation.

Something had obviously gone wrong. No one was calling him back. His mind reeled with the possibilities, the most likely of which was that he had blown his chance all to hell.

He tried the next day, again with no results.

So at the end of his second day back from New York, much of it spent staring alternately at the lake and his telephone, a cold beer and a burger at a local sports bar sounded like just the ticket.

Later that night, as he drifted off on the couch, nausea hit like a scud missile. The eleven-o'clock news was wrapping with a story about a group of legislators in Arizona proposing the state excuse itself from the union, and the possibility of a pandemic outbreak of swine flu. In spite of the news, Gabriel had felt just fine. Until now.

He certainly wasn't drunk after two beers. His money was on food poisoning. Or maybe the dreaded swine flu had arrived in central California.

After throwing up he collapsed fully clothed onto an unmade bed, not bothering with the covers. He was unconscious before Letterman finished his monologue.

Within minutes he was dreaming of fire.

PERHAPS THIS WAS hell. The thought actually occurred to Gabriel as he gagged for breath, his recent rejection of faith, such as it was, suddenly floating above him like a judgment. Smoke clouded his vision, burning his throat, tasting of ashes. When he tried to raise his head the room spun like a county fair ride, the picture rolling madly, the remote out of reach. The coughing made him retch, the heaving dry and painful. The heat was almost sensual in the way it wrapped him in the inevitable.

Somewhere in the smoke, a shadow stirred.

Walls flashed, strobes of orange, even through closed eyes. A dull roar filled his senses, the happy humming of Satan himself, strolling through a sea of fire.

This wasn't hell, because his eyes beheld an angel.

Lauren emerged from the flames, gracefully floating. Her face was a mask of dark intention, boring down, hair flowing as the boiling air around her stormed. Focus ebbed and swayed. She was there, then she was gone, dissolved into vapor.

And then she was holding him. He was elevating, rising into smoke, to wherever angels fled.

So many hands. Propping him up. Holding a mask to his face. Fitting his arm with a sheath. Penetrating him with a needle.

Gabriel's eyes fluttered. He could feel his cheeks burning, too close to the sun. And yet, a cool breeze was here, too, God given. Red lights flashed, piercing his brain.

And in the distance, his house was burning down.

Gabriel tried to emerge from a fog of incomprehension. Enough to realize he was lying in the street in front of his yard, that the pavement was wet and cold. That there were trucks, lots of them, lining the street, lights flashing, filling the night with questions. And that a crew of very serious emergency workers were tending to him, smothering him with oxygen, taking his blood pressure, shooting him full of hope.

"Lauren . . ."

One of the firemen shouted, "Get the ambulance, damnit!"

Someone answered, "Two minutes out."

"Where is she . . ." Gabriel tried again, this time drawing a look. It was clear they wanted him to remain calm.

"Were you alone in the house, sir?" asked one of them.

"Yes . . . no . . . where is she . . ."

"Where is *who,* sir? Was someone else in the house?"

A disembodied voice said, "He lives alone. Wife died a few months ago, poor bastard. Her name was Lauren."

Gabriel looked up to see his neighbor, a lawyer he'd never much cared for, talking to a fireman. When the man saw that Gabriel was watching him, he moved closer and said, "I got your back, buddy. Don't worry about all this, I'll take care of it."

Gabriel had no idea what he meant. The two had barely spoken in all the years he'd lived here.

They checked it all again, his pulse, his blood pressure, his ability to focus on a moving pen light. He could hear them talking, as if he were invisible, or perhaps dead. They marveled that he was here, that he'd made it out alive.

That the house was mostly gone.

As he tumbled back into the void, he heard someone say they had no idea how he made it out of there on his own.

Washington, D.C.

NO MATTER WHO summoned whom, Larsen always arrived first. It was he who did the summoning today, extricating Simon from a breakfast meeting with a senator. The senator was seeking an obscene amount of campaign money, which she would get in exchange for votes down the line that served the agenda of The Brethren, so she didn't mind the intrusion. Simon could have brought a hooker to breakfast and it would have been fine with her.

Besides, Simon hadn't really been listening all that closely. He had been doodling on his paper napkin, feigning interest, lost in another world. The pattern on the napkin was composed of dots, all of them arranged in a three-dimensional cube. Next to the cube he had written a name: *Mordecai.*

Larsen was waiting in the elbow of the Vietnam Memorial, shielded by the tallest part of the structure, lost in a terrible roster of names. The area was deserted, the tour buses not yet having arrived. A light mist was falling, creating an appropriately gloomy ambiance.

Larsen greeted Simon with his usual poker face, a man who took himself and his work very seriously. They rarely shook hands. Despite the intensity of their work and what resided at its heart, the two had never really connected as friends.

Which made it easier for Larsen to lie today. If he played this right, he might just get through unscathed.

"You found Gabriel Stone," said Simon. He wore the same London Fog he'd worn for years, ever the eccentric billionaire with no sense of style. Other than a housekeeper and an accounting firm, he didn't surround himself with sycophants and bodyguards, the fact of which added to his mythology. In their eleven years of working together, Larsen had never observed a trace of ego in the man.

Larsen held Simon's eyes. "You won't like it."

Simon simply nodded, a signal to continue.

"He lives in California, forty years old, recently widowed. Straight shooter, pays his taxes, no record of any kind, no visible political agenda. Recently unemployed, a loner."

This was all true. But Larsen had known these things for well over a week now.

"So we have nothing that explains his name in the code. Or why he's on your watchlist."

Larsen bit his lip. "Oh, we have plenty on both counts."

He withdrew a computer disk from his pocket, held it out.

"A little light reading," he said, his attention turning back to the black marble wall as Simon took the disk. The reflection made it easy to watch the perimeter and his companion with equal discretion.

"What is it?" asked Simon, looking at the disk as if there might be something to see.

Larsen visibly squirmed, a contrived look of concern.

"Gabriel Stone has written a novel. Big money deal, on a fast track for publication before the election. That timing is critical."

Simon felt the rate of his pulse suddenly spike. At the very heart of everything were words someone had written down.

"How did you acquire this?"

"We screen everything before it goes to print. Even submissions that don't make the cut. Looking for red flags, codes, anything remotely treasonous. Once in a while we find an idea we can use. I just ran the name on the database and the file popped back at me."

Larsen rarely talked this openly about his role in the Central Intelligence Agency and the access to classified information it afforded him. It was this very pedigree that drew Simon to the man in the first place. That, and his enthusiastic participation in The Brethren.

Simon pocketed the disk. "You've read this?"

Larsen nodded.

"Then perhaps you can tell me why Gabriel Stone's name was found in the code."

Larsen drew a deep breath, impressing upon his companion the weight of what he was about to reveal.

"The book is an apocalyptic thriller. A Revelation rip-off, complete with obligatory Middle East conflict and White House intrigue and a preponderance of floods and earthquakes. Guy wrote some pretty convincing armchair prophecy, passing it off as lost scripture. Specifically, Revelation ten, four."

Simon inhaled audibly. "The seventh thunder of Patmos." Then, in a whisper, he added, "Fascinating."

"Reads like a timetable," Larsen continued. "Bikini Island, Hiroshima, the '47 Israeli convention, all three of the Kennedy deaths, nine-eleven, it's all there. Plus some."

"What's the downside?"

"An assassination subplot."

The two men locked eyes.

"A bomb, targeting a presidential candidate."

Simon closed his eyes. "God help us."

"Oh, it gets worse. It goes off in a new hotel, planted a year earlier during construction. The whole thing was perpetrated by the President's men and made to look like a terrorist act. Like that DeMille book that drove us nuts. The President survives, of course, then goes on to find the terrorist sect behind it all, the members of which conveniently martyr themselves in the process. He then reveals himself as a New Age agnostic who is pulling strings from behind the scenes, and with the help of those close to him, denouncing God and leading the world into darkness. The story ends as the press is reporting the appearance of a man many believe to be the resurrected Jesus Christ."

Simon was shaking his head. He had never seen Daniel Larsen of the CIA quite this distraught.

"Please tell me he doesn't show up in Provo."

Larsen wasn't amused. At least he didn't have to lie to Simon about the book. All of what he'd reported was true.

"It gets worse. In Stone's book, in addition to working for the White House, the men behind the bombing belong to an ultra-right-wing, politically powerful pro-Christ organization. When the President shows his true colors, they jump ship, believing him to be the Antichrist, and that his wife is the false prophet. They join a sect of martyrs who try to bring them down. People who believe their instructions come from ancient scrolls kept secret by the Catholic Church."

Simon's eyes fluttered as he mumbled, "Jesus." Larsen wasn't sure if it was a prayer or an expletive.

Larsen cast a glance from side to side, an occupational habit. "We have to stop this. While we can."

Simon looked up with alarm. "What are you suggesting?"

"I'm suggesting this book is too close. It casts a dark light on the Brethren. People will start asking tough questions we won't want to answer. Not only that, it'll sideswipe the election."

Simon glared at his protégé. "This isn't about the election, Daniel."

"Not for you, it isn't. The president in the novel is an obvious personification of my present employer."

"What are you saying?"

"It would appear that someone's already trying to stop it."

Simon's eyes squinted with sudden urgency.

Larsen saw his opening and charged in. "Stone's agent and his publisher are dead. Murdered in what was supposed to look like a car hijacking. The book itself is gone, wiped from the publisher's system."

Simon's eyes were suspicious.

"It wasn't me, Simon, give me a break."

Simon nodded, but the expression remained. "Hypothesis?"

"Somehow the White House got wind of this, put a hitter on it before the thing gets legs."

Larsen watched Simon take this in. He felt his heart skip a beat, hoping it didn't show. He had hired McQuarrie to kill Stone and eliminate the manuscript. It was he who was protecting his President, and he was doing it on direct orders from people higher up the chain.

Simon chewed at his lip, processing what he'd learned. He finally said, "We must find this Gabriel Stone, protect him until we understand what this means."

Obvious disapproval crossed Larsen's face.

"I don't understand that position. Stone's book could kill us. I say we step back and let whoever else is nervous take care of this for us."

"Stone's name is in the code, Daniel. We have to honor that."

"The man may already be dead. We both believe in God's will. Let's see how it turns out before we risk everything we've worked to put in place."

This was the moment he'd been crafting. If things had gone right, if McQuarrie had completed his mission, then the story would tie itself into a nice little bow. Stone would be dead, the Columbia Center would soon be destroyed as planned, the President would be reelected, and, from Simon's perspective, someone who just might have been the Antichrist would be out of the picture. He'd given Simon the disk with Stone's manuscript in the hope that he'd realize just how dangerous it was.

But with or without his approval, Gabriel Stone was going down. If this wasn't God's will, it was certainly that of the reelection committee. The nice thing about working with Simon was that he believed *everything* was the will of God.

Simon closed his eyes, obviously praying. Larsen watched, sensing his objective was at hand.

"Nothing simple about this one," he offered.

Nearly a minute of silence passed. Larsen checked his watch and the perimeter with equal frequency, trying not to stare at the man who thought of himself as his mentor.

"This requires counsel," said Simon.

Larsen nodded. It wouldn't be the first time he had been subordinated to the illusive higher powers from whom Simon took his divine marching orders. If those powers had any sense of self-preservation at all, they'd see that the book had to be stopped and the author taken out. Larsen was relying on it.

"Of course. Just say the word, it's done."

Simon was backing away, realizing he had to go to Israel to apprise Uriah of the situation. Tonight.

"As soon as The Word speaks to me, I will let you know."

By then, thought Larsen, with any luck the decision on Gabriel Stone's fate would be well out of Simon Winger's hands.

Haifa, Israel

URIAH'S APARTMENT COMPLEX was on a bluff overlooking the quiet Technion campus, the lights of the ancient city of Haifa visible in the valley, the dome of the local mosque dominating the skyline. Gerson's seemingly ageless wife, Evelyn, had excused herself after sharing the meal she had prepared, leaving them to wine and private conversation. "My angel" was how Uriah referred to her. Simon believed it an apt moniker.

Simon waited until she was out of the room to begin.

"Your young protégé Mordecai appears to be somewhat of a genius," said Simon. "Like his mentor, only better looking."

"He thinks you are insane." Uriah shot back, his face stoic. "And I must concur. But at least he humors you."

"My model will work. It is of God."

Uriah nodded with a smirk. *A square upon a square . . .* he should have seen it himself.

At that moment the sun disappeared over the harbor's horizon, casting a pinkish glow. The magic hour, God's pastel pallet.

"So many have died," said Uriah, his voice weary.

"Perspective," replied Simon. "It is our sanity."

They sipped their wine simultaneously.

"And now," said Uriah, "you believe it to be over."

"What do the scrolls say?"

"I have found nothing beyond the final name."

The final name. Not Gabriel Stone—that was another issue altogether—but a name culled from the secret scrolls of John. A man they would manipulate into being at the Columbia Center at the precise moment of truth. And because it was the final name offered in the scrolls, both men believed their work was done.

That man's name was Armand Brenner.

"Tell me about this *novel*," said Uriah, who had been waiting to ask this all day. The last word was spoken with distaste.

Uriah's tone made Simon nervous. Like many old men, Uriah was irrevocably set in his ways.

"The book reveals the seven thunders that were shown to John on Patmos. A fiction, granted. But a dangerous one."

"These visions were meant to be sealed."

"So it is written. The question is, sealed until *when?*"

Uriah shot his friend a look. "Are you suggesting that *now* is the time of their revelation to us? Through this book?"

Simon recognized the challenge.

"Gabriel Stone's name is in the code, Uriah, next to the words *thy will be done.* This cannot be discounted."

"Just as all who would become the Beast are named in the scrolls. Perhaps this Stone fellow should be vanquished, too."

Once again it was old versus new, Torah versus Jesus.

"*This* is different."

"Is it? God's angel on Patmos commanded the visions be kept secret. To violate that command is blasphemy."

Simon sipped his wine, praying for patience.

"The visions Stone describes are obvious signs of the end of days. Monday-morning quarterbacking, I'll grant you, things we know, events we have witnessed. But the seventh thunder, as Stone had reinvented it . . . that is most disturbing."

Simon had read Gabriel Stone's novel on his laptop during the flight over. The theology was flawed, the politics dangerous, but he found the outrageous gall of the story quite compelling. Especially the seventh thunder, which sent shivers down his spine for its parallel to the present reality.

"So you say," said Uriah, also striving for patience.

"He writes of a plot to assassinate a presidential candidate." His voice lowered. "A bomb, Uriah, planted in a hotel."

Simon watched to see if the professor had a reaction. He didn't, other than the words "Disturbing, I'll grant you."

Simon went on to explain other parallels in the book. When he was done they locked eyes, acknowledging the risk.

Uriah's face tightened. "Who is this man?"

"That is the question we must answer. For now, he is the name in the Bible code hidden behind the Book of Revelation. And because of that, he is part of it. Whether *he* even knows it or not. His book cannot be coincidence."

"Coincidence," said Uriah, "does not exist."

"We must look at this carefully," said Simon. "And we must act with the greatest of deliberation."

He would tell Uriah about the death of the literary agent and the editor some other time. The old professor had enough on his mind; better not to burden him with the politics behind the emerging conspiracy. Perhaps, as Larsen had suggested, it was already out of their hands.

Uriah leaned back and regarded the sky, as if the truth was written there. "Hear me, Simon. If this Gabriel Stone has written a book that interferes with prophecy, or worse, if it interferes with what we have set into motion, then he must be dealt with. Conclusively."

The specifics of *dealt with* required no elaboration.

And because in their world there were no coincidences, it was precisely then that Uriah's mobile phone began to ring.

Mordecai was ready.

Auburn, California

THE TWO OLDER men flanked Mordecai at either shoulder as he sat before his keyboard in the darkened lab, a large plasma-screen monitor in front of him. A graphic model of the Hebrew character matrix he had created was displayed in several colors, spinning in a silent, three-dimensional ballet.

"The one real challenge to your model is the vectoring. It's a bitch, if you'll pardon my American slang."

"Vectoring?" asked Simon.

"The direction of the coded word within the grid. It can spell itself out going backwards, up, down . . . and with the addition of a third dimension, in an infinite number of directions within a spherical array. It's theoretically possible to even have arcing traces, or those that follow geometric shapes, such as the letter *S*. The possibilities are nothing short of infinite, requiring infinitely powerful technology."

"Quite appropriate," said Simon softly.

All three men stared at the screen. They needed a moment for the sheer magnitude of the task before them to sink in.

Uriah said, "The chase, Mordecai. Let us cut to it."

The young programmer smiled as he keyed in instructions. The image on the plasma blinked away, replaced moments later by a screen too dense with text to understand at a glance.

"I almost missed it," said Mordecai. "Normally the codes appear as discrete formations, usually in different arrays. These formations are linear, like sentences without a period. You have to stare at it awhile. When you do, you recognize two linear vectors, intersecting symmetrically."

"Mordecai . . ."

Uriah's tone was harsh, but he stopped short when Simon placed a hand on his shoulder.

"There are five formations here. Each with the same ELS, with no separation between them on their respective vectors."

He looked directly at Simon now.

"And they are only visible within your expanded cubical model. You are to be congratulated."

It should be doubled into a square; a span shall be its length, and a span shall be its width . . .

Simon nodded his own subtle thanks. As he did, he felt something twist deep in his stomach.

"You'll love this part. The ELS on these hits is quite interesting. There are precisely six hundred and sixty-six spaces between each letter in this sample."

Mordecai let this sink in before continuing.

"One vector reads horizontally, the other vertically. And get this—the point of intersection of the vectors is at the precise geometric-center point of the matrix."

He paused, his face flush with adrenaline.

"Gentlemen, this array was *designed*."

Simon and Uriah exchanged another look. Whatever was happening in Simon's stomach was accelerating its pace.

Uriah said, "Tell us the words, Mordecai."

Mordecai swallowed hard, closed his eyes for a moment, as if remembering the sequence of keystrokes. Then he turned and entered the instructions.

"On the vertical, and taking the liberty to add the appropriate spaces between words, the first formation reads, *gabriel stone*. Directly beneath it are the words *seven thunders book*. And beneath that, still descending on the vertical, are the words *behold the hand of god*."

Simon heard Uriah inhale audibly, holding it in frozen contemplation. As he watched his friend, he felt a trickle of ice descending along his spine.

"And the horizontal?" asked Simon.

Mordecai delivered his answer with a tiny smile.

"The first is what appears to be a date—*tenth month, eighth day* and then the word *columbia*. After that are once again the words *thy will be done.*"

Now it was Simon's breath that froze.

"What is it?" asked Uriah, seeing Simon's body tense.

"October the eighth," said Simon, as if to himself, "is the date of the National Prayer Luncheon."

"At the Columbia Center Hotel," whispered Uriah.

Simon muttered the words "My God."

Mordecai honored the silence that followed, while the two older men stared solemnly at the words on the screen.

"There's one other thing," he finally said, his voice barely audible, like someone interrupting a prayer.

"The vector array has a definite shape. Not only is the intersection of the vectors at the precise center-point of the matrix, it appears as a recognizable geometric grid. One we see every day."

"What is it?" asked Uriah, more breath than voice.

Simon already had his eyes closed in prayer.

"A cross," said Mordecai. "The vectors which contain these coded messages form a perfect cross."

SIMON FLEW ALL night, which was his preference on his trips to Israel. The Gulfstream was outfitted with a queen-sized bed, and he found the monotony of the engines comforting. That and a handful of Valerian root was all he required.

On this particular flight, however, he had stirred. His mind was squaring off with a question that had no apparent answer, one with stakes that gave no quarter. The code was clearly revealing that the Columbia Center bombing was part of the prophecy, that it was to be God's catalyst in lighting the apocalyptic fuse. On that count, then, they were on solid ground. But the role of Gabriel Stone and his book was less clear.

The book would seem to be a threat, since for all intents and purposes it exposed the whole thing to the world. Which, in a logical turn, meant it should be stopped, as Daniel was suggesting. Then again, why, and in what way, was the author's name positioned as part of it? What could *behold the hand of God* mean here? Was it a warning about the book, or was it telling them to leave it alone?

Faith told him to leave Gabriel Stone and his book to God, to let destiny unfold. The real question, then, was this: what was his own role in the unfolding of this prophecy?

Was he supposed to figure this out now, alone and with no further help from the code?

He prayed, but on this night nothing spoke back to him.

Which was why, in the morning hours after his arrival home, and as he finally drifted to sleep in the brownstone that no one in this upscale Georgetown neighborhood full of millionaires suspected was occupied by a *billionaire*, he was alarmed to hear someone ringing his doorbell.

THE CHIME SOUNDED three more times before Simon finally reached the door. He wore a royal blue bathrobe better suited to a boxer than a gentleman of leisure.

He leaned down and squinted into the peephole.

His visitor was a woman, about the age of the daughter he never had. Tall, quite lean, and stylishly dressed in a beige suit, nicely cut. His first guess was that she was a congressional aide or a White House courier, come to deliver something for his eyes only, most likely a request for a contribution. This happened frequently, but usually at the mansion where The Brethren held court. But other than a purse she had no packages.

He opened the door, sensing something strange about the moment.

Her eyes were from a Botticelli painting, unflinching, a muted blue. She smiled like she knew something that was about to make him happy. Or, if she were evil, as though she knew his fate.

Such beauty could deliver either outcome.

"May I help you?" He conjured his own smile, but his mind was too full of questions to allow it to be convincing.

"No," she said. "But I believe I can help you."

The woman was in no hurry to continue, content to size him up, allowing him to do the same.

"Do I know you?" he asked. He had the sudden feeling he did, or at least that he had seen her before. There was a strange sense of comfort to be found in just looking at her.

"No," she said, the smile dissolving.

A jolt of adrenaline fired through Simon's veins as she moved for her purse. He had no way of defending himself, and doubted that he could get the door closed if such action was required. Many times his associates had begged him to hire a houseboy or even a bodyguard, but Simon valued his privacy and was content to let God protect him.

She took a photograph out of her purse and handed it over. The face of a young man with bright red hair and glasses stared back at him, a shot taken candidly at a restaurant or bar.

"Do you know this man?" she asked.

He stared. It was familiar, but that was all.

"I'm not sure," he said, handing it back. He could feel her eyes burning into him.

She returned the photo to her purse without offering further explanation.

"What is this about?" he asked.

She studied him a moment, her eyes empathetic, as if she sensed his confusion.

"You are Simon Winger," she proclaimed.

He nodded slowly, realizing that something akin to fear was making the hair on his arms stand on end. But it was not fear, more like an awareness of an impending crossroads. Perhaps what John the Divine felt that day on Patmos, peering two thousand years into the future of mankind.

"Your mother was a nurse before she married your father at the age of twenty-two. She died giving birth to your only brother, who was killed by a land mine in the Korean War. Your father inherited a meat-processing company before he was thirty, in the year you were born, in fact, which he parlayed into one of the largest food-distribution conglomerates in the nation. He died of stomach cancer before his fortieth birthday. You finished school living with an aunt, who unsuccessfully contested the estate that put the whole thing into your name when you turned twenty-five. You ran the show for ten years, then sold out to a private syndicate, taking stock options that over the next ten years multiplied sixfold. You got into the high-tech sector early, invested a lot of venture capital in companies destined to go public before turning the whole thing over to a money manager when you reached fifty, and they've done rather well for you. In fact, you've survived the recession of the past few years rather nicely, divesting your real estate and going liquid in the stock market with what some might call exquisite timing. Through all this you've worked as a philanthropist, one of the most sought-after lunches in town. Yet only a privileged few know of your true wealth, which you take great pains to conceal."

She stopped, as if to gauge his reaction. His jaw gaped slightly, but other than that he hadn't moved.

"And, of course, you love and serve the Lord Jesus Christ. You consecrate that love through your affiliation with the group that some call The Brethren, in addition to other alliances which are less known."

Something unspoken passed between them.

"Who are you?" he asked again, his voice suddenly weak. A wave of urgent fatigue flooded into his limbs.

Her smile was gentle. "A friend."

"I don't have friends," he said.

"That's quite sad."

"Something I've chosen. Necessary to my work."

She nodded, as if she knew what he meant. Even though there was no way that she possibly could.

He waited for her to speak, but she just smiled. She was beautiful, her face innocent yet wise, her eyes deep yet warm.

"Why are you here?" he asked. "Please. I'm not feeling well."

"To give you what you want," she said.

He squinted. "Why?"

"I think you know," she said. She just smiled, as if there was more to tell.

"No," he said, his voice barely audible. "I really don't."

It was impossible to look away from her. His attraction was not remotely sexual, not even in an innocent sense of fatherly admiration. It was deeper than that, as if he were regarding something holy. Or something unthinkably evil.

He desperately needed to lie down.

"Matthew six, verse six," she said.

Although he knew the verse, his mind was suddenly, and strangely, blank.

The young woman then said something to him. She simply uttered it, without qualifiers or context. After a moment he realized it was the name of a hospital and a town.

As she did she reached out and touched his wrist, her skin warm, her eyes steady on his.

"What is your name?"

"My name is Sarah," she said, withdrawing her hand.

Then she turned and walked away, into the late-morning sun, which suddenly blinded him in a way he knew he would never understand.

SIMON WINGER WENT into his den and, upon reaching his desk, quickly jotted down the name of the hospital. Then he picked up his beloved Bible, already lying open, flipping to the ook of Matthew, chapter six, verse six.

And read aloud.

But you, when you pray, go into your inner room, close your door and pray to your Father who is in secret; and your Father who sees what is done in secret will reward you.

He felt the touch of something on his skin, sending tiny rivers of ice to the very marrow of his bones.

He had just been rewarded with the whereabouts of Gabriel Stone.

Washington, D.C.

THE BROTHERS WERE praying, standing in their traditional circle, arms linked in a chain of Christ's love. That evening there was a contingent of West Coast Christian business leaders coming for dinner, with the brothers serving as waiters and hosts. This would be followed by a discussion of global politics led by Franklin Moss, friend of presidents and kings, whose father had founded the organization.

Simon stood to the side, though he prayed with them in spirit. Only today his eyes were open, watching Daniel Larsen, who stood among the younger men. Larsen was leading the prayer today, asking God for the courage to fight for Christ in arenas where the battle seemed lost, for the courage to confront evil in all its forms.

The guy was good. In eleven years, Simon had never observed a crack in the man's icy facade.

Brother Daniel opened his eyes without breaking the rhythm of his sentence. He saw that Simon was motioning with his eyes to join him outside.

A few minutes after the prayer concluded and Franklin Moss had begun to talk, Brother Daniel slipped quietly from the room.

The air was chilly as they walked, an early fall having arrived in Washington. Both men were dressed casually, as if ready for an assault on the first tee.

Simon began by briefing Larsen in detail about the trip to Israel, though as usual the location was not disclosed, nor were the players. Larsen listened quietly, offering nothing in response until he sensed that Simon was done.

"You didn't call me out here to discuss Bible codes and software upgrades."

Simon drew a deep breath, summoning the patience that enabled him to endure his deadly efficient associate.

"I need your reassurance that you can pull the plug on Columbia, and quickly," said Simon. "On a moment's notice. Right up to the very instant, if necessary."

Larsen didn't respond right away. These were the words he'd hoped he'd never hear from Simon Winger, and though he appeared to be thinking about the question, he was in fact trying to calm his nerves.

"It's not like you to seek reassurance," he finally said. "Especially from me."

"We've never had stakes this high. And we have only a short while. It may go right down to the wire simply to understand what the codes are telling us."

"Too much is in play to suddenly doubt the source."

"Christ battled doubt, even on the cross."

"Jesus Christ wasn't planning to blow up a building."

Simon winced, as if hearing it put this way somehow diminished its place in the divine order of things.

"Nor was his fate reversible," Simon shot back. "Ours is. We have always labored within a belief that we would one day be stopped, the prophecy fulfilled. That we would step aside so the true Antichrist might come to power, according to God's will."

"And you believe the time has come? Please."

"I have no choice but to consider the possibility. As do you. The hotel is named in the code. Whether it is meant to be destroyed, or to be saved, is unclear."

Larsen was glad that Simon could not see his grimace. Debating faith with Simon Winger, or anyone within The Brethren for that matter, was a waste of energy. To believe in Christ, as they did, was to be *right*.

"The device has an abort protocol. Once engaged, the thing is about as dangerous as a microwave oven. The abort is nonretractable, so you must be certain."

"And what if your field operative is dead?"

"That contingency has been covered."

"And what if *you* are dead, Brother Daniel?"

"Is that what you found in your coded message from God? Tell me now, I have unused vacation time."

"Humor me," said Simon, his patience wearing thin.

Larsen drew a calculated breath. "If I'm dead, then it is you who will make that call. A mechanism is in place for that. Dare I say, one of us had best stay healthy."

"God willing," said Simon. Both men knew his words were intended as more than a trite colloquialism.

BACK INSIDE THE mansion, Daniel Larsen went to the deserted top floor and locked himself into a bathroom. He withdrew his mobile phone, punched in a number, then a code. He paced as he waited for his voice mail to respond.

Nothing. He was hoping for a message from McQuarrie, confirming that the deed had been finished. That Gabriel Stone was dead, and that the Columbia Center plan could proceed.

McQuarrie always called, always confirmed.

But not today.

Which meant that Gabriel Stone was still alive. It was as if God himself were protecting him.

Book Four

*A*nd when the fourth thunder sounded,
I beheld the summer moon,
and upon it were the footsteps of man.
Know then, the days of tribulation are nigh,
and false prophets will seduce many,
though only those who follow He who created all
will rise in glory unto heaven.

"WHISPER OF THE SEVENTH THUNDER"
by Gabriel Stone

- 3 1 -

THEY GAVE HIM drugs he did not want to force him into sleep he did not need. In the brief moments he was awake they took his blood pressure and temperature with a deft, robotic efficiency.

He had not been burned and he had not inhaled an intolerable quantity of toxic fumes. They'd moved him from the ER to ICU—all of his personal and insurance data had been retrieved from his wallet, which survived the fire thanks to the fortunate fact that he had fallen asleep in his clothes—and then six hours later to a regular room with less enthusiastic care and a better television.

No one was buying his story, that someone had dragged him out of his burning house and left him on the front lawn for the ambulance to find. A fire investigator had been the only visitor allowed—several concerned neighbors had been turned away—and while the man seemed satisfied with his responses, he seemed more concerned with Gabriel's visit to a local bar that evening, the details of which were hazy at best.

Observation, they called it. Making sure his brain had emerged from the flames unscathed. And until he told them what they wanted to hear, it seemed he was going nowhere. There was no day, no night, only an endless series of vital-signs tests and pale smiles.

Mostly, there was sleep. And a distant awareness of his own mortality.

HE HEARD THE voice, waking him from darkness. A cool touch connected him to a world that was all too real. He perceived a scent, fresh and light, reminding him that he was a lucky man, very much alive.

He opened his eyes. A young nurse he'd not seen before smiled down on him, her hand resting on his forehead.

"Mr. Stone, you get to go home now."

He noticed that the IV lines had already been disconnected from his arm, and that his street clothes were waiting for him on the chair.

"Home?" he asked, suddenly cognizant enough to wonder what this meant.

The nurse stepped back to pull the sheets away, urging his legs over the side of the bed.

"You're being released," she said, picking up his chart now.

"Something I said?"

"Friends in high places, from what I hear. There's a car waiting for you out front."

"Who's in it?"

"I wouldn't know. I assumed you would."

As he dressed—the scent of fire wafted from his shirt—he could feel an emerging clarity of thought, like a dizzy spell winding down, and he was suddenly giddy at the realization that this chapter of the nightmare was about to conclude.

In his pocket Gabriel found a business card from his neighbor the lawyer. He had no idea how it got there.

He was looking forward to seeing who was in the car.

GABRIEL DIDN'T NOTICE a slight man with wire-rimmed glasses sitting in the ER lobby as he was wheeled through, the face partially hidden behind a newspaper.

That man, in turn, didn't notice a lovely young woman with long blond hair sitting across the room, facing the window as she read a paperback. She didn't appear to look up when Gabriel was wheeled through, nor when the slight man got up and left moments later.

But she was watching, using the glass in front of her as a mirror.

THE CAR WAS actually a luxury SUV, the back door open and waiting. Standing next to it was a trim young man Gabriel had never met, dressed more like a caddy than a hired driver. The fellow offered a smile and a hand-shake, then nodded an acknowledgment to the young nurse as she helped Gabriel to his feet.

It was mid-evening, the sun just now surrendering to shadows. A strange time for a hospital to release a patient.

"I will never dis my insurance company again," said Gabriel, taking a moment to steady himself as the driver held the door open. "By the way, who are you?"

The man leaned close, barely moving his lips.

"A friend. Get in, Mr. Stone." His expression was reassuring. "That's not a threat. More like a lifeline."

Gabriel peered inside. An older man with thinning hair sat in the front seat, looking straight ahead, speaking quietly into a mobile phone.

The man with the wire-rimmed glasses turned right out of the sliding glass ER door, walking behind the SUV that was waiting under the portico, his head turned to avoid eye contact.

He had to run the final steps when he saw the Escalade pulling away, the heads of three occupants visible as silhouettes. He snatched his phone from his pocket and deftly clicked a photo. Maybe Larsen's techies could do some-thing with it, see who it was that was bailing Stone out.

He froze as he yanked open the door to his rental car. All four of his tires had been rendered flat. Short of hot-wiring the car in the next stall—not a good idea with the hospital security vehicle less than a hundred yards away—he was done for the day.

This was a new wrinkle, indeed. Or it was a just a bad break in a business skeptical of coincidence. Someone was onto him. First his mark survives the fire, then this.

The mission had been compromised. He would have only one more shot, and it would have to happen soon.

He would kill Gabriel Stone himself, face-to-face.

- 32 -

Auburn, California

THE STRANGER IN the front seat half-turned and smiled at Gabriel, the phone still at his ear as he held a finger aloft to indicate he would be just a moment. He was nonthreatening in a fatherly sort of way, wearing a mauve sweater and smelling of cologne. His hair was a wispy gray, and what there was of it was meticulously combed.

As he clicked off the line, he pivoted and extended a hand over the seat. "Gabriel Stone. A pleasure, sir."

"I take it you're not my insurance agent," said Gabriel.

"My name is Simon Winger," said the man. "This is Brian."

The driver nodded without averting his eyes from the road as the SUV headed out of the lot.

"Does this come with a side order of explanation, too?"

The older man cracked a knowing grin, as if he'd heard and seen it all.

"Indeed it does. Normally in a situation like this I would preface it with a plea to open your mind and try to believe what I'm about to tell you. But after what has happened to you, I imagine your mind is about as open as it can be."

Now it was Gabriel who nodded solemnly.

"Ever heard of Salman Rushdie?" asked Winger.

"Of course. The writer."

"Then you know what happened to him. He wrote a book that ruffled the wrong religious feathers, and a death threat was put on his head. A *fatwa*, they called it."

"They never got him, if I recall. He's still out there writing books nobody reads."

"Know what happened to the book they *did* read? *The Satanic Verses*?"

Gabriel shook his head. The book hadn't exactly been at the top of his must-read list.

"Through the roof. Were it not for the death threat, chances are *no one* would have read it. That's just an opinion."

Gabriel nodded again, realizing he was more nervous about this than he thought. From the way Winger was staring, it was obvious.

"There are some—not many, but some—who believe the death threat was a *strategy*. A contrivance, hatched in the publisher's marketing department and leaked to the press with all the stealth of an election rumor."

They turned onto I-80, heading east.

"I don't think I like where you're going with this."

"Dead writers sell. Especially when their books strike a timely chord with great controversy. They sell even better when their death occurs under suspicious circumstances."

Gabriel stared at Winger as if it were he who was threatening his life.

"Who are you?"

Winger and the driver shot each other a quick glance.

"A fan," said Winger. "Of your book."

"You're in publishing?"

"You could say that. I have an interest in one of the oldest houses in the business."

Winger told him which publisher it was. Gabriel had heard the name. He'd known of it since grade school, where it appeared on many of his textbooks over the years. Their fiction department was even bigger than their scholastic division, with some of the biggest author names in the business on their list.

"I have a publisher," said Gabriel. "At least I think I do."

There was a quick meeting of the eyes between the two men in the front seat.

"I'm afraid you don't," said Winger. "Wyatt Veerman is dead. As is your agent."

Gabriel stared ahead, an entire semester of human biology conducting a sudden lab experiment inside him.

"You obviously didn't know."

Gabriel just shook his head slowly, eyes fixed, remembering the meeting in which Veerman had tried to retitle the book.

Winger and the driver exchanged yet another glance, as if they'd anticipated his reaction. A game was in play, though the dimensions of the field remained a mystery.

"I'm sorry," said Winger, "this is happening very fast. Listen to me. Nothing that has occurred has been an accident. Not to them, not to you. Certain forces are determined to block the publication of your book, and as you can see they will stop at nothing to accomplish that objective."

"Wait," said Gabriel, holding up a hand. "Are you saying my house burning down was no accident?"

"I believe that is the case, yes."

"Are you with the federal government?"

"I'm just a guy who is trying to protect your book. And you."

"And I'm just a guy who wants to take this straight to the authorities. In fact, I'd appreciate it if you'd pull over."

Brian didn't seem to hear or care.

"We have a lot to discuss before you go that route."

"Really? Excuse me, you're saying someone tried to kill me? End of discussion."

"I'm also saying I'm here to help you. If you'll just slow down, hear what I have to say."

The two men sparred with their eyes for a moment. Gabriel could sense nothing in Simon Winger's countenance that seemed remotely threatening. Indeed, the man was positively fatherly.

"At this point one has to ask," Gabriel said, "why? What's in this for you?"

Winger's face changed, summoning patience.

"Let's just say I believe your book is an important contribution to the literature of the times. And not for political reasons, if that's where you're headed."

"Spiritual reasons, then."

Winger nodded, his mind already having moved on.

"I believe the people behind this were intending to eliminate you before the publication date, make it look like the work of a Muslim extremist group. With the publicity already in the pipeline, it would have blown it through the roof. Posthumous publication of a controversial political novel in an election year, the author martyred for his beliefs . . . It would have made *The Da Vinci Code* seem like a regional cookbook."

Gabriel's head was already shaking. His words emerged very slowly.

"*They* were going to kill *me* . . . and now *they're* dead? That's some marketing strategy."

Winger nodded. "Whoever had them killed is trying to wipe the book off the map *before* it surfaces. A different agenda altogether from Veerman's. They're competent, well-funded. Most certainly a contract agent, probably offshore. The idea was to eliminate all known copies of the manuscript. Including the one on your computer. Which, from what I understand, melted in the fire."

Gabriel thought a moment. "Call Google. I use gmail, it's on their server after I emailed it to my agent."

"It's not, actually. And they can't explain why. They say *you* must have deleted it."

Gabriel's face drained of what little color remained. "It's over, then," he said, barely audible.

"Maybe not."

"I don't have another copy to give you."

"I already have a copy of it, Gabriel."

But Gabriel didn't seem to hear. After a moment of distant thought he turned and looked behind them. "You think someone was at the hospital?"

"We have no idea. We have to assume that if they weren't, they were close."

"After all, *you* found me, right?"

The driver's eyes shot toward Winger, but the older man didn't respond. He was looking directly at Gabriel.

"You're not worried they'll come after you, too?"

Winger's expression was complex, conveying his empathy with the question concurrent with a certain level of patient judgment concerning its absurdity. As if to suggest he might be vulnerable was ludicrous.

"I am not, no."

Gabriel just nodded, saving this one for later.

"What about the other submissions Kathryn made?"

"There were no other submissions. She and Veerman were in on this from the beginning. They were blindsided."

"What about the editor? Barry something. I met him at . . ."

"Barry Lincoln is dead. A convenient heart attack upon hearing of Wyatt's death. The rest of the staff would have no way of contacting you, and wouldn't unless someone told them to. Any computer records with your data have been wiped clean."

He let this sink in, then added, "It's as if you were never there."

Gabriel's heart was thudding. He could feel the weight of his iPhone in his pocket—also fortuitously in his pants pocket the night of the fire—where Sarah Meyers of the NSA was one autodial key away.

"That makes no sense. I'd have just submitted it elsewhere. Started over with another agent, another publisher."

Winger's head was already shaking. "You're forgetting one small detail. You'd be dead. Without anyone on the New York end throwing up a red flag, two seemingly random deaths on opposite coasts would not be connected. Maybe down the road, but doubtful. Frankly, the people behind this couldn't care less either way. The election would be long over with, their ties to the killer long since terminated."

Gabriel covered his eyes with his hands. He wished he were back in the hospital, beneath a blanket of sweet narcotic insulation, awaiting his next visit from the nurse with no name. He was empty, scooped hollow, and rushing into the sudden vacuum of his vaporized dream came the past, a cold slap of solitude.

In another time he'd have offered up a little prayer for help. But he'd burned that bridge, and he wasn't sure he was ready to swim across that particular river yet.

- 33 -

GABRIEL WATCHED THE familiar landscape cradling I-80 as they drove east, up the hill toward Auburn. He felt Winger's hand touch his wrist, which still bore a bandage from the extracted IV. He looked up to see that he was being offered a water bottle. He took it, the water soothing on his throat.

"I know how this all sounds," said Winger, "but I believe your book may be prophetic. Ordained by God, in fact."

Gabriel snorted an involuntary laugh. "Right. I wrote it on my dining room table."

"Perhaps you were not alone in that room," said Winger.

A chill assailed Gabriel, the memory of feeling that he was indeed not alone as he wrote, the recurring dreams of Lauren, the ease with which the words poured from him. He had passed it off as that feeling a writer gets when he *knows*, when it's *there*. When that happens, when the writer feels more like a conduit than a source, there's always more going on than the touch of pen to paper, or more timely, fingers to keys.

The SUV pulled off at the Highway 49 exit, turning north. The road would pass through Auburn toward the Lake of the Pines, where he used to have a life.

Winger again touched his wrist.

"I want your book, Gabriel. I want to publish it. Name your price. I am also offering you protection from the people who have done this, and I'm offering you the pursuit of justice against them."

He paused, then added, "I'm giving you your life back."

Gabriel audibly inhaled. He closed his eyes, as if to better absorb the words, perhaps even savor them. But in fact what he was feeling was rage, his existence having been violated in a way that demanded consequences.

At least in the world according to Gabriel Stone.

He suddenly snapped back to reality.

"I don't even know you. You could be the bad guy. I should be talking to the police." Or, he failed to say, to his new friend Sarah, the lovely NSA agent.

"I can assure you, you shall."

Gabriel shot Winger a look full of questions.

"What does your heart tell you?" asked Winger.

Suddenly, inexplicably, Gabriel's eyes filled with tears. He had to clamp them shut and turn his head, the pain as physical as it was rooted in the past. It was not rage this time, though his rage had merely stepped aside for a moment.

"My wife used to ask me that," said Gabriel, barely audible.

"It's called faith," said Winger. "It announces itself in the quiet of your heart. It is the wise man who listens."

The SUV drove past the Lake of the Pines turnoff without slowing. Gabriel said nothing, though he felt his pulse accelerate as the place he used to live receded into the distance.

It was dark now, making it easy for him to hide behind a stoic expression.

They traveled ten miles farther toward the community of Grass Valley, where a prepaid room in an off-road motel had been reserved using an assumed name. To his great surprise Gabriel saw that his car was already parked in the lot, waiting for him, the key on the floor. Winger's only explanation was that he was a man of varied means.

Winger produced an envelope containing five thousand dollars in cash, enough, he said, to tide Gabriel over until he could return with his credibility in tow, not the least of which would be a contract and a briefcase full of proof that he was, in fact, the savior he was claiming to be.

A telephone number was scribbled onto the envelope, in case something urgent came up.

Winger explained that it would take a day or two of banging heads in New York to get the process under way. In the meantime Gabriel would be safe here in Grass Valley, as long as he remained under the radar. Winger assured Gabriel that the police had been advised, in case they needed to talk to him about the fire investigation, or even the New York murder of his publisher and agent, should his name come up. In fact, this was the only reason Winger was leaving him in the area. He would have much preferred to whisk him to safety on his private plane, a plan the local authorities wouldn't consider cooperative.

If Gabriel remained patient and faithful, he would be greatly rewarded. As soon as Winger arranged things in New York, he would send the plane for him.

They stopped a few stalls away from Gabriel's midsize BMW, a two-year-old five-series. Brian got out, opened Gabriel's door.

He didn't move at first. He stared down at the envelope in his hands, fat with Winger's cash, then closed his eyes.

He held out the envelope.

"I don't understand," said the older man, slowly taking it from Gabriel's hand.

"Neither do I," said Gabriel as he got out of the SUV.

"Until I do, I can't take your money. Thanks for the ride."

Special Agent Sarah Meyers probably wouldn't have approved. This was a chance to plug in, see where it might lead. But that was the trouble with this blind-faith business. While you had your eyes shut, someone just might be picking your pocket.

As he walked toward his car, he heard Simon call after him. "Don't be a fool. They'll come for you. You have to let someone help you."

Gabriel just waved. Without turning he said, "They'll have to find me first," not sure if Winger could hear. Then, in a quieter voice, he added, "And God help them when they do."

If his salvation was meant to be, and if salvation's name was Simon Winger, Gabriel would find the man when the time came. Until then, he had to sort this out in his own mind. He'd put his life into the hands of the only person on the planet he could trust. Himself.

When you're ready, *you* find salvation. It doesn't find you.

He watched the SUV drive away.

Gabriel had memorized the telephone number written on the envelope. It was a 202 area code—Washington, D.C. Not exactly a hotbed of publishing, or even the epicenter of religious consciousness. In Gabriel's opinion, most of what originated there were lies.

Milwaukee, Wisconsin

FOUR HUNDRED OF the faithful and true crowded into the ballroom
of the historic Pfister Hotel in downtown Milwaukee to celebrate Armand
Brenner's forthcoming ascent to power. Armand Brenner—Gulf War hero,
football player, devoted husband, the first candidate born of Jewish blood to
seriously contend for the highest office in the land—had delivered the campaign rhetoric crafted for him with his usual panache, and the party minions
ate it up. All the while he wondered why the great bulk of this effort and
money went into sucking up to those already enrolled, when it was the fence-
sitters that promised the best return on these investments.

The polls had him up by six percentage points over the incumbent President. Many believed his wife, Charlotte, would become his chief of staff,
adding to the already significant outrage of the political far right, which this
time around had been cast to the sidelines, and which highly disapproved
of his running mate's mixed bloodline. In any case Armand Brenner was, as
his director of publicity had labeled him from the beginning, the savior of a
brave new nation.

Brenner was standing arm in arm with his wife and a few local campaign workers as they pressed the flesh with practiced glee. He marveled at
Charlotte's way with the common folk, the warm glow on her already olive
complexion, her ethnicity vague while lending an exotic elegance to her obvious intelligence. It made him smile to think that none of them knew the bar-
racuda she really was. The room was awash in joyous noise, including music

from a live salsa band just audible over the passion of a crowd that had been plied with cases of Costco's finest champagne.

He smiled at the notion of ethnicity. It had served him well thus far.

No one paid attention as the candidate's top campaign officer slithered through the crowd and tapped him on the shoulder. When Brenner leaned close, Alex whispered, "Upstairs, two minutes. This is huge."

The expression on Alex's face told Brenner the summons was non-negotiable. And if he'd learned one thing along the road that led him here, it was to never challenge Alex when that expression was in place. He kissed Charlotte on the cheek and made his way out of the room surrounded by security guards.

He could feel her eyes, which had been described by one panting journalist as "a supernova of compelling smoke," burning into his back as he left.

That journalist, Brenner had often thought to himself, had no idea how right he was.

BRENNER'S BODYGUARD REMAINED outside the doors to the health club that occupied the Pfister's twenty-seventh floor. Through the windows the view of the Lake Michigan shore three blocks away was spectacular, the waterline rimmed with jewel-like lights. Alex looked out at them, as if appreciating the panorama.

But Brenner knew better. Alex, who defied categorization up to and including gender—other than Charlotte, he was prettier than any of the women in the Brenner camp—hadn't noticed a view, spectacular or not, in years. The man's mind was consumed with strategy, the minutiae of power, and the presidency was within their grasp.

"Wyatt Veerman is dead," said Alex without turning.

Brenner weaved through the monolithic exercise equipment to stand next to the lord and master of his campaign. Veerman had been a friend and a significant contributor. And more recently, the recipient of a great deal of money to conduct a highly sensitive piece of business on their behalf.

Alex had handled that particular transaction. The less Brenner knew, the better.

"How?"

"Murdered. He and the literary agent who brought him the book were killed in some kind of carjacking thing."

Alex continued to stare out with eyes void of expression.

Brenner knew about the book, but only to the extent that it was harmful to the interests of the President. From that he could easily intuit why someone had killed to stop it. If published, it would become a sort of sociopolitical virus that would play right into their hands. The book painted a picture of an incumbent administration so threatened by the leading candidate—a thinly veiled version of Brenner himself—that they would resort to assassination to take him out. The book's publication and the publicity campaign to launch it would be tailored to the promulgation of this perception. The book not only painted the incumbent President as a jackass, it made him out to be a killer, insulated by sycophants willing to die for him.

The deal with Veerman had initially been Charlotte's.

The two had been friends in college, and when Veerman was pitched the book he contacted her immediately with what at first seemed a political football, but quickly became a political landmine. She had to distance herself before it got legs, but only after entrusting the plan to Alex, who in turn issued a green light. Alex finally briefed Armand Brenner, but only the part about making the current administration look bad.

There were other aspects best left unspoken.

Wyatt Veerman had promised that the book would be on the shelves before Election Day, cutting the normal ramp-up time to a fraction of what it normally required. He had been promised an under-the-table fortune to get it done.

With any luck, it just might help Armand Brenner win. Especially the dark ending of the story, which Alex had crafted. The writer of the book would die suspiciously concurrent with the book's publication, giving the novel immediate blockbuster cachet in the marketplace. Alex had started to tell Charlotte about it, but with a smile more appropriate to a snake spying a nest of baby mice, she had told him it would be best if he kept the details to himself.

"Obviously," said Alex, "someone wants the book stopped."

"Is the author still alive?"

"We don't know."

"So why is it obvious? Maybe it was a robbery." Alex now turned to look the candidate directly in the eye.

"The editor of the book dropped dead at his desk. Heart attack, supposedly stress-induced at hearing the news of Veerman's murder. You tell me, Armand. I call it obvious."

Brenner stroked his chin as he thought a moment.

"Sounds like wet work."

Alex considered this. It was amazing how well those steel-gray eyes masked any fear or anger. "Don't be ridiculous."

"Who, then?"

Alex paused, not bothering to answer. The answer had implications that cut much deeper into the destiny of the world than the White House.

"That's the question, isn't it."

"We aren't the only ones who have a stake here," said Brenner. "Maybe it's not the White House. Could be some other radical right wing faction that wants to protect the President. Alex paused, then said, "The religious right wing."

Brenner grimaced, then nodded. "They're doing it because . . ."

"Because maybe the book comes too close to something they already have planned. They have to shut it down to protect themselves, keep their game in play."

Brenner nodded thoughtfully. "An assassination plot with my name on the ticket."

Alex nodded solemnly. Brenner was following his lead, just as he had hoped.

"Many like you, and many not at your level but nonetheless promising, have died. You've heard the theories, some kind of cult dedicated to eliminating anyone who challenges the will of God. If this book meddled in things they consider sacred, then they just might consider stopping it."

"You've read this book?"

"No. But Charlotte has read coverage. She told me it complements our objectives, but she wasn't specific. She has to be careful with this conversation because of her relationship with Veerman. The press is already sniffing around that puddle."

Brenner paced in front of the window, hands clasped behind his back, a black silhouette against the night.

"An assassination plan is in motion," he offered, playing it through. "Suddenly this book comes along, exposes that plan, and they have to bury it before it goes public to accomplish their goals."

Alex smiled wickedly. "You think they want you dead enough to risk it?"

"Ask Wyatt Veerman," answered Brenner dryly.

A moment of quiet followed. Brenner realized Alex was way ahead of him, simply waiting for him to catch up.

"So it follows," Brenner offered cautiously, "that the book itself will tell us what we need to know. And that it is in our best interests to take it public. Whether it incriminates the administration or the Jesus people, it stops their plan and puts blood on their hands. We win either way."

Alex now turned to face Brenner. "There is no book. If they've taken out Veerman, the agent and the editor, it stands to reason the book itself is gone. Especially if it's CIA. That's the point of it all, Armand. Closure."

Brenner nodded, but not in agreement. "Maybe not. There's always the author."

"If he's still alive."

"What do we know about him?"

"Nothing."

"But there are ways to find him."

"There are always ways."

"We find the author, we find his book. We call in some favors, get it published. We're right back where we started."

Alex nodded, rubbing his chin. Brenner had no idea how right-on he was. The author dies suspiciously, the book becomes a bestseller. End of problem.

Just as he and Charlotte had planned all along.

Alex drew a deep breath, closing his eyes dramatically.

"Let me think," said Brenner, as if he was suddenly in command of this situation. "My guess is the guy is already dead. We go sticking our dick into this, we risk exposure."

Alex turned and smiled. He slowly ran a finger from the corner of Brenner's eye, down his face, and then across his lips. Brenner's eyelids fluttered slightly, his breathing shallow. But he didn't move away.

"We wouldn't want to stick our dick into anything dangerous now, would we, Armand."

Then Alex walked from the room, leaving Armand Brenner to ponder the monstrous stakes of it all, including the ever-present truth that there were significant powers in play committed to his destruction.

Just as other powers, perhaps even greater than those, were at his side to deliver him from harm's way.

GABRIEL KNEW HE had to get the hell out of Dodge. After a sandwich and a random tour of town to ensure that he wasn't being followed, he took a circuitous route west toward Marysville on a rural two-lane highway that would expose anyone behind him. From there he headed south into downtown Sacramento, where he parked his car in a familiar lot and walked three blocks to a hotel where he'd occasionally lunched with clients.

The hotel business center offered high-speed Internet, and with his laptop in ashes this was his connection to reality. All the news services had the story—the bodies of New York publisher Wyatt Veerman and literary agent Kathryn Kline had been discovered in their car the previous day after what appeared to be a robbery in midtown Manhattan. In a bizarre twist, an editor who worked for Veerman dropped dead of a heart attack upon hearing the news.

Later, Gabriel slept fitfully, his mind on fire.

In the morning he availed himself of an ATM in the hotel lobby—he had no choice if he wanted to remain mobile, and he'd already used his credit card for the room—then rented a car. He checked out, leaving his car in the anonymous downtown garage, not wanting to cast a shadow in the same place for too long. From here on out he'd use cash only, sleeping in the car if he had to.

On the road he called to arrange for an appointment with his neighbor the lawyer.

Sooner or later the New York police would want to talk to him, and he needed to understand his options. The first available opening was right after lunch, meaning he had several hours to suffer through.

He knew precisely what that suffering should be.

He called the hospital. After several minutes on hold he was connected to a friendly admittance clerk who told him his discharge indeed appeared to be somewhat unusual. Approval had come after a call from the hospital administrator himself, who had phoned in from a Hawaii vacation. A favor for a friend, or so went the unofficial office buzz. No doubt Simon Winger held shares in the company that ran the hospital, too.

THE GATE GUARD at the Lake of the Pines greeted him with a sad smile. Because Gabriel was in a rental he had to stop and check in manually, rather than use the bar-coded drive-through that was the normal routine. He'd have preferred to enter unnoticed, but he was stuck with the rules of this game.

Moments later he was driving into a nightmare.

His house and the adjoining shrubbery had virtually blocked any view of the lake, but now the water was fully visible from the street. Half the structure was gone, a pile of blackened charcoal that appeared to have been trampled into rubble. Nothing was recognizable, it was all just slabs of carbon and black dust. The structure was seemingly torn in half, the side with the guest bedrooms remaining intact, the interior gaping open like a battlefield amputation, dripping with insulation and shards of torn wood. From the moment he emerged from his car he could smell the decomposition of his life, a biting sensation that quickly transcended scent to become taste.

As he stared at the devastation, his mind saw Lauren.

The house and everything in it had been hers. He was merely occupying her space after she was gone, preserving what he could. The emotion was overwhelming. He'd been in a sort of avoidance mode, the book keeping him busy, the solitude insulating him from the pain. Friends and former coworkers had called, some repeatedly, but he had remained conveniently occupied.

But there was no stopping the memories now. Entire chapters of his life crunched beneath each step as he walked through the ash. A picture frame, now empty, that used to hold a montage of vacation photos. Brass candle holders, which Lauren collected at each port of call. She came from money— hence, this house on the lake—but never allowed it to be a factor in her unconditional support of his dreams. She had been patience to his urgency, calm to his storm, reason to his impulsive drives.

He stood among the dead memories for half an hour, completely motionless. And he was not sorry he came.

Closure sometimes required a bullet to the brain.

A NEIGHBOR WHO had been watching through partially open shutters would later remark to her husband, the lawyer who had given Gabriel his card on the night of the fire, that Gabriel looked determined, even energized, as he drove away in a car she didn't recognize.

A man, perhaps, with a purpose.

GABRIEL STUDIED THE face of the man he hoped might help him. For the past forty minutes Michael Land, his neighbor and now his lawyer, had listened to Gabriel's story, leaning back in a plush leather chair, elbow on the arm, chin in hand. Other than a nod offered at regular intervals he hadn't moved, hadn't offered a single expression of surprise or disapproval. He was disturbingly handsome—Lauren once said he was the best-looking man on the Lake—with a thick head of *GQ* hair and a UL-approved tan.

Behind every lawyer joke was an underpinning of public perception, and everything about this guy screamed *asshole*. But watching him now, and in context to his unsolicited offer to help, Gabriel realized the perception was of his own creation. He had been jealous of Lauren's opinion, compounded by a prejudice against the word *attorney*.

"Good story," said Land, leaning back in his chair as he folded his arms. "And I'd like to help. But frankly I'm a small-town guy, and I'm not sure how much I can do for you."

"What does one usually do in situations like these?"

This made Michael Land smile, lighting up the office, which was located above a strip mall, one of the tenants of which was his preferred tanning salon.

"Like *these*? You're shitting me."

"I want it on the record, for starters."

Land nodded. "Of course. In case something happens. I become your champion, take it to the press."

"You can take your fee out of my vast estate."

"I'm not charging you, Gabe. Connie and I feel terrible about what's happened. Lauren was an angel."

Connie Land and Lauren frequently shared coffee on the deck, no doubt discussing how gorgeous Connie's husband was.

"Sometimes these fire settlements get nasty," said Land, "especially when there are issues of arson."

"You don't have to do this."

"Least I can do. Here's what I think. The fact that your home was destroyed in an act of criminal mischief gives you legal recourse somewhere down the line. Not to mention the pursuit of justice and the inevitable insurance implications. Second, you've been told by someone you don't know that your life may be in jeopardy, that there may be parties seeking to harm or even kill you, which is an entirely different legal realm, one that requires the involvement of various police and investigative agencies. Talk to them now or talk to them later, doesn't matter, it sounds like they're definitely in your future. Then you say a beautiful but mysterious NSA agent approached you, asking for your help just before she disappears. And lastly, you've got a shot at getting your book back into the game with this Winger fellow, which otherwise, given the death of your publisher and agent, seems like a doubtful outcome. That about sum it up?"

"About."

Land chewed at his upper lip.

"Legally and ethically," he finally said, "I believe you are obliged to call in the proper authorities, who will no doubt be interested in anyone with information regarding the New York deaths, not to mention potential arson charges. Pragmatically, though, just between us Pinesmen, I like the Winger option. Play this out, see what surfaces. You can always call in the dogs later on. Nothing incriminating or ethically compromised about waiting until they find you. Might even be a book deal in this. It's all so Grisham."

Gabriel thought it was more Ludlum-meets-Hal-Lindsay, but then lawyers do tend to stick together.

"If I'm around to write it."

Land, who was scribbling a note, didn't respond.

Gabriel cast a glance to the wall behind the desk, which was covered with framed diplomas, honorary citations, and a few pictures. A Little League team wearing jerseys bearing his name. Michael Land shaking the hand of a pre-governor Arnold Schwarzenegger at a local fundraiser. Land and his wife accepting his Pinesman gavel at an award dinner.

Gabriel smiled. It was good to have an advocate.

"I need a lead, some proof. And I'd say a million-dollar house reduced to briquettes is a good start on proof. And this Winger guy smells a lot like a lead to me."

Land turned both palms up and smiled. "There you go."

Gabriel drew a deep breath. "I went to the house this morning."

Land's nod was empathetic. "Connie told me. She saw you."

"It's gone. Everything I had."

"You're alive, Gabe. Maybe you should focus on that."

"I'm glad I did it. It's time to move on."

Gabriel suddenly realized his new perception of Michael Land was part of that very process. Maybe what doesn't kill you makes you stronger.

Again Land said, "There you go."

Land leaned back again, the hand on his chin and his soft eyes fixed on Gabriel, totally in the moment.

Gabriel said, "You must think I'm one mitt short of a full infield."

"Not at all. I think you've had one too many brush-back pitches lately. As your lawyer, and as your friend, all I can tell you is what your options are. It all boils down to this—watch your ass. Don't talk to the police before talking to me. Call me with anything, anytime. If you see someone following you, and if you can do it safely, get a license number, maybe even confront whoever it is. Unless you feel threatened, in which case I suggest you run like hell. Carry a camera and a recorder. And for God's sake, don't lose your phone."

Gabriel shrugged. "And then what?"

"See where it leads. If nothing else, you got what you wanted today."

"Which is?"

The lawyer stood and offered Gabriel a warm handshake. "You're on the record, my friend. Anything happens to you, I've got your back."

As he drove away, Gabriel hoped that he hadn't just pulled his new friend into the crosshairs with him. And he wondered which side of those crosshairs NSA Special Agent Sarah Meyers resided.

Citrus Heights, California

GABRIEL SLIPPED THE key into the door of his room at the LaQuinta Inn. He'd returned to the Sacramento area and, after making sure his stashed BMW had gone unnoticed, abandoned the sleep-in-the-car strategy and checked in here. He reasoned that by the time they traced him through his credit card, a notion he found hard to accept despite his circumstances, he'd have moved on one way or the other. He then headed out for something to eat, hoping to divert his mind from his situation.

But none of that mattered now.

As soon as the hotel room door closed behind him he felt something cold and hard pressing behind his right ear.

"On your knees."

A hand pressed him down, the pressure behind his ear bordering on pain. The voice was smooth, low pitched, with a terrifying self-assuredness.

"Scoot to the bed. Put your forehead on the bedspread."

The man moved with him, both points of contact unaffected. The voice was bolder now, the tone of a small man talking big.

"You scream, I shoot. I have a silencer, so no one will hear. Nod if you understand what I'm saying."

Gabriel nodded quickly, his forehead in full contact with the bedspread, which smelled of stale smoke.

"Tell me your name," asked the intruder.

"Harold Lipshitz," said Gabriel. The response was followed by a quick kick between his legs, causing his full weight to collapse onto the bed and his dinner to rise in his throat.

A moment passed, presumably to allow Gabriel's breath to return. Which it did, though the nausea remained.

"You know who I am," he breathed through the pain.

"Here's the script, Mr. Gabriel Stone. In a moment I'm going to step back to the door. I'll use the gun if you don't do precisely as I say. Do you understand?"

Gabriel nodded as best he could.

"You will remove your wallet, keys, and watch and put them on the nightstand. Then you will take off your clothes and get into bed, naked. Do it all from a kneeling position. Go."

"How am I supposed to get into bed if I'm kneeling?"

"Do not fuck with me."

Gabriel reached into his pockets, fumbling for a moment.

"Slower," asked the man.

Gabriel extracted the items and placed them on the nightstand as instructed. Then he removed his jacket, taking care to stay prone on the bed, followed by his shirt. He kicked off his shoes, then reached behind to tend to the socks, perceiving the outline of a man at the very periphery of his vision.

"Eyes forward," barked the intruder.

The pants were harder, requiring him to raise each knee in an awkward dance. Then his shorts, equally awkward. Only now, with his bare ass staring up at his new companion, did his thoughts wander toward heretofore unacknowledged fears.

He yanked back the covers and scrambled face-first onto the sheets, pulling the bedspread up to the middle of his back as best he could while facing down.

"Turn over," said the man.

As he turned, Gabriel regarded his captor for the first time. His first impression was the size of the man, noticeably smaller than himself. Had he known this moments earlier he might have chanced a move. The guy had a receding hairline and cold black holes for eyes framed by wire-rimmed glasses.

Both men glared, sizing up the situation. The stranger wore a take-your-best-shot grin, reading Gabriel's mind.

"Who sent you?" asked Gabriel, his voice surprisingly bold.

The intruder smiled wider, igniting deep crevices on his face. "You won't believe me."

"Try me."

"God sent me."

Their eyes held fast. The man's smile faded away to add weight to the answer. There was no sarcasm in it.

"Did God tell you to kill my publisher and my agent?"

The man didn't respond.

"Did God burn my house down, you emaciated little fuck?"

This prompted the smile to return.

The stranger reached into the pocket of his jacket and produced an object, which he held out toward Gabriel. It was a clear flask of liquor, half of the contents already gone.

"I don't drink."

A sudden rage formulated behind the man's eyes.

Gabriel watched him rein it in with a frightening force of will.

"But you *will*. Then you will sleep. There will be no pain. There are several ways we can do this, none quite this easy. I say again, and for the final time—drink. Please."

Gabriel squinted at the flask. "I get it. I'm committing suicide. Makes a sick kind of sense, actually."

It really did have an obscene logic to it. Easily acquired prescription narcotics, washed down by easily acquired booze. Reliably fatal in the right quantities. And, as the man just said, painless.

Gabriel tried to snort a defiant laugh. Buying time.

"Widowed writer loses his book deal, then his house burns down, all in one week. He cracks, can't take it anymore, gets a cheap room where nobody can recognize him, finishes it." He paused, then added, "No one who knows me will buy it."

The man considered this a moment, which lasted long enough to cause Gabriel's heart to race even faster.

"Neither will the attorney you saw today."

The surprise on Gabriel's face amused the man.

"I knew you'd go back to your house, that's where I picked you up after the hospital. I followed you to his office. And if I may guess at what you told him, he'll have no choice but to corroborate the fragile state of your emotional health."

Gabriel squinted, realizing he had but moments to save himself. And the solution was clear. Suicides don't look like they've been in a street fight. And they don't shoot themselves with silencers. If he couldn't escape, he'd at least make this difficult, leave the police with something to work on.

The man with the wire-rimmed glasses again read his mind.

"There are a lot of ways to kill yourself," he said. "This is clean, easy for you, easy for me. If you'd prefer a bloodbath with slashed wrists, or a broken neck from a botched shower hanging, we can go there. Up to you, my friend. I assure you, whatever you choose, they *will* believe it."

So much for the street-fighting solution.

Gabriel drew a deep breath, as if sudden terror was restricting his windpipe. His hand trembled as he slowly reached for the bottle, a feeble whine emanating from his throat, an internal cry to stop. He had to sit up slightly to reach it, his tormentor remaining at arm's length.

Gabriel made his move. He lunged forward, snagging a tight grasp on the smaller man's wrist, which he yanked toward him with all of his strength. He made sure to twist to the side in case he got a shot off, rolling his body to add weight to the move, his eyes riveted on the gun.

But the smaller man surprised him. He released the gun from his grasp and surrendered to the force of Gabriel's maneuver, the deadly instinct of a trained Special Forces operative.

Gabriel's untrained instinct was to go for a headlock, intending to break the little bastard's neck. He would fight for his life with everything he had. Suddenly, inexplicably, it was worth fighting for.

But the smaller man had skills. Before his body landed on the mattress he had his hands on Gabriel's throat, steel fingertips digging purposefully between straining tendons, finding their target, which at a touch shot bolts of agony through Gabriel's frame, freezing him, draining him of strength. Unable to breathe, see, or even move, Gabriel found himself helpless on his back, the man's elbow buried deep in his solar plexus, fingers sunk to the knuckles into the sinewy anatomy of his throat.

The other hand was on his jaw, and with a surgical-like intrusion behind the jaw muscles, forced it open. In the seconds it took to incapacitate Gabriel the man had heaved his weight on top of him, immobilizing Gabriel's legs. Somehow, without compromising his advantage, the assassin momentarily freed a hand to reach into a pocket.

Gabriel tried to bite down, but the grip had somehow paralyzed his jaw. He tasted latex, followed by the sting of a needle buried deeply into the soft tissue under his tongue.

Waves of ice shot out from the point of entry. But only for a moment. Long enough for Gabriel to hear, as if coming from the end of a long tunnel, whispered words carried on breath sour from its own festering need.

The man said, "Thy will be done, motherfucker."

As the darkness enveloped him, Gabriel prayed the one-touch mobile connection he'd enabled as he'd fumbled in his pocket while undressing had gone through.

- 38 -

Chico, California

HE WAS LOST in the light. Carried by it, cradled in it. Loved. Lauren emerged from the light, floating, enveloping him in its embrace. For a moment he forgot everything that was, lost in all that is. The light was warm, it was liquid, he breathed it in, he soared in its vastness.

And then the light began to pulse. It focused to a point, surrounded by black as it moved, bisecting his vision.

Fingers were at his eyes, holding the lids open. He became aware of the object from which the light came, moving left to right, right to left. A pen. Held by a hand, in a familiar room. And then a face, smiling at him, calling his name.

Lauren.

No. Another face entirely. A face of perfect flesh, flushed with concern.

The face of the woman who had pulled him from the fire.

Gabriel sat up with a gasp, but was quickly pressed back down to soft sheets by gentle hands. He was breathing heavily, as if he'd just sprinted upon the scene.

"That was close," said Sarah Meyers. She sat on the side of the bed, stroking his forehead. As before, she was stylishly dressed, more country club wife than federal agent.

Suddenly he smelled vomit. He glanced to the side and saw an ice bucket next to his head, half-filled with dark fluid. Moments later he realized where he was and from where the fluid had come.

Another cheap hotel room. Different colors and angles than the one in which he had been nearly killed. She had reached him in time and taken him away.

"You attempted to take your own life by chasing Percodan with Southern Comfort. At least, according to the bottles your friend left on your bedspread."

"You know who he was?"

She shook her head, as if she wished she did.

Gabriel rose to his elbows and studied the room. Next to him on the sheets was what amounted to a mobile clinic: blood pressure cuff, latex gloves, a syringe kit and a vial with no label, several bottles of pills.

"You a nurse, too?" he asked.

Sarah smiled shyly. Or perhaps humbly.

"NSA survival training. Fingers down the throat, a little heart medicine and a little luck . . . here you are."

He squinted as he continued to survey the room, which was spinning. He flopped back down on the mattress and closed his eyes.

"How are you feeling?" she asked.

"Drunk."

"Nice move with the phone," she said, smiling approvingly. "How did you know I'd followed you here?"

"I didn't."

They locked eyes. The obvious questions were best left for later.

"So . . . is this a rescue, or a hostage situation?"

Sarah seemed saddened by the question. "You called. I came. What's next is up to you. All you have to do is ask."

"And ye shall receive."

"Something like that."

His smile tried to counter her darkness. "I'm asking." He paused, his expression sincere. "I need your help, Sarah."

She nodded. Suddenly the gentleness left her face. Her eyes were alert, as if she sensed something ominous.

"What is it?" he asked, just now noticing that the first light of dawn was seeping in through the drawn curtains.

"We have to get out of here," she said. "Now."

-39-

Washington, D.C.

TRAFFIC ON THE bridge connecting Arlington to the monuments was at a standstill, something about a movie shoot dealing with the crash of an airliner two decades earlier shortly after takeoff from what was then known as Washington National Airport. By law the production company could not hold traffic for more than ten minutes, so they had to make each take count.

Daniel Larsen flinched when his phone rang. He'd selected "76 Trombones" as his ring tone, a riff he'd learned to hate since it almost always meant bad news. Such was the nature of his job—national security was a bitch these days.

"Larsen."

"We have a problem." It was McQuarrie, that sing songy sarcastic tone that defied the inevitable weight of the words.

Larsen's stomach flipped. "You got my message last night?"

"No. Not in time, at least."

"Jesus."

"Relax, Danny boy, your guy's alive."

Larsen had called McQuarrie, leaving him an urgent message to abort his efforts where Gabriel Stone was concerned. He had a better idea, one that served his objectives in an even more devastating manner. But McQuarrie hadn't called back.

"Status," he said.

"I took a shot. The only way this flies, given the fire fuckup and the possible connection to New York, is if Stone kills himself. Distraught writer on the brink, yada yada yada."

"But you didn't get to him," said Larsen.

"Oh, I got to him. The staging was perfect. I departed the scene uncompromised, leaving the mark as good as dead."

"And?"

"Someone intervened."

"Who?"

"I was sorta hoping you'd tell me. Given the heat, I didn't stick around to watch the fireworks. I assumed they'd find his body in the morning. I called the motel at nine, they said the guy had checked out. As in, paid his bill and departed the premises intact. Someone's onto you."

"It doesn't matter," said Larsen. "In fact, it's perfect."

"As long as I get paid, it's perfect."

"Listen to me. This is important. Stand down on Stone. Are we clear? It's off."

"Your dime, pal."

The traffic began to inch forward. The guy in the next car was so distraught Larsen could see the veins in his forehead.

Larsen said, "I have more work for you."

"I'm busy."

"I'll double your end."

"My schedule just cleared."

"Meet me in Tucson tomorrow, eleven a.m., Pima Air Museum."

"Tucson? I hate Tucson."

"Deal with it."

The line went dead.

It took several minutes to traverse the length of the bridge, one lane of which was choked with location trucks and the film crew. The going remained slow as the cars dispersed around the Lincoln Center into the maze of the Washington grid, off to meet lobbyists and balance budgets and generally kiss the collective ass of the incumbent suits. Larsen drove behind the Lincoln Memorial to the north side of the mall, finding a parking spot near the new World War II memorial.

A bit of a hike to the Washington Memorial, true, where his next appointment would be waiting. But it was suddenly a very nice day indeed, in a business in which nice days were few and far between.

40

DANIEL LARSEN HAD to laugh. It was overcast today, and despite the mild temperature his counterpart was wearing the ever-present London Fog and a bad hat. The collar was turned high and he wore last decade's sunglasses, scanning the crowd around him for familiar faces. Recognition, it seemed, just wouldn't do.

The two men didn't shake hands as Larsen arrived at his side, standing at the chain fence that surrounded the monument.

"I'd ask how you are," opened Larsen, "but I've seen the polls."

Several straw polls had Armand Brenner ahead of the incumbent President by as much as eight percentage points.

"Reelection's a bitch."

The man Larsen called by his first name only, Brock, was badly in need of a personal shopper and a diet. He was squinting up at the 502-foot pinnacle as if he'd just gotten off a tour bus.

"Comes with the lease," offered Larsen. "You take enough tough stands, you piss somebody off."

Brock made a face, weary of the small talk. "You asked to see me."

"I have an update. Somebody's helping Stone."

"You're a deputy assistant director with the CIA, and you can't tell me who it is?"

Larsen took the arrow with an impatient nod. "We can make this work *for* us."

Brock nodded, skepticism all over his face.

Larsen moved closer, lowered his voice. He covered his mouth with his fist as he spoke.

"I have a proposal."

"You always do."

"We wanted to take Stone out, for obvious reasons. The device goes off, people die, suddenly there's a book out there pointing fingers at the administration. The public's gullible, they'll buy it. At least enough to pull votes. We cannot take that risk."

"The public is *perceptive* is more like it."

"My point. Work with me here. What if we paint Stone as a political right-wing psycho, a Bible-thumping extremist. We plant some phone records, contrive some testimony, he looks like Lee Harvey Oswald if we want him to. We can even design an Al Qaeda connection if that's what it takes."

Brock nodded again, the skepticism fading.

"So instead of a martyr trying to warn us," continued Larsen, "we have ourselves a bona fide perp with visions of glory. A psycho who wrote it all down for posterity because he knew he wouldn't survive to tell his story."

The nodding slowed, the eyes glazed. "You're suggesting we lay Columbia on this guy?"

Now it was Daniel Larsen who nodded. "I've already pulled my field op. Stone's untethered."

"A little presumptive, don't you think?"

"Brilliance trumps presumption. Stone is running, but we'll find him. Hell, we don't have to find him. We just make sure his book gets published and the dotted lines are all in place."

The man who worked across the street at the White House began to pace, two steps in either direction, hands behind his back, his collar masking his mouth from curious electronics.

"What if we connect him to the Brethren, too?"

"Better idea," said Larsen. "It wouldn't work to pitch him as a Brother in good standing, too many people able to testify he was never there. Better idea is to position him as a wannabe."

Brock nodded, lost in thought.

"Strengthens his motive. He was trying to sell his Antichrist line to The Brethren, they didn't buy it, so he went solo. Got his pound of flesh with his ticket to heaven."

"It's interesting."

The pacing continued for half a minute. Then Larsen said, "He's the perfect patsy."

The other man stopped, standing close to Larsen, facing the White House a few hundred yards away.

"I'll run it by them."

As he walked off, Larsen called after him.

"I need to know by tomorrow morning. It's pay or play after that."

Brock just raised a hand without looking back, one finger pointing skyward in casual acknowledgment. Then he pulled his collar tight around his neck and headed across the street.

41

Interstate 5, Central California

IT WAS JUST after dawn when they departed the Chico motel room where Sarah had taken him to recover from the attack, and while still groggy and nauseous, he felt good enough to ride. They were on I-5, heading north in a rented Lexus.

He had pressed the issue of their hasty departure, and was content though cynical about her answer: whoever had tried to kill him would check back on the results, and Gabriel didn't want to be anywhere in the vicinity when that happened.

He watched the onion fields pass for a long time before venturing his next question. All the while Sarah's eyes were as intent on the rearview mirror as they were the road.

"Mind if I ask where we're going?"

"North."

He waited for an elaboration that didn't come. After a few minutes he closed his eyes, still feeling the opposing cocktails of narcotics that vied for his consciousness.

He had allowed her to squire him away without knowing the true color of her uniform. But she had come when called, then pumped him full of God knows what to save his life. That bought a lot of slack in the game of dodging the next bullet.

The fact was he had absolutely nothing left to lose.

Sarah suddenly smiled, as if reading his mind.

"You have more questions," she said without looking over.

"A thousand or so."

"I suggest you begin, then."

"Happy to. Who are you, really, and why are you in California? How was it you were at my house at the precise moment it was about to burn down with me in it, how did you get in, and why did you leave me on the lawn instead of coming forward?"

When he paused she said, "That's it?"

"Just warming up. Who is trying to kill me, *why* are they trying to kill me, who killed my publisher and my agent and why, and what is it about my book that makes people so freaking nervous? How are you connected to Simon Winger, and what does he want?"

She nodded, duly amused. "Would the beginning be okay?"

"Perfectly," said Gabriel, easing back against the leather headrest and closing his eyes.

"I haven't lied to you. My name is Sarah Meyers. I teach religious history and theology at NYU. I also work for the government."

"So which is it?" said Gabriel. "*Doctor* Sarah Meyers of NYU, or *Special Agent* Sarah Meyers of the NSA?"

"Both, actually."

They drove in silence for a few awkward seconds.

"I've been at NYU for five years," she finally continued. "Before that I was a police officer in Denver. Which is what qualified me for the NSA job."

"Of course it did," Gabriel interjected. "Why the NSA?"

"They came to me."

"It's a strange combination of skills."

"Makes sense when you understand my story. I shot and killed a robbery suspect. Turns out he was only fifteen. If that doesn't cause you to confront your notions of God, nothing will."

She paused, expecting Gabriel to respond, which he didn't.

"So, I went back to school, got a few degrees, landed the jobs. Long story, not relevant. What is relevant is that I'd been working with a grad student, a brilliant kid, on his thesis. And that's what ultimately led me to you."

"So I was right. You *are* off the clock."

She swallowed, suddenly uncomfortable.

"That picture you showed me in New York," he said, "the guy with the red hair. That was your grad student?"

She nodded.

"So you're a religious scholar and a spook. Guess the Tea Partiers killed all that separation of church and state malarkey, eh? God, guns, and good whiskey."

"I embrace all types of belief systems. I believe there are veins of truth in all the major religions, at least the ones that deify a creator. Not so crazy about the ones waiting for a comet to cruise by. I also think none of them got it completely right."

"Now, *there's* some common ground for us to work from."

"And by the way, your patio door was unlocked."

Gabriel studied her, sensing a myriad of complexities.

"My thesis was on the commonality of major theologies. It's not that I think there's anything in the Bible that's overtly wrong, per se. In fact, I think it's all there, perhaps more than meets the eye."

He remained quiet as she gathered her next thoughts.

"Organized religion is the problem. Not God, whatever you call him or her. Certainly not Jesus. It's *people*. We've messed it up for thousands of years, and it's getting worse."

He let that hang between them for a moment. Then he said, "Tell me about your grad student."

"There's a group of men in Washington who like to think of themselves as soldiers of God. Literally. They're all about power, about evoking change in the world, no wimps allowed."

"Scary."

"Quite. Like any elitist group, they've fostered a mystique, which by definition makes them a target for left and right wingers alike. Religion is a political football, Gabriel, and these guys play tackle."

"Let me guess," he said. "Simon Winger's the starting quarterback."

"We'll know soon. You'd be surprised who these guys have signed up. They control massive amounts of money and resources, and their connections are more important than any lobby working in Washington today. They've got senators, congressmen, governors, mayors, police chiefs, major industrialists, ex–military brass. You name it, they're represented. It's like a stock exchange for reciprocation."

"*Very* scary."

"Ever heard of the National Prayer Luncheon?"

"Can't say that I have."

"A very big deal. These guys run it. Three thousand invitees, including world leaders and people of influence. For the past twenty years it's included the President and his wife, too. This year they're even inviting the opposing candidate."

"Covering their ass?"

"Like I said, they're as political as they are holy."

"So how does this relate to your grad student?"

Sarah drew a deep breath, a nerve hit. "Matthew had successfully infiltrated The Brethren."

Gabriel whistled, just under his breath.

"He was writing his doctoral thesis, contending that their political agenda is a corrupting influence on their spiritual manifesto. While turning over rocks toward that end, he stumbled onto something. Something big."

"I smell a bestseller. He told you what it is?"

Sarah swallowed, hesitating before answering.

"Matthew is dead. Heart attack in the hospital recovering from a hit-and-run. He was twenty-two years old."

A sudden wave of nausea washed over him.

"He'd hinted at something for a few weeks prior to his accident. He mentioned the possibility of a subcell of the group, a radical infrastructure that operated under the auspices of The Brethren, but with a darker agenda. Even the Lord has dirty work to be done, he told me, and these were the guys who were doing it. If the rest of them were foot soldiers, these guys were Navy SEALs."

Gabriel now felt a chill assault his spine. He had written about a similar secret sect of religious zealots in his novel. For the first time since his life had begun to crumble, he had a hint of what this might be about.

"Matthew didn't have a heart problem," she said softly.

The look of pain on her face made him want to inquire about the nature of their relationship, but he hesitated. Sarah stared straight ahead, gripping the wheel with bloodless force.

"You're wondering what this has to do with you," she said.

"My book," he responded.

She nodded. "When I last spoke with Matthew, he said he'd heard about a novel in the publishing pipeline, something that was making the brass at The Brethren very nervous. Supposedly the book had a plot that paralleled something on their radar, something that threatened or exposed what they're into."

She paused, drawing a deep breath.

"He asked me if I'd ever heard the name of Gabriel Stone."

She turned and looked at him now, her eyes moist. "So you see, I have questions for you, too."

AT MIDMORNING THEY stopped for breakfast. Huddled over smoothies in a corner booth, Sarah asked more about Gabriel's book. For ten minutes he walked her through what was recently worth two million dollars.

Sarah listened without the slightest twitch.

"My opinion?" she said, not waiting for approval. "Bombs in buildings has been done. Bruce Willis saves the day, available on DVD. Religious sects with a dark agenda, rent *Stigmata*. But inserting history into scripture, now *that's* interesting. That's what people want. It's what makes your book dangerous."

"I kinda like dangerous."

Sarah cast a glance around the café. "Here's the question you have to ask yourself. What if you were *right?*"

Their eyes engaged, the room suddenly smaller.

"Sarah, I made it up. It's *fiction.*"

"So you think. But what if you nailed it? What if there *is* a plot to put a bomb in a building, and what if Matthew stumbled on it? He hears your name, contacts me . . . then he dies."

Gabriel pursed his lips and nodded solemnly.

"You haven't answered all my questions," said Gabriel.

Sarah sipped through a straw, her eyes intense.

"The university has incredible resources. Took me all of six minutes to get your address, phone, and credit history."

"Wow. Big brother goes to college."

This made her smile.

"The school has contacts at all the major publishing houses. A few calls, your name comes up. Now I know the house, the title, and the approximate date of publication."

Gabriel nodded, eyebrows furrowed.

"When your publisher and agent were killed, it didn't take a Ph.D. to conclude that you were next. So I flew out here, followed you around. Pulled you out of that fire, saw you drive away from the hospital in an SUV. I was watching your room when I got your covert call from the LaQuinta, and here we are."

"That's amazing if it's true."

She nodded, eyes downcast. "Everything I say is true. Always."

They finished their drinks at the same moment.

"So what do we have?" he asked.

"An opportunity," Sarah said thoughtfully, "and an obligation. Take your pick."

"Run through both," he said.

"Opportunity. Another publisher is still interested in your book. We see who comes out of the woodwork, be ready for anything. At best you get a pile of money and a career, at worst we put a stick in the spokes of something potentially ugly."

"And maybe learn what happened to your student," he added.

She nodded. "Obligation. If there is a bomb out there, or any other plan that comes close to what you've written, then as citizens of the planet, not to mention my oath to the National Security Agency, we have an obligation to try to stop it."

"Which means, we call in the troops."

"I *am* the troops. Right now, my superiors would laugh us out of the waiting room. You have no idea how many threats like this come up in a given year. What does your lawyer say?"

"You know about him?"

"I was parked four stalls down from you."

"Did you happen to see a skinny guy with wire-rims?"

"No one was anywhere near you."

"I'm on the record with my lawyer. And he knows about you."

"A good move."

It was then that Gabriel noticed a shift, a sudden distance in Sarah's eyes, bordering on sadness.

"What is it?" he asked, his voice low.

Her eyes landed on his with unflinching resolve.

"Do you believe in Providence? In God?"

"Loaded question."

"I mean *really* believe. Not with your head, your Sunday school stories, but with your heart. With all of it."

He held her eyes. "I don't know," he said.

Her smile was sad. "Something is going on here, Gabriel, something huge. What you do about it, how you react, may have implications far beyond yourself."

"Now you're scaring me."

"You have to believe in something to be scared."

He started to respond, but stopped. His big struggle since Lauren died had been with lies. Now, having survived two attempts on his life, he had to acknowledge that the most blatant lies of all may have been the ones he was telling himself.

Sarah waited, letting him feel the moment.

"Where there is light," she said softly, "there is also darkness nearby. Behind or below. Somewhere close, looking for an opening. Where there is good, there is evil. We get to choose."

Gabriel smiled. "Thank you."

She barely nodded. "We have a chance to prevent a tragedy."

Gabriel reached into a pocket and took out his wallet. From it he withdrew a piece of paper, a telephone number written from memory on stationery from the LaQuinta Inn in Citrus Heights.

"What's that?" she asked.

"That, my lovely guardian angel, is our chance."

- 43 -

Weed, California

THIS, THOUGHT GABRIEL, was truly no-man's-land. A gap between worlds belonging to ranchers and hermits. The airstrip was forty miles north of Mt. Shasta, a black monolith looming over them in the light of dusk. From I-5 the airstrip resembled a dark stripe in a pasture, lined with dim lamps that glowed in the evening haze. There was no control tower, and the only planes on the tarmac were small Cessnas and a couple of recycled crop dusters.

Simon Winger had personally answered Gabriel's call. He seemed genuinely delighted with Gabriel's decision to move forward with their business arrangement, and it appeared he had no idea what had transpired since their face-to-face two days earlier. Gabriel would fill him in, but that part of the story could wait.

Sarah stood next to him as they waited for the plane, which Winger had arranged. Their eyes scanned the dusk sky for lights, but they heard it before they saw it. The jet emerged from the clouds with flaps and gear extended, executing a low-level fly-by on its downwind leg. It turned gracefully a half mile out, returning to kiss the pavement with a graceful flare.

As they watched the plane taxi she said, "I'm not coming."

He'd assumed that she would accompany him to New York, into the mouth of the beast. His eyes betrayed his disappointment.

"I thought . . ."

She touched his arm. "There's work to be done."

The jet was heading straight at them, dramatically out of place, an eagle among ants, filling the air with thunder. It was an older Cessna Citation, bearing no identification.

Gabriel stared at the jet, reconciling what she'd said. He assumed she'd use the time to check out Simon Winger. And perhaps she had already realized something that was just now occurring to him—if she were with him upon arrival in Washington, Winger might have *her* checked out first. Perhaps, Gabriel concluded, it was best to let this woman do her job.

"As long as the team reconvenes," he said.

The airplane pivoted. Then the hatch lowered as the turbines wound down to idle.

"That's your cue," she said.

"One more question."

She waited with raised eyebrows.

"Who are Phillip Reilly, Michael Cobb, and Daniel Hergert?"

These were the names she'd asked him about at the deli near the Cathedral of St. John the Divine. Gabriel had jotted them down as soon as he returned to his room that day.

The question jarred her. She stared into him, confirming they were names with stories to tell.

"You're good," she said.

"Who are they, Sarah?"

Her expression told him the answer was not easy.

"When you know that, you will know the reason I am here," she said. She leaned closer, near enough for him to feel the heat of her breath on his ear. "Have faith, Gabriel."

She began walking toward the Lexus.

Gabriel watched for a moment before heading toward the jet. At the base of the stairs he stopped to look back. The Lexus was already turning onto the access road, heading for the freeway.

The sudden loneliness was suffocating. It was a familiar pain, held at bay only by a thin strand of hope. But soon pain gave way to anger, one salving the other. He was on a quest, and it was righteous. Someone had burned down his house, and they were trying to destroy his work and his life.

They were messing with the wrong writer.

– 44 –

MCQUARRIE WAS WAITING under the fuselage of a massive helicopter that served as the gate awning for the Pima Air Museum Visitors Center. One call to the local Agency office had rendered the area deserted. But the museum had nothing to do with this meeting. Its proximity to the desert did.

Larsen pulled up in a rented sedan, leaned over, and opened the door. "Get in."

McQuarrie took off his sunglasses to inspect the interior.

"Should I be worried?" He was obviously being sarcastic.

"We're meeting someone," said Larsen.

As McQuarrie got in, he casually reached into his jacket pocket and flipped off the safety on his nine-millimeter Glock.

They merged onto the 10, thick with morning traffic. As they headed south, Larsen said, "You've been compromised."

"That's pretty impossible," McQuarrie shot back. He had his arm perched casually on the back of the seat, his hand directly behind Larsen's head. A flick of a practiced wrist and he could snap the man's neck like a toothpick.

"Nervous?" said McQuarrie. "You look nervous to me."

"Your account code has been frozen. I need to pay you the kill fee in cash."

"Awkward. And highly suspicious."

"It's necessary. You'll get over it."

"Where is it?"

"In the trunk."

McQuarrie scanned the terrain, an infinity of dust. "Perfect day, don't you think?" Then he turned and looked at Larsen. "Who are we meeting?"

"Your next cutout. I've been compromised, too."

Both men knew what this meant—the end of their working relationship. Any further contact between them would put their mission, and their lives, in jeopardy.

"Why here?"

"Because the people we want you to kill are here."

"Gotta love the wet work. Bad hours, good pay."

It had better be. He'd hold out for more money than his usual fee. After that he and Joan would fade away.

"When it's done you'll chill out in Mexico for a while. These are hot targets, there'll be repercussions."

"I choose where I disappear. Not you."

"Whatever. I pay you, we kiss good-bye, have a nice life."

McQuarrie nodded, returning his attention to the road. What he'd just heard was fine with him. And it was good for Daniel Larsen, too. Because McQuarrie had a rule, and it was about to kick in: if a handle made him nervous, he made that handle vanish. Not exactly good for customer relations, but it was real peace of mind in the long run.

He smiled, picturing Joan lying by a pool. She loved Mexico, always had. Almost as much as she loved the money. There were darker depths to this woman than he knew, and he was looking forward to exploring them.

THEY TURNED OFF onto a side road just a few miles past the Titan Missile Silo that was now a tourist trap. It was the only one of the fifty-seven once-lethal Titan sites that remained assembled, its cadaver missile still in the bay and its warhead, rendered impotent, resting on the ground near the five-thousand-ton cement lid that once hid it from satellite surveillance.

"Just out of curiosity," McQuarrie asked, "what was the nature of the compromise?"

"Never thought it would happen in your lifetime, did you."

"I have my standards."

"Stone worked with a police artist, drew up a pretty good comp of your face. There's an APB out statewide. You're famous in California, my friend. Over the years we've been seen together around town, so I'm shit, too."

"There goes my inauguration tickets."

"After this next gig we'll take a breather, then work you offshore for a few years, maybe get a surgeon involved. You're too valuable to lose."

"Make me look like George Clooney and you've got a deal."

The car stopped behind a rocky knoll a mile in from the highway, out of the eye line of anyone but the local snakes.

"How many faces have you had?" asked Larsen as the car came to a stop on the gravel.

"On my fourth," he said.

"Strange business."

"I get better looking every time."

Larsen got out and headed for the trunk, but McQuarrie beat him there. Larsen arrived to see a gun was pointing at his forehead.

"Don't do this," he said.

"Give me the keys."

Larsen hesitated, as if he might defy the instructions.

Then, straightening, he said, "I need the deactivation code first. That's the trade."

McQuarrie chuckled. "I've already got your money. Now all I need are the keys. Which I can take from you."

"Wrong. You kill me, my people will find you. It's all downside, my friend. Take the money and live to work another day, or take the money and run. Your call."

McQuarrie squinted, the sun directly in his eyes. Then, wearing a smug expression, he said, "Just fuckin' with ya. The code is four four three, five five six."

Larsen's mouth moved silently as he memorized the code. He pulled out the keys and tossed them to McQuarrie, who snatched them from the air without moving his eyes.

"No reason to cross you, Daniel. I'm not stupid."

Larsen's eyes were suddenly distant. "You're some piece of work. No wonder we cut you loose."

"You cut me so they could use me in ways for which they wouldn't be held accountable," said McQuarrie. "Now step away."

Larsen shook his head as he moved back.

McQuarrie grinned. "How do you think I've lived through four faces? On your knees, hands behind your neck, facing away."

"These are new slacks, asshole."

"Send me the bill."

Larsen nodded, then turned his back and lowered to his knees. Satisfied, McQuarrie pocketed the gun as he unlocked the trunk. The lid rose with a squeak.

Two shots rang out—more like quick pops—one bullet hitting McQuarrie in the forehead, the other in his right eye socket. The agile young agent who had been hiding in the trunk sprung out like a cat, standing over McQuarrie's body as he pumped four more rounds into the already dead man's chest.

Larsen rose to his knees, dusting his pants as he walked past the body without so much as a glance. He snatched the keys from the trunk lock and moved to the driver's door.

"Bury it deep. No surface trace."

"Yes sir," said the young agent, taking off his jacket in anticipation of an hour of hard work in the midmorning sun, followed by a God-knows-how -long wait for his extraction. One had to pay one's dues in this business. At least he got to be the trigger this time out. That was sweet.

Larsen waited behind the wheel, mobile phone in hand. He had several calls to make, a full complement of shiny new wheels that needed to be set in motion.

"Four four three, five five six," he said aloud as he punched in the first telephone number, simultaneous digitations being an integral part of his training.

Then he laughed, waiting for someone to answer. If it weren't for his dirty pants, this would be a perfect day indeed.

-45-

MORDECAI SHOOK HIS head as he stared at the screen. The American's idea wasn't exactly brain surgery. It was no more complex than stacking bricks, forming them into a perfect square. Only in this case, each brick had hundreds of thousands of pieces of data, multiplied geometrically when cubed.

It had taken Mordecai two days to format the program and add a basement full of the world's most muscular memory chips to get to a point where a beta test was feasible. Once formatted, he'd tested the program with a search for known code arrays, including those he'd recently deciphered from the three-dimensional scans.

Typical technology evolution. Last week his three-dimensional matrix was the bomb. Now it was old news.

Nonetheless, given the sheer mass of this new model, he was still looking for a wisp of smoke in a hurricane.

Mordecai was actually ready by mid-evening, but the next day was his birthday. How cool would it be to unearth the greatest biblical secret in the history of the world on that day.

So, as his digital watch flashed midnight, Mordecai pressed the button.

He had expected the first hit, if it was there, to take up to an hour to find. But the world's fastest computer, navigating silicon with the most advanced deciphering algorithm ever written, took nearly six hours to find the next coded item.

A short electronic beep jarred him out of a power nap.

He rubbed his eyes and focused, squinting to be sure his eyes were not playing tricks. He had watched the program flail away at the cyberspace he had created, like a pressurized garden hose let loose, seeking direction but finding none. There had been false starts and dead ends, but finally the computer had found something.

With any luck, it would be a name.

There were sixteen letters in this newly discovered array. They matched an obscure item found in the target database, which he had downloaded prior to the beta test using the sum of all data utilized in every previous test ever done on this project, plus a downloaded database of every holder of every political post known to man since the advent of recorded history. There were over ninety thousand target words and names available.

It had just landed on one of them.

He was indeed staring at a name. Each letter had been found precisely six hundred and sixty-six counts deeper into the matrix than the one before it.

He felt a chill wash over him, as if something evil had licked the base of his neck.

WHEN MORDECAI SPOKE the name, Uriah Gerson felt ill. He was sitting at the breakfast table with Evelyn when the call came. He kissed her on the forehead and started to leave. When she expressed alarm at his haste, he told her that *the one* they had been waiting for had been at long last identified, and that his work had been validated.

He told her the name, but for Evelyn it held no meaning.

He left her with a gentle smile, thinking how very much he loved her innocence.

URIAH SPED TO the lab with the realization that the Columbia Center bombing had to be called off. Because the name they had found would be staying at the hotel the night before the Prayer Luncheon, a fact unknown at the moment of the plan's inception. Unlike the first target, the newly identified person must survive to step into the shoes of prophecy.

The faith of Uriah Gerson and Simon Winger had been rewarded. God had told them to back away, to allow the visions of the Book of Revelation to blossom into fact.

As guided by the secret scrolls of John, they had killed all those who would falsely ascend to the throne of the Antichrist. Satan's spawn, a desperate attempt to thwart the inevitable timetable of God. But that work had finished.

The name that Mordecai had extracted from the code belonged to the *true* Antichrist. This person, according to the Word of God, *must* survive, as revealed to John two thousand years before.

And as revealed to them now.

HE WAS STANDING IN the elevator at the computer lab when it happened. In an instant Uriah Gerson learned the answers to the burning questions which had consumed his life. And that his work was just.

Because, in a flash of unearthly white light, he was staring at the face of God Himself, consumed with love.

The truth was nothing like he expected. It was infinitely more beautiful.

THE BOMB COMPLETELY demolished the Technion computer sciences building at the Israel Institute of Technology. While vehemently denied by the Israeli government, it was acknowledged among the intelligence agencies of the world that the device had been thermonuclear in nature, small but effective, most likely detonated manually by a suicide bomber posing as a student.

This, too, had been hidden in prophecy. But no one would find it, because the only computer on the planet capable of finding and deciphering that code had been vaporized into a fine mist.

There were no survivors. Nor were any of the proprietary software programs and hardware prototypes salvaged. Everything within and near the perimeter of the premises had been vaporized in a white-hot fission flash. The death count was only eighteen, given the early hour of the explosion. Among those who perished were Professor Uriah Gerson and the brilliant doctoral candidate who worked under him, Mordecai Rosen.

That afternoon, the Tel Aviv newspaper *Ha'aretz* received a letter from a rogue splinter group of ex–Taliban revolutionaries working out of Syria, claiming responsibility. In the name of Islam, they promised further and even more extensive attacks on all who supported Israel and her heathen cause.

The greatest fear of the free world had materialized. Nuclear weapons had fallen into the hands of terrorists. It was, believed many who ascribed to biblical prophecy, yet another sign that the beginning of the end was at hand.

Book Five

And when the fifth thunder sounded,
my eyes beheld the dead in a time
twoscore years hence the fallen king,
a legion which numbered in the thousands of thousands
in all kingdoms of the Earth,
a plague spawned in the land of Eden
by the angel of liars to smite innocent and unclean alike,
though their ways had become common,
and upon their lovers and their children
and their children's children was the plague made.

"WHISPER OF THE SEVENTH THUNDER"
by Gabriel Stone

-46-

Washington, D.C.

THE SMALL JET banked over the Potomac on its final approach to Reagan Field, the monuments visible in the distance. Gabriel pressed his forehead against the glass, thankful the lonely all-night trip was over.

The plane taxied to the civil aviation terminal across the runway from the commercial passenger buildings. A black Town Car was waiting near the point at which the plane would apply brakes and cut power.

The hatch lowered. Gabriel emerged into morning sunlight, happy to be standing upright after five hours in a tube. He was looking forward to seeing Winger again. He had many more questions than before, and much more context within which to ask them.

The rear door of the Town Car opened, seemingly on its own.

He wished he had a minute to himself between rides. He wanted to call Sarah, ask a few more of those thousand questions on his list. If she was about to embark on a background check of the other players in this game, she would likely be doing it here. Close enough to help if he needed her.

Winger wasn't waiting in the limo's backseat. Instead Gabriel was greeted by a surprisingly youthful man wearing an old man's suit. The kid looked as if he should be washing and waxing the vehicle for ten bucks and a sandwich.

"Welcome to Washington," he said. "Ryan Healey."

Gabriel shook his hand, which had all the tensile rigidity and warmth of a day-old omelet. "Gabriel Stone. I was expecting Mr. Winger."

Ryan Healey pushed a button that automatically shut the door behind

Gabriel. This definitely wasn't Kansas anymore, or rural Sacramento, either.

"Mr. Winger sends his apologies. He's been called out of the country on an urgent matter."

The limo headed off quickly. The driver didn't bother to turn, but Gabriel could see that he was older, perhaps Winger's age. This, too, struck him as odd.

"I guess I'm confused," said Gabriel. "We were supposed to talk contracts. I spoke with him yesterday."

Ryan Healey smiled, expecting the comment. "He'll be back in a day or two, I assure you. In the meantime, Mr. Winger believes you'll appreciate the accommodations he's arranged for you. And I have the contract for you, which you can peruse at your leisure. Please feel free to forward it to your lawyer. If you need anything, I'm at your disposal. Here's my Skype name."

He handed Gabriel a card. The only thing on it was "Hunter666."

An odd handle, that. The buzz in Gabriel's head subsided slightly, though the loose ends were suddenly tightening around his throat.

"Mr. Winger believes it's important to get your book into print at the earliest possible date."

Gabriel was surprised by this. The rush implied the same agenda that was driving Veerman's schedule—the election. As the limo headed into town, the distant Washington Monument stabbing into the sky to their right, Gabriel wondered why Simon had not mentioned this.

The good guy sharing intentions with the bad guy. Interesting.

The ride took fifteen minutes, most of it consumed by the final six blocks as they entered Georgetown. Healey tried for small talk, asking all the requisite gracious host questions, but Gabriel's mind was reeling. He had come for answers, and what he got was a wannabe George Stephanopoulis and an excuse.

He was deposited in what Healey had called a "discreet boutique hotel" on M Street, just a few hundred yards away from the bars and clubs that made this neighborhood notorious, and from what he'd read, close to some obscure enclaves for the rich and politically paranoid.

As Gabriel was about to exit the limo, Healey handed him a large envelope.

"Your contract and some expense money. Go out, enjoy our city. No one other than me and Harvey here know where you are. Except Mr. Winger himself, I should add. We'll be in close touch."

Healey again offered that freshly embalmed handshake. Gabriel mindlessly wiped his palm against his jeans as he stood on the curb, watching the Town Car blend into the chaos of the Georgetown rush hour.

A SUITE HAD BEEN prepaid by a third party, with no check-out date specified. Gabriel gave the bellman a five, tossed his bag onto the bed, and tore into the envelope.

Another "Hunter666" card was clipped to the contract, this time with Healey's phone number. Between it and the contract was an envelope, unsealed, which at a glance contained a half-inch stack of mint-crisp twenties.

Gabriel scanned the documents, his head pounding too hard for a detailed read. He recognized the name of the publishing company, referred to here in the unabashed legalese as "the buyer" or "the publisher." He scanned the headings, looking for the words *advance against future royalties*.

He found it on the second page. Winger was offering him a one-million-dollar advance. And that was just for the hardcover, a more prestigious edition than the trade paperback Veerman was planning. Plus another million dollar advance for the mass market paperback rights, payable immediately, something even Gabriel knew was rare.

Winger wanted this book very much indeed. The question was, why?

Gabriel tossed the contract on the bed and flopped backwards onto the mattress, suddenly energized. But within moments the elation ebbed away, replaced by an awareness of the cost thus far—the deaths of Kathryn and Veerman, the destruction of his house, the sense that he was no longer in control of his life.

And, that he was alone.

For a moment it had almost seemed real.

- 47 -

Library of Congress
Washington, D.C.

IT WAS TEN in the morning and Sarah hadn't returned his call. Out west it was only seven, too early to hear back from Michael Land. Gabriel had faxed him the contract from the hotel's business center before heading out.

After a croissant and overpriced coffee, Gabriel took a cab to the Library of Congress, across the street from the Capitol. The library was divided into three buildings, requiring a map and an abundance of time, neither of which he had. His intention was to search out three names—Phillip Reilly, Michael Cobb, and Daniel Hergert.

His first stop was the Madison Building. A helpful little man working in the first-floor research room sent him across the street to the Jefferson Building, where the library's computer research center was located. If the article database didn't yield results, he would delve into as yet undigitized microfiche from the U.S. Census Bureau, looking for birth and/or death data.

He would also search for anything he could find out about Simon Winger.

By noon he had found the three names Sarah Meyers had provided, knowing that he would investigate. But strangely, there was virtually nothing on Winger.

The telephone in his pocket rang, eliciting an evil stare from a librarian who looked like she needed a night out.

It was Sarah. She was in town, and as he suspected she was close by. She wanted to meet him on the steps of the library in thirty minutes, anxious to hear what he had learned.

Hanging up, Gabriel was certain that she already knew.

THREE TIMES THAT morning Gabriel had been hit with the familiar sensation of being watched. In the library's computer reference room, full of cubicles that were occupied at all times, he'd twice looked up to see an attractive woman with dark hair looking right at him. The third time he glanced up he saw her leaving the room.

This was more than coincidence. He'd already seen her earlier in the lobby of his hotel. She'd glanced away then, too.

Outside, Sarah was coming up the steps, dressed like one of the federal drones that swarmed these streets.

"You look pale," she said, extending her hand in a businesslike greeting. She'd pulled him from the fire, literally and figuratively, and suddenly she wanted to shake his hand.

"Isn't flushed the opposite of pale?"

Her smile was that of schoolgirl caught off guard.

"How'd you do?" he asked.

He was looking forward to hearing her news about Simon Winger, hoping she'd been more successful than he had.

"Eat first?" she asked.

Lunch was as good an excuse as any to get out of there. Because next to the door, looking through her purse with a contrived urgency, stood the dark-haired woman.

THE PIZZERIA ON a nearby corner was crowded, junior bureaucrats on a lunch budget. Gabriel brought two slices of thin-crust Genoa and two soft drinks back to the table. He cast a glance around in search of the woman with long dark hair, thankful she wasn't there.

At least that he could see. A sixth sense told him that they were still within her line of vision.

Sarah looked up and smiled as she took the food.

"You first," she said, already digging in.

Gabriel took a thoughtful sip of his drink. "Tell me why you asked me about those names in New York."

Sarah didn't wait to swallow before answering. "Same reason I showed you Matthew's photograph. To see your reaction."

"A little technique you picked up in spy school?"

"Something like that."

He nodded. "You knew I'd check them out. What I don't understand is, if you're really with the NSA, you already have a file on those guys. Only conclusion left is that you wanted me to find out who they are for myself. Question is, *why?*"

She chewed thoughtfully, casually took another bite.

"Maybe I didn't know where you stood. Maybe Matthew was right, your book was dangerous to the people he was watching, which means the author might be dangerous, too."

"So now you know. I'm harmless."

"Hardly." She took another bite, grinning. "Tell me what you found. Then we'll talk about what it means."

He reached for his notepad from the empty chair next to him. He reviewed the data for a moment.

"Phillip Reilly. Twenty-year-old British law student, killed in a bus bombing while on holiday in Jerusalem in ninety-nine. Part of a well-known old money family with political ties. One magazine said he was on a fast track toward a Parliamentary seat, if he could learn to hold his tongue."

He looked up at Sarah. She was nodding, though her eyes remained on the food. He had been right—she already knew.

"Michael Cobb. Eighteen-year-old from Florida, also from money, nephew of a U.S. congressman and headed to Harvard, pre-law. IQ near two hundred, concert pianist, ran the hundred in ten flat. Died May of ninety-four, complications stemming from HIV. He wasn't gay, though, far as anyone knew. Got it from a transfusion during an appendectomy. Friends claimed he was set on becoming the President of the United States before he was thirty-six, and they believed him."

Sarah said, "Go on," again without looking up.

"Daniel Hergert. Lawyer from Idaho, two-time loser in congressional races before the age of thirty. Committed suicide with painkillers and booze, no note. Friends thought it was suspicious because he'd just gotten engaged and seemed happy. Very politically outspoken, lots of enemies. And get this—the guy studied for the priesthood before politics."

He looked up from his notes.

"Three dead rich guys. All politically ambitious. Then again, you knew all that, didn't you?"

Gabriel's intense gaze caused Sarah to look away.

"So let me ask *you*," he said, "did *you* find anything?"

She bit her lip, her eyes elsewhere. "Yes."

That was all she said. Gabriel turned his palms to the ceiling and shook his head.

Her eyes snapped back to him. "I can't tell you."

"That's crap."

"Yes it is. And you're getting warm."

She watched him process her words, saw a dance of rage and confusion behind his eyes.

"Who do I work for, Gabriel?"

"You know, that's a terrific question."

"Answer it."

"Supposedly the NSA."

"Meaning . . . what?"

"Meaning . . ." He paused, frozen with realization, his eyes huge. "It's classified. You can't tell me squat."

She was nodding. "Meaning . . ."

"Meaning you're legally bound by your job description. On or off the clock, you can't go there." He paused, making sure that she was still nodding. "But there's no law saying I can't investigate for myself."

"Is it still crap, Gabriel? Or am I helping you?"

His face melting into a knowing smile. "You're waiting for me to catch up."

"Let's walk," she said, her eyes surveying the room as she got to her feet.

48

THEY DEPARTED THE restaurant and headed down a busy street toward Sarah's rental car, which she'd parked under some trees three blocks from the Library of Congress.

"Tell me what else you found." From her expression Gabriel could see she already knew his answer.

"Nothing substantive on the Brethren. A few churches by that name, but nothing in Washington and nothing with an elite roster or a political agenda. There were several pieces about the National Prayer Luncheon, none mentioning a sponsoring entity."

Once again Sarah was already nodding.

"They're good," she said, her eyes on the sidewalk.

"Simon Winger is a myth. I was sure the name's a pseudonym until I ran a scan on an obscure search engine that focuses on offshore published media. Holdover from my agency days. One article in an obscure radical British rag, now defunct, claimed there was a conspiracy perpetrated by wealthy right-wing psychos who were killing off anyone who threatened their political and religious agendas, which to them were one and the same. Daniel Hergert was named as a potential victim, claiming his suicide was staged, that he was killed in the name of God. And of course, there were the Kennedys, all three of them, Sadat, even that Hamas leader supposedly killed by the Israelis a couple of years ago. Paranoid stuff, even by my standards."

Sarah asked, "What's that have to do with Winger?"

The tone of her voice told Gabriel that he was right about what he suspected. She knew everything.

"Coincidence one—the writer was American, a former editor working for the publishing company in New York that Winger claims to control. A sidebar article said he was working on an exposé at the time, that he had names and connections that corroborated his conspiracy theory, but his bosses killed the article."

"So," said Sarah tentatively, "we find the writer."

"Great idea. One problem, though, and it's called coincidence two—the writer is dead. He was in the north tower on September 11. And besides, the magazine is out of business."

Gabriel watched her, sensing a shift that had more to it than a consideration of the facts. He had caught her in a contradiction with the story of her friend's fate.

"Too much, too soon?" he offered.

Sarah looked away. "I don't know what you mean."

"I think you do. You wanted me to uncover the names, you wanted me to know how mysterious, how dangerous, Simon Winger may be. You don't cross the federal line, you get a partner in figuring this thing out. What you weren't counting on was me finding that article, much less the name of the guy who wrote it. Hell, maybe the NSA doesn't even know about my little search engine."

Sarah began fishing her keys out of her purse.

"Which brings me to coincidence three, and it's a dandy. The deceased author's name was Matt. Matt Pascarella."

She had no reaction to the news.

"Matt. As in *Matthew.* As in, your supposedly dead-of-a-heart-attack friend. Which was it, Sarah? A heart attack or a terrorist attack?"

She snapped her eyes onto his.

"It doesn't matter," she said. "And it doesn't change anything."

"You're lying to me. Lying changes everything."

"Sometimes it's *necessary.*"

Everything in his programming screamed at him to run, yet he desperately wanted to give her the last possible benefit of the significant doubt that was now in play.

"I need you to trust me, Gabriel. I'll tell you anything you want to know. Off the record, of course."

"When?" he asked.

But she didn't get to answer.

At that moment a windowless van appeared, stopping in the traffic lane abreast of Sarah's rented car. Simultaneously, a huge black man wearing a Wizard's warm-up and sunglasses came up behind them, thrusting an arm around Sarah.

Before he could react Gabriel felt something hard pressing against the back of his ribs.

"Inside," barked the man, who had four inches and sixty pounds on Gabriel. He propelled them toward the vehicle, the panel door of which slid open as they approached.

When he pushed them inside, they were greeted by a woman holding a gun. She had been driving, but had climbed into the back, leaning against the opposite sliding door.

The door slammed shut. The defensive tackle from the sidewalk trotted to the front and climbed in behind the wheel. Without looking back he slammed the van into gear and took off, the momentum of which threw both Gabriel and Sarah to the floor.

The woman with the gun simply stared. She had long, straight hair and an olive complexion that screamed third world. Gabriel recognized the face, then the clothes. As he stared, the dark-haired woman from the library said, "Hello, Gabriel." And then she smiled, raising the gun to eye level.

49

THE VAN PULLED away, commencing one of those suspended moments in which the game could spin either way. The eye contact was intense, the woman delivering hers with a sly smile fortified by the gun.

"Who the hell are you?" Gabriel finally asked, his back now pressed against the metal slats of the van's side.

"Who the hell is *she?*" snapped the woman, flicking her eyes to Sarah for the briefest moment.

"Old friend," shot back Gabriel.

"Guy like you needs all the old friends he can get."

"What do you know about a guy like me?"

"Everything," said the woman. This began another few seconds of intense quiet, all eye contact and posturing.

In a less hostile voice he again asked, "Who are you?"

"Not important. What is important is the fact that I was married to the man who has been trying to kill you."

Sarah and Gabriel swapped a quick look.

"Relax," said the woman. "I'm not here to finish his work."

The woman smiled slowly, an element of sadness evident beneath the harsh veneer. She relaxed the gun to a more comfortable angle, now pointing straight at his chest.

"My husband is dead." The woman was watching them carefully. "He left behind explicit instructions about how I am to conclude his business with you."

The van turned and accelerated into heavy traffic, inertia forcing them to struggle for balance. It would have been the ideal moment for Gabriel to make a move, especially in light of what he'd just heard, but it was over quickly.

"How did you find me?"

"My husband had friends. Some of them have access to certain government databases, one of which included flight plans filed all over the country. Yesterday a private carrier filed a flight plan from a rural strip in California to Reagan. One of his other friends saw you get off that plane and called me as he followed you, including here."

She looked smug as she watched Gabriel sort it out.

"Who hired him?"

"I honestly don't know. Nor do I care. But I do know *why*."

Gabriel and Sarah exchanged looks. "Feel free to share," he said.

"I intend to. There's a new hotel here in Washington, a very big deal. The Columbia Center. You've heard of it?"

Gabriel shook his head as Sarah nodded hers.

"It's about to open," said Sarah.

The woman nodded back. "Tomorrow, in fact. What you need to know is this—there is a bomb hidden in the infrastructure of that building. I know this because my husband put it there. The device draws power from the building itself, which means it can remain active indefinitely, even in the case of a power failure thanks to a lithium backup. And here's the part that should interest you—it's wirelessly linked to the house state-of-the-art digital network, in the event a deactivation code is required."

"Reach out and kill someone," said Gabriel.

"I hope you're taking me seriously, Mr. Stone."

"You didn't mention your husband was a *traitor*, too."

The woman's eyes turned cold, and for a moment he thought he'd pushed too hard.

"Don't be so quick to judge what you don't understand."

"You got *that* much right, I *don't* understand. Top of the list is, what the hell does *any* of this have to do with me?"

Her expression softened, control regained.

"Nothing, and everything. My husband's employers believed that you were a threat to the successful completion of their plan, the politics of which I don't really understand, either. Something about a book you've written. Based on the obvious fact that you are still alive, I must assume you are protected by people with significant resources. He said that would be the case, too."

Sarah chimed in with "You have no idea how significant."

The woman ignored Sarah, keeping her eyes fixed on Gabriel.

"My husband left me with very specific instructions. If something happened to him and you survived, it could only mean that he was betrayed. In which case, he wanted to make sure you had the option to stop these people before the bomb is detonated."

"*Me?*"

"I will show you how to do it."

Gabriel and Sarah both stared at the woman in disbelief.

"Why don't you just do it?" he said.

"I wish it were that simple. The deactivation code transmission must be made on the hotel property itself, using the hotel's house phone. A failsafe designed to prevent remote intervention if the plan was compromised. The people behind this may know who I am. You can see why I can't just walk through the door and dial in a code and then walk back out."

"So why *me?* I'd say I'm in the same boat."

"My husband said it was your choice to make."

"I don't understand."

"You will. You see, he believed that the only way he would be stopped from killing you was if his employer realized you were of more value alive than dead. That you were, in fact, a perfect patsy for the bombing. Whoever comes forward with the deactivation code will be, by implication, the person *behind* the plan. Your coming forward to stop the bomb is as good as a confession that you were behind it in the first place. Of course, the bomb may go off anyway for all I know, in which case you won't be there to argue your case."

Sarah suddenly said, "Some sense of humor, your husband."

The woman smiled at her.

"He said that's how he'd do it, if it were his plan. As it was, he was just the triggerman."

Suddenly the plot of Gabriel's novel crystallized as the link to the reality before him. At first they—whoever *they* were—feared it might expose their plan, that it hit too close to home. Now they intended to use the book to cover themselves, make him look like it was all his idea in the first place. All they needed was to put him on the scene.

Which was precisely what this woman was trying to facilitate.

Gabriel squirmed, sore from sitting on the metal floor. He remembered Simon Winger asking him if he was alone in the room when he wrote the book, which at the time seemed like a strange inquiry. Now, it seemed quite insightful.

Perhaps, while he was ignoring God, God was writing him a script.

"How do I know this code of yours won't actually set the thing off? The patsy walks in, blows himself and the hotel all to hell, gets immortalized in the process."

"You don't. Interesting notion, though, don't you think?"

"What prevents me from taking this to the police as soon as you let us go?"

"Be my guest. I'll be someplace sunny with more money than I need. You do what you have to. The police are already looking for you."

"Fine. I'll just hand over the code, let them call it in. I'll take my chances with my side of the story."

"And in the meantime, the people who killed my husband detonate the bomb and several hundred people die while you're eating jail food. You still get blamed."

"I'll take my chances."

The woman was suddenly red faced, not a good thing in a person holding a gun. "I don't think you understand me here. If you go to the authorities, the people behind this will know, because they *are* the authorities! What part of this am I not making clear?"

There would be no simple choices today.

Gabriel glared darkly at his host. "Thanks for the rock and a hard place, lady. What, exactly, did your husband think I'd *do* with this information?"

"He thought you'd be smart. Dig around, find out who's behind this before you expose yourself. He wants revenge, you want justice. Two sides of the same coin. You *do* want justice, don't you Mr. Stone? Isn't that what you'd choose?"

Gabriel saw that Sarah was staring at him. Everyone wanted to know what he'd do now.

The woman reached into the front passenger seat. Again, Gabriel could have easily moved for the gun, but it didn't enter his head now. The story had become more intriguing, and any sudden movement might send the house of cards tumbling.

She turned back and handed him an unlabeled DVD disk in a clear plastic case.

"My husband is the one in the cheesy rent-a-cop uniform. I know because I shot it myself. The other two men are your ticket out of this. Find them, tie them to the hotel, and you've got a bestseller on your hands. One you can write from your deck instead of an isolation cell. Either way, Mr. Stone, you're famous. And you'd better hurry. You have less than twelve hours."

Suddenly the van pulled over to the side of the road. They had been weaving through busy traffic, and Gabriel hadn't noticed that they'd crossed back into town on another bridge. In fact, they'd already departed Georgetown and were well into downtown Washington.

It had been only four days since his house had burned, two since this woman's husband had tried to facilitate the illusion of his suicide. And yet his old life seemed a distant memory, one that was vague and meaningless. Suddenly the fate of hundreds of lives rested on his shoulders.

The woman slid open the panel door. Then she held out an envelope.

"Choose wisely. You only get one chance."

The gun came back up to eye level, the barrel flicking at the door.

Gabriel took the envelope as he and Sarah stepped out onto a crowded sidewalk. The van sped away before the door had fully closed.

Gabriel saw Sarah's eyes sweep skyward across the street. He followed her line of sight, his own eyes narrowing in the brightness.

Before them was the Columbia Center Hotel and Conference Center. A huge banner hung over the entrance courtyard announcing the grand opening, and the inaugural event that was its centerpiece.

The National Prayer Luncheon would be held there the next day.

THE STRUCTURE WAS a monochromatic weaving of glass and steel, polished to a chromic sheen made all the more surreal in the afternoon sun. Like the tallest buildings in the city that weren't designated as monuments, the Columbia Center had been restricted to twelve stories, but made up for it with a four-block sprawl of architecturally interlocking modules, each connected by tunnels and bridges.

Standing in its shadow on the opposite sidewalk, Gabriel tore open the envelope. An index card inside bore three lines of data, all neatly typed. The first was a telephone number. The next two were what appeared to be access codes. The word "engage" appeared after one, "void" after the other.

Sarah stared at him, then grabbed his arm and began escorting him down the sidewalk. Gabriel kept his eyes on the building, as if it were daring him to return.

"Keep walking," she said. It was a mile or so to her car, which he assumed was their destination. They would go back to his hotel, regroup, watch the DVD, develop a plan.

But Sarah couldn't wait that long.

There was a copy center a block ahead. Where, for twenty cents a minute, you could rent a computer that played DVDs.

Sarah didn't ask to see the code, and Gabriel didn't volunteer.

THE IMAGE WAS amateurish, captured from a cheap handheld camera positioned about a hundred yards away from its target. They knew this
because the opening shot was a wide angle from the Lincoln Memorial—a
column occasionally appeared at the side of the frame—looking down over
the steps toward the mall reflecting pool. People milled about under umbrellas in a gray mist, paying no attention to the camera, which panned slowly.
But suddenly it zoomed close, clearly showing the face of a man dressed in a
nondescript gray suit near the water's edge, his eyes nervous. There was no
sound, adding a surreal touch.

"Know him?" asked Sarah.

"No."

A moment later the man was joined by a mall security guard who was
much shorter, wearing wire-rimmed glasses.

"But I know *him*," said Gabriel, his adrenaline spiking. "The rent-a-cop.
That's the guy who tried to kill me."

Sarah's eyes remained fixed on the screen.

At first it seemed to be a chance encounter. The guard's initial words
were delivered with a smile, but the man in the suit didn't seem pleased.
It was odd how the suit kept covering his mouth while his eyes constantly
scanned the area.

"Guy's a pro," said Sarah. "From the trade."

The security guard kept his eyes riveted on those of his taller companion
as they talked, a trace of amusement evident.

Sarah said, "He knows he's being taped by his wife."

The suit handed something to the security guard, which he deftly
pocketed without so much as a glance.

After another moment—a paranoid one for the suit—the security guard
cast his eyes directly toward the camera and nodded. The suit then squinted in
the same direction, as if trying to find something the guard had just pointed
out to him. A moment later realization dawned, his expression that of a man
about to be hunted down.

As the guard turned away, still grinning, the image quickly shifted. There
was a moment of black, one of the monument's massive columns in the
frame, then another moment as the lens auto-focused.

Then it shifted slightly, stopping on a man standing in shadows, holding
a camera of his own. He, too, had been shooting in the direction of the pond,

possibly even the same conversation they'd just witnessed.

The image zoomed closer to the new guy's face.

Gabriel gasped.

"What is it?" asked Sarah.

The man suddenly turned toward the camera, his expression alarmed as he realized he was being photographed.

The image smeared and then went to black. As if the operator had hit the off button simultaneous with the first steps of a hasty flight.

"Go back," said Gabriel, leaning closer.

Sarah positioned the cursor and clicked. The image reversed. When it reached the moment of the man's surprise, Gabriel said, "Hold."

His chest pressed against her shoulder, allowing her to feel as much as hear the sudden acceleration of his breathing.

"That's him," said Gabriel. "That's Simon Winger."

THEY RETURNED TO Gabriel's suite to weigh their options, which suddenly seemed few. The truth was, neither of them knew what to do next. Simon Winger was *involved*, but to what extent, and with what intention, was impossible to call.

Sarah wanted to watch the DVD again on her laptop, so Gabriel took the opportunity to grab a shower. As he steamed himself, doubts began to lick at his reasoning.

He heard her scream his name.

He grabbed a towel and emerged wet from the bathroom. Sarah leaned forward over the desk, staring at the screen.

"Watch this," she said, hitting a few keys to reset the image. The scene shifted to the base of the Washington Monument, the camera panning up as if to establish this location. When the pan leveled, it zoomed to the image of two men having a conversation near the base. Their body language was awkward, eye contact avoided, a little too much distance between them, as if to create doubt in the mind of an onlooker that they were actually speaking to each other. One covered his mouth while the other had the collar of his coat pulled high to cover his.

One was the suit from the previous sequence. Apparently the camera operator had followed him here after the near-miss with Winger. Which meant this was all about insurance for the assassin, just as the woman in the van had implied.

She froze the image at a point when the newcomer's collar had blown to the side, revealing a distinctively square jaw.

"Recognize him?"

Gabriel squinted. The face was still blurred.

"Maybe this will help," she said, striking a few keys. A grainy but suddenly familiar face filled the screen.

Something hot and foul spilled into Gabriel's stomach. His breath froze as Sarah turned to look at him.

"Jesus H. Christ," whispered Gabriel.

"Not exactly," Sarah answered.

The man on the video was a regular on the evening news. The face of power. It was Brock Carter, special advisor to the President of the United States. A few months earlier, in addition to his duties as a heavy-handed enforcer on the President's Cabinet, Carter had assumed the leadership of the committee to reelect the President. He'd been all over the news for years.

Somehow, if this footage was to be believed, Brock Carter was involved in a plot to bomb the National Prayer Luncheon.

Haifa, Israel

THE SYNAGOGUE WAS quiet as a tomb. Dusty light streamed in through stained glass, illuminating years of patina and wear on rows of sparsely populated wooden pews. Every footfall, every muted sniffle of pain, echoed through time and space. Candles illuminated an elaborate altar, the only source of light.

A solitary woman sat at the end of a pew, flanking the center aisle. Her head hung beneath a black veil, her body stooped over so that her face was in contact with the pew in front of her. She rocked slightly, back and forth in unison with her breathing, which had the tempo of deep sleep.

Simon Winger stood at the back and watched. He had known Uriah for more than half his life, had considered him a mentor before realizing they shared friendship as well as a common goal. Uriah had brought him into God's work, had opened the ancient secrets to him, all with the blindest of faith.

When Simon saw his own name in the scrolls, written there by the hand of John the Divine nearly two thousand years earlier, he could make no other choice. Everything that had happened to him in his lifetime—great wealth, access to power, Uriah's friendship—was merely a means toward an end of God's design.

Together they had literally changed the world. They had bridged the chasm between Testaments, between Jew and Christian, erasing it entirely as they did the bidding of the Lord. There was only one reality, simple and pure, and it defied all dogma and religious bias. At the center of that truth, amid the rattling of the swords of the pretenders they would smite, there was always but one prophecy, one Christ, one Antichrist.

One Truth. Whose time had come.

Simon walked slowly down the center aisle, his soles gritty on the ancient tiles. He stopped when he was abreast of the woman, hoping to sense an awareness of his presence in her posture or breathing. His eyes were heavy with grief.

Several moments passed before he heard her say, "Simon."

He touched her shoulder, leaving his hand there for a moment. She did not move, other than to reach up and place her hand on his. He moved to the pew in front of her and sat, turning back to face the mourning wife of Uriah Gerson.

Evelyn raised her head, trembling hands pulling back the veil. A smile rallied through swollen red eyes, the face of a seventy-five-year-old woman who had seen many things, who understood much more than her husband realized.

"There are no words," said Simon softly. He had wept on the flight over, but his tears were now dry.

"Thank you for coming so quickly," she said.

He nodded. She had called him personally with the news of the bombing and of Uriah's death. Before the newswires had picked it up, the suspected nuclear aspect of the incident was destined to become one of the top stories of the decade.

She had alluded to important business left unfinished.

"So much has been lost," she said. "But the work remains."

Indeed. Uriah's precious computer, the scrolls themselves, were both gone. Mordecai was with Uriah in heaven. God in His wisdom would have to find a way to light Simon's path.

"It is upon you now," she said, her voice frail.

"I know that," he said, unsure what she meant.

"He spoke of a name," she said, her eyes burning.

"Uriah gave you a name?"

She nodded. "The code revealed it to Mordecai. Uriah said it was the name of the chosen one, the foretold, for whom you have been praying. That of the true Antichrist."

Simon felt something constrict in his soul. All of the decades, all of the fallen, had passed in quest of this name.

"What, precisely, did he say?" asked Simon, placing his free hand on hers. "The exact words."

She smiled slightly. "He said you were right. That Mordecai had created your cube, and at its heart there awaited the unholy name of names."

Simon nodded, on the precipice of madness.

She said, "It is not whom you believed."

She whispered it. And in an instant, everything was suddenly rendered clear.

Gabriel Stone had been right. Not about his story, or the flawed theology residing at its heart. But rather, about what had seemed like a brash and insignificant aside, a heretical supposition intended to fire his fiction with controversy.

Gabriel Stone had foretold the destruction of the hotel. And, perhaps unwittingly, identified the Antichrist, as well.

Maybe the Holy Ghost had indeed been at his side all along.

At all costs the Antichrist, the last in a series of pretenders to this throne, must be allowed to live on to assume this dark destiny, as written by God himself.

The Seven Thunders had commanded John to seal what he had seen. When the time had come, the key would be turned. That time was now. And Gabriel Stone was the key.

Now Simon had one more task before him.

The Columbia Center bombing had to be stopped. Because the truly anointed Antichrist, the fruition of God's promise, would be there.

- 53 -

39,000 Feet Over the Atlantic Ocean

THERE WAS NOT the slightest sense of motion as the sleek airplane floated through a liquid void above a black sea, a few dozen knots shy of the speed of sound and only a hundred miles west of the coast of Spain.

He used the time for reflection. All along, as guided by Uriah's interpretation of the secret scrolls, they believed the name of their final target, the man who would be the Antichrist, was Armand Brenner. A man who, if the polls had merit, was about to assume the office of the President of the United States. A man who had been cleverly manipulated by The Brethren to be present, along with his staff, at the Columbia Center when the bomb went off in the middle of the night, the fact of which would minimize innocent fatalities.

Soon, unless he acted swiftly, they would kill the wrong man. Armand Brenner, their target, was *not* the Antichrist. And now, in a twist of divine irony, his mission was to make sure *no one* died that night at the Columbia Center.

Of all the scholars and martyrs and prophets across twenty centuries of prayerful expectation, only an innocent named Gabriel Stone had gotten it right.

He waited until the breakfast hour on the eastern seaboard to dial Daniel Larsen's secure line. Despite the logistics of satellite telemetry and secure encryption protocols, the ringing was immediate and clear.

"Yes." His traditional frosty salutation.

"Brother Daniel," Simon greeted him.

Simon heard the receiver being muffled, as if Larsen were dismissing someone from the room before speaking.

"How was it?" he said when he came back on.

Simon had briefed Daniel prior to leaving for Israel. Larsen had already sat in on several meetings about the bombing in Haifa, and was intrigued with the possibility that Simon's contact had managed to leave behind something of value, even if it was only a verbal message from the dead man's widow.

"Tragic," said Simon. "We need to talk."

There was a moment of silence as a brief crackle of static compromised their connection. Then, suddenly, the line went perfectly clear.

"Daniel, listen to me. You know our work has always been based in faith. About preparing the way."

"One man's faith is another's laundry list. You listen to voices, I put soap into the machine."

"The answer has been revealed, Daniel. Faith and patience have been rewarded." He paused. "We know the name."

"The name."

"The prophesized one. Hidden deeply in the code."

"Brenner," said Larsen with a matter-of-fact tone.

Simon paused, then said, "No. It is someone else."

Silence signaled Larsen's reverent appreciation for what this meant. At least that's what Simon wanted to believe.

"This changes everything."

"I would say so."

"Our work is finished. The Antichrist must survive. This is God's will. You must silence the bomb."

Another moment of quiet passed. One man was praying, the other calculating.

"Daniel?"

"I'm here."

"Do you understand what I just said?"

"Yes."

Simon smiled. For all his cold efficiency and brusque mannerisms, Larsen was above all a brother in Christ.

"God in heaven be praised," Larsen said, his voice flat.

"God be praised indeed," Simon echoed.

"Who is it, Simon? Please, I must know."

"It is best you don't. For now."

Larsen had always been involved on a need-to-know basis, and he need not know the name to stop the bomb. Simon would tell him the name of the Beast later, when this was all safely behind them.

"You have the disarming code?"

"Of course. I will do it myself, tonight."

Simon knew that the disarm code had a fifteen-minute active window, beginning precisely at two o'clock in the morning. If no code was entered, the bomb would go off at two-sixteen.

"I'll call when I land. There *is*, however, one more thing."

"I'm listening, Simon."

"Gabriel Stone. If you find him . . . he is not to be harmed."

Simon closed his eyes, hoping to pass the final hours of the flight in a deep sleep. The world was about to plunge into a tunnel of darkness, with the true Antichrist casting a false shadow of hope. What a complex emotion it was, rejoicing that the will of God was at hand, and knowing that it meant the end of life as he knew it. Anxiety gnashed at his stomach.

But the anxiety was caused by something else entirely.

Daniel Larsen had rolled too easily. His tone was too conciliatory, his words too perfect. Something was wrong, and Simon had less than a day to find out what it was.

Langley, Virginia

DANIEL LARSEN SAT in what appeared to be a typical corporate board-room, a long table of marvelously finished Brazilian wood surrounded by plush leather thrones, three of which were occupied by men who stared at him. Profit margins and dividends, however, were rarely discussed within these walls.

Two of the men were agency royalty, but even they felt impotent before the superior force among them: Brock Carter, special counsel to the President of the United States and chairman of his reelection committee. Balding and bloated, his suit in need of pressing, he wore the impatient scowl of a tired detective straight off a New York cop show. It was a known fact that this man had not smiled since 1982, on the day his daughter married a software prodigy who would one day own an NFL franchise.

Larsen clicked off with an understated flourish. They all knew it was Simon Winger who had interrupted their meeting, and they had listened carefully to Larsen's side of the conversation.

"New problem?" said Larsen's boss, a surly little man who hadn't smiled since 1988, on the day his divorce was final.

"Simple fix," Larsen said. "I'm on it."

"Stone is in town?" Carter asked, tired of this Simon Winger business. The old coot had been getting in the way for years, and Larsen's 'simple fix' was long overdue.

"Yesterday," said Daniel. "We picked him up at his hotel and have had eyes on him since. He's with a woman."

"Get an ID on her. Is Stone positioned?"

"Definitely. Anyone who checks will find calls to a Berlin bank known to do business with Afghani and former Iraqi militants. There are also calls to various hotels, paralleling the known travels of an Al-Qaeda operative who will be apprehended before the week is over and silenced before he can refute the confession we've written for him. There are other details, but mostly there's the book. Reads like a diary confessing to the crime."

"Status?" the CIA honcho barked.

"We have a copy. When we break the news of Stone being the trigger, it'll go wide in paperback within two weeks."

This required no further explanation. A major New York publisher owed them favors, especially given his dicey situation with the IRS, which the agency would happily remedy.

"What if people don't buy it? If they think his bogus theology is as bad as his prose?" said Carter.

"People filter newspapers, but they believe books. Hell, half the world thinks Jesus and Mary Magdalene are living in a condo in Istanbul thanks to a goddamn book."

Brock Carter nodded his satisfaction, then stood. His eyes went to each of the men before him. "Gentlemen, on behalf of the President of the United States, thank you for your work."

They watched him leave the room. Normally he traveled with an entourage, but today he was alone.

By tomorrow the man who sought to replace the President in the White House would be dead. The world would be outraged, most of all the President himself. Within days, mobilized by the President's passion for swift justice, the terrorist perpetrators of the horrible crime would be located and dealt with harshly. The President would be praised for his bold and righteous protection of the nation.

And he would take action against the perpetrators of what would be the most heinous act of terror in history.

It would all happen before Election Day. As if it had been ordained on high.

Other than the men in this room, no one who knew the truth would be alive to tell it.

-55-

GABRIEL HAD SAID nothing when he saw Brock Carter on the laptop screen. Suddenly, without a word, he returned to the bathroom, leaving Sarah alone with Carter's face.

"What are you doing?" she yelled through the door.

"Getting dressed."

"Talk to me, Gabriel."

"I'm done talking."

She stood up and went to the door, leaning against the jamb with her arms folded.

A moment of quiet followed. Gabriel was digging through his bag to find a pair of clean shorts, his energy building by the second. His fascination with Sarah had blinded him to what he should have seen long ago.

"Are you going to the police?"

"Somebody has to."

"Listen to me. They'll throw you in a room, bring in waves of interrogators more interested in proving you wrong than in listening to what you have to say. That's how it works."

"Not with the DVD in my pocket. I turn over the codes, then it's on them."

"It'll always be on *you*. No matter what happens."

"That's your take. My take is that it's the only choice."

"You can go to the hotel tonight, enter the code yourself."

"Right. All that does is make *me* the trigger. A dead one, at that."

"If you go to the police, you'll lose your only window of opportunity to stop it."

He was buckling his pants now.

"I would think it's *your* window of opportunity, Sarah."

For the first time in their acquaintance, Sarah appeared on the verge of anger.

"That DVD is just a bunch of suits talking in the mall."

"What choice do I have?"

"I don't know. But I know this—while you're pleading your case to the cops, the bomb goes off."

"Maybe. You have a better strategy?"

"I'm going with you. Flash my badge."

"Not a chance."

"Why not?"

He paused. He said, "Because you're off the clock," in a voice tinged with sarcasm.

There it was, his doubt exposed.

"Why are we sitting here in a hotel room," said Gabriel, "kicking it around, when the bomb is supposed to go off . . . when? Tonight? Tomorrow? Wouldn't the NSA want to see this evidence? Something's wrong with this picture, Sarah."

As he was pulling on his socks, he recognized one of his many emotions as disappointment. Once again someone he wanted desperately to trust was making it difficult.

"I have contacts at the FBI," she said.

He was working on his shoes now. "I suggest you call them."

"I thought we were together on this?"

"You haven't told me everything."

A pause. Then he heard a tiny voice say, "No."

He felt his heart skip a beat. When she spoke again, the sound was even more distant.

"You're a good man, Gabriel. You have a good heart. Listen to it. Everything depends on what you hear there."

He emerged from the dressing area adjacent to the bathroom, stuffing his wallet into his Dockers.

But Sarah was gone. As was the laptop and the DVD.

Book Six

*A*nd when the sixth thunder sounded,
my eyes beheld the falling of towers
and my ears the wailing of men,
and the new Babylon made war
with those that had been deceived by false prophets,
but like a snake the prey was made lost,
war rendered fruitless,
and many died in vain.
Take heed, all who behold the book of secrets,
for the age of prophecy is at hand.

"WHISPER OF THE SEVENTH THUNDER"
by Gabriel Stone

- 56 -

THE INTERVIEW ROOM at the Georgetown precinct was lined with cork walls full of holes and dotted with waiting pushpins. The only window was in the door itself, facing out to the opposite wall of the hallway, also beige. A faint ghost of smoke still lingered a decade after what the incumbent lieutenant back then had called "that goddamn no smoking ordinance" had gone into effect.

Gabriel was sure the door was locked. He couldn't bring himself to try it during the forty-five minutes they had made him wait alone. This was after nearly two hours of "the interview phase," which bore a disturbing similarity to every suspect browbeating he had seen on television.

He told them everything. He gave them the codes, which he had copied onto a piece of hotel stationery, stashing the original in his shoe. Then he told them a second and then a third time, as if the story were too complex to comprehend in one pass.

And now he feared that Sarah may have been right. It was after nine and they were still looking at him as if he were speaking Chinese.

A huge bald man with several chins entered the room, accompanied by the officer with whom he'd been debriefing since he arrived, who closed the door after them. His tie was loose, and there were traces of dried sweat visible on the white collar. He wore no jacket, his shirtsleeves rolled up, one a turn higher than the other.

"I'm Lieutenant Cerotsky," the man said, avoiding eye contact and a handshake as he sat down. He had a file with him, which he plopped onto the scratched green tabletop with unnecessary flourish. "Here's the deal. Hotel security says these numbers you gave us don't exist. And they don't recognize these so-called codes."

The two men locked eyes.

Gabriel turned to the younger, more familiar cop. "Have you guys heard a word I've said?"

The junior officer diverted his gaze.

"NSA says they have no agent named Sarah Meyers."

Gabriel didn't move.

"We couldn't reach Mr. Simon Winger, but then, no one can. He's one of the most powerful and respected people in the city. Of course, you already knew that, right? A regular target for whackos looking to smear the name of people with influence in this town. Happens every day. You catching the scent of my signal fire here, Tonto?"

Gabriel stared with unflinching eyes.

"*Your* name did come up on the wire, though. Nothing serious. Lost your wife, and just maybe you burned your own house down."

Gabriel felt his skin beginning to get hot.

"On yeah, there's a little matter of the New York Police Department wanting to ask you a few questions. Something about a phone call placed from your mobile phone to that of a woman who was killed in a high-profile robbery couple of weeks ago."

"Am I under arrest?"

Gabriel saw the two badges shoot each other a look.

"No. You can go. Please do, in fact. There's the door."

Gabriel looked at them with disbelief.

"I walk in here with a bomb threat, with the New York police wanting to talk to me, and you're letting me walk?"

Cerotsky and the young cop exchanged a glance before turning their attention back to Gabriel.

"I don't recall hearing that you were instigating any kind of threat at all. Quite the contrary, way I hear it. Just a good citizen, trying to protect the public interest, which we do appreciate. And the New York thing, that's just peripheral to a closed case. Nobody cares."

The two officers now exchanged another glance, this one tinged with humor, the sharing of a secret.

"Listen," said Cerotsky, "you're about the sixteenth Columbia Center bomb story we've heard in the last ten days. There's more security people in that place than there are parking spaces, let me assure you. I suggest you go back to your hotel, get a good night's sleep, then check out early, get a flight, and return to your little fantasy world. We've got your number, and yes, we've got your fingerprints, in case we need you to help us solve any impending national emergencies. But frankly, Mr. Stone, we don't need you coming in here and wasting our goddamn time on a bunch of paranoid delusions. We square on that?"

Gabriel slowly rose to his feet. His eyes bore into the fat lieutenant's, who responded with a sarcastic grin. Then he turned and stepped toward the door.

As he was leaving he heard the younger officer mumble, "What the *hell* was that about?"

Gabriel stopped, turned back.

"It's about a guy trying to do the right thing. That's it. Put that in your report."

Then he walked out of the room, wondering where Sarah had gone, and why.

WHEN HE LEFT, the younger officer looked at Cerotsky with complete confusion.

The lieutenant continued to stare at the door as he spoke. "Interagency courtesy. CIA wants him cut loose. My guess is they'll pick him up on the street, cover him through the night. Precautionary stuff, pretty routine."

Cerotsky stared at the door, his head shaking.

"That goddamn Jesus luncheon brings out the nut jobs every time."

SIMON WINGER OPENED the door to his house to find Daniel Larsen, his Brother in Christ, standing on his front porch, hands pocketed like a nervous teenager arriving for a first date. Another man waited at the base of the stairs, where Simon knew he would remain during this meeting. He was huge, with a face incapable of compassion. Their eyes met briefly as Larsen brushed past into the foyer. Simon closed the door and followed his guest into the study.

"Thank God for civil aviation," Larsen said as they entered the room, feigning a sudden interest in the books that lined Simon's walls. They were mostly standard religious texts, with a smattering of relevant history.

"You must be tired," he added without looking at Simon.

Simon took a seat behind his massive oak desk, regarding his visitor with a combination of curiosity and wariness. Larsen had never been to his home before, and with their dark business finished, Simon assumed this was simply Daniel's impatience to know the name of the Beast, which he had withheld during their previous conversation.

"I don't believe for a minute you came here to inquire after my jet lag."

Larsen turned from the books and faced his old friend. "I needed to see you. Given what we've just done, it just seemed . . . *right*."

"Given the path we've traveled," Simon shot back, "I think you owe me a better line of crap than that."

Larsen nodded an acknowledgment of Simon's cynical insight. He seemed nervous, something Simon had never observed in him before.

"I just need to talk to someone. All the killing, then my operative turning on me that way. I had to kill a man I thought was my friend."

McQuarrie. Simon pictured the face of the man Larsen had killed. He had seen him that day in front of the Lincoln Memorial, when he had followed Larsen and shot a few pictures of his own. It was always good to cover one's backside when the stakes got this high.

"You've killed men before."

Larsen's eyes flared with sudden anger.

"Not by my own hand."

"It is not my forgiveness you require," said Simon.

Larsen smiled slightly, drawing a deep breath as if to banish the emotion that had threatened to overcome him. "What happens to us," he said, "as the world begins to burn?"

"We live our lives. We watch the word of God come to pass. And we cling to faith as we wait."

"I've read the prophecy, too. It's terrifying."

"You have proven your devotion. Now you must embrace it. We must be strong. God awaits you with open arms."

Larsen went back to the rows of books, running his finger over a few leather spines. Simon knew the business at hand had not yet been broached.

"The President's people aren't happy," Larsen said, as if this was an afterthought of little consequence. He withdrew one of the books and began flipping through it with contrived nonchalance.

Simon narrowed his eyes, the moment at hand.

"The irony here is that our President hates the goddamn Muslims even more than he does Brenner. If it's a holy war God wants, the President is a better soldier than Armand Brenner ever could be."

Simon felt his nerves come alive. Brenner's survival meant the President's defeat. And he knew that Larsen was a passionate advocate for the President.

Larsen snorted a contemptuous little laugh. "Of course, you have your codes and your scrolls to tell you what *is*. But then, like the rest of scripture, the best we can do is apply an interpretation, isn't it. The word of God may be infallible, but what about the men through whose filter those words pass? Is it still *faith* if you believe what you feel in your own heart, rather than in the words of others? Words in a book? I think it is. It has to be."

Simon had a ready answer for that—the divine guides the hand of those who would translate The Word—but stopped short.

A figure appeared in the doorway to the study. It was the agent posted outside, a former college lineman who was known to teach hand-to-hand combat to CIA agents when he wasn't guarding Daniel Larsen's life. His massive hands were opening and closing, his face void of life.

"The president is a great man," Larsen continued. "Armand Brenner is a pawn. He cannot be allowed to win this election."

Simon lowered his eyes to the floor and said, "You worship the wrong god, my friend."

Suddenly Simon felt an iron grip on his shoulders, pushing him down, pinning him to the desk. He opened his eyes to see that Larsen had moved close as the thug agent held him in place.

"Even this," said Simon, speaking through a jaw barely open because of the force against the back of his skull, "will be forgiven."

He felt a needle penetrate the soft tissue behind his earlobe, where the jaw bone curved upward.

Digitalis. It causes irregular heart rhythms that soon, depending on the dose, result in a myocardial infarction. Should someone stumble upon the victim prior to death, any good doctor would inject more digitalis to counter the arrhythmia, leading to a quick and somewhat painful death by toxicity.

Larsen pocketed the syringe, his mouth inches away. Simon could smell liquor on his breath.

"You have me at a disadvantage," he said. "Because in a moment, you'll know for sure if that is indeed true. Or if we've been fools, you and me and your dead Israeli friend. That wasn't us, by the way, in case you're wondering. Either way, the world will have to wait for your Antichrist to start a world war."

A few seconds later the iron hands released him. Simon tried to sit upright, but there was no muscular response at all. He felt himself sliding off the desk over which he'd been pinned, the floor rushing up to meet him.

He closed his eyes, wanting the darkness to come on his own terms, wrapped in prayer.

But instead he saw light, brighter and hotter than anything the world could offer.

And then he heard the voice of an angel.

"CAN YOU HEAR me?" the angel asked. "Mr. Winger, can you hear my voice?"

And then the angel slapped his face. Twice.

Simon Winger's eyelids felt as if they'd been sewn shut. He had to arch his eyebrows to separate them, and when he did the ambient light in the study made him squint. His heart beat like that of a bird, its panicked wings struggling for freedom.

The angel had hair of gold. She wore a formfitting t-shirt with a DKNY logo above her left breast, and her perfume smelled of a stroll through Neiman Marcus, where the angels surely shopped.

Simon was lying on the floor of the study next to his chair, from which he'd fallen as soon as Daniel's goon let go of him. He remembered that much, how it seemed as if the room was melting, but nothing at all of their hasty retreat.

"I know you," he said, barely audible.

The woman kneeling beside him cradled his head on her leg, looking at him as if his revival was something of a miracle. Given his role in the unfolding of prophecy, that wasn't such a stretch.

"My name is Sarah."

In an instant he recognized her, from her visit a week earlier to tell him the whereabouts of Gabriel Stone.

"How did you get in here?"

"Your front door was wide open."

Simon noticed that the lamp on his desk was on its side, his papers strewn about the floor. As if he'd collapsed there, clutching at anything for support.

"Please, tell me what this means."

"It's a long story, Mr. Winger. Can you sit up for me?"

She pushed his shoulders forward in an effort to help him. He tried flattening hands against the floor, but a wave of nausea slammed him as he approached vertical. She sensed this and allowed him to return to the floor.

"But you know me," he said.

She smiled. "No one *really* knows you, do they."

He looked hard at Sarah, this angel who would save him, hoping to see something dark lurking behind the ice blue portals that were her eyes, a subtle indication of duplicity in the unfolding moment. But the smile and the eyes were both sincerely warm, bold enough to defy any need for agenda or conspiracy.

"How did you . . . bring me back?"

She nodded toward the floor next to him, where she'd left the syringe that contained Digibind, the drug that binds digitalis and reverses the symptoms of toxicity.

Simon stared at the syringe. "There are many conclusions I would like to draw. Should I?"

"There will be time for conclusions later. Right now we should get you out of here."

He made another strained attempt to stand. Sarah put her hands under his arms to help him rise from the floor.

"What time is it?" he asked, suddenly more alert.

"Five to ten," she said without checking her watch.

He grabbed her wrist as he plopped into a chair.

"Why are you here?" he asked.

She gently removed his grip, then took both of his hands into hers, the way a lover does when asking for something. The last woman who had touched him this way was his wife, moments after she emerged from a coma as if to say good-bye, minutes before she died in his arms.

"You are a man of God," she said, "You labor behind a shield of faith stronger than anyone can comprehend. You have been tested, you have failed and you have prevailed, all without precisely understanding the consequences of your actions."

Simon's eyes inexplicably filled with emotion as he listened. Seeing this, Sarah's grip on his hands tightened.

"I know your sacrifice, your doubt, your great witness to God. I know your heart, Simon Winger. If you need a reason for my being here, then that is enough."

Simon swallowed hard. His pulse and breathing had slowed, and a warm tingle now radiated through his flesh, something akin to the goose bumps of children at their first glimpse of God's glory, of adults who behold a miracle.

"Who are you?" he asked, the context rhetorical.

"Someone who wants what you want."

"Only Uriah could know these things," he said.

Her eyes sparkled. She was, Simon suddenly realized, the most beautiful woman he'd ever seen.

Her expression shifted as she said, "Unless we leave now, the one you seek to save will die tonight, along with many innocent souls."

Simon winced in pain. "Why should I believe what you say?"

"The same voice that has led you here speaks to you now."

He felt his skin prickle with an electric sensation, the touch of the unseen.

"I have something you need," she said.

"I require nothing."

Sarah was already shaking her head.

"You need Gabriel Stone to deactivate the bomb," she said. "And I know how to find him."

GABRIEL WALKED BRISKLY down M Street toward the hotel, still furious from his visit with the local police. They had blocked his best option, or at least his safest. Only a darker choice remained. The evening was warm, and the street was clogged with tourists and resident partiers swapping venues.

He could turn his back on the truth, let God settle his own score. It wasn't his fight. Or he could step into the deep end, do the right thing, perhaps at the cost of his own future.

At that moment the iPhone in his pocket rang. The caller ID read *No Number Available.*

"Sarah" was how he answered. Somehow he knew.

"Where are you?"

"M Street, walking back to the hotel. You were right . . . they didn't buy it."

"They will, and soon. I've got Winger."

He paused, making sure he heard this correctly.

"You went to the FBI?"

"No. I found him on my own. They tried to kill him, so he's more than a little willing to talk. I'm calling in my agency and the FBI now."

"How the *hell* did you pull this off?"

"Never underestimate a fed in high heels. Listen to me, this is going down fast. They'll want to meet with you. I'll cut a deal, you provide the code, tell them everything you know, they'll try to keep you out of it. Or at least out of the center of it. You're a peripheral player, nothing more."

"The FBI doesn't negotiate complicity."

"They do when they've got someone else signing a confession. Winger says he'll attest to your innocence."

"Winger's confessing?"

"Singing his heart out, but he's demanding neutral ground. There's a Hampton Inn on the airport property at Dulles. Get there fast."

Gabriel ran the next half hour through his mind.

"We have to talk first. Just you and me."

The line was silent.

"The police made a call. The NSA says you don't exist."

Silence.

"Talk to me, Sarah."

Her voice was hushed. "They call it ghosting, Gabriel, but the program has no official name. There's nothing about it on paper. Certain agents, those without family or visible roots, are rendered more effective when they simply disappear. Sometimes they go so far as to arrange a death, a funeral, the whole charade. That's why you won't find anything on Matthew, either. Nine-eleven was a perfect opportunity to ghost him. That's all I can tell you. You have to trust me."

"The old blind faith line again."

"That's how it works. You get to decide if you want to ride along or let the truth pass you by."

Now it was he who was silent.

"I think you know. I think you've known all along. This isn't about bombs and hotels and missing grad students. This is about you. It's time you decided who you are."

Then the line went dead. No good-bye, no admonition to be careful. Just the mad, enticing poetry of a ghost.

He glanced at his watch. An hour, give or take, to the Hampton Inn, then who knows how long with the feds. That left roughly three hours to get to the Columbia Center and put an end to some psycho's definition of God's will.

He wondered who, in the end, would be placing that call.

- 60 -

THE BELLMAN INTERCEPTED Gabriel as soon as he set foot in the lobby of the airport Hampton Inn.

"Mr. Stone?"

Gabriel nodded. He was handed a room key and pointed toward the elevators that serviced the hotel's four floors.

The place was completely deserted. Gabriel suspected this was by design, adding to the storm of reluctance in his stomach.

He took the elevator to the fourth floor and found the room. He knocked on the door, bringing no response. He slipped the key into the lock, turned it. Pushed the door open.

The lights in the room were all on, but no one was there. He checked the bathroom to be sure. He was alone.

Gabriel closed and bolted the door, then hooked the chain. He leaned against the wall and waited. For what, he wasn't sure.

One thing stood out immediately. A laptop computer sat open on the coffee table in front of a small herringbone couch. It was Sarah's laptop, no mistake about it. The screen was already illuminated. As Gabriel approached he read two words centered on the screen: PRESS ENTER.

He sat down, staring at the screen for nearly a minute. He then pressed the Enter key.

A video window appeared. On it was the frozen image of Simon Winger. He had been sitting in this very room, on the same couch Gabriel was now using. The lighting was bad, just the available ambiance of the room.

Gabriel positioned the cursor over the *Play* button and tapped the mouse pad.

Winger began talking to him.

"I apologize for my absence tonight. And for the rather dramatic pretense necessary to bring you here. The time has come for me to disappear from this stage. In my heart I believe this to be the will of God, both in terms of my own future and of yours."

On the screen, Winger took a deep breath as if to collect his thoughts. Gabriel saw his eyes drift to the side, perhaps making eye contact with someone else in the room. This would be Sarah, or maybe the federal agents she had summoned.

"By now you know more than you would have chosen for yourself. I am here to explain, and dare I say, defend. There is indeed a bomb at the Columbia Center hotel, deep in the infrastructure of the lower parking levels. There isn't enough time to find it, much less manually disarm it. I am responsible for this device. And when I tell you why, I hope you will at least understand, if not forgive."

Winger paused again, this time taking a drink from a glass that had been out of the frame. When Gabriel looked around the room, he saw an empty glass on the nightstand, and that the bedspread was ruffled, as if one or two people had recently sat there.

People who might, in fact, be waiting nearby.

"You must be wondering what all this has to do with you. The answer is nothing, and everything. And thus, there are two stories to tell, unfolding in parallel, converging at this very moment. The ending of both is yours to write, Gabriel. Which is why it is necessary for you to understand. Only with understanding will your heart be opened and your courage fortified. You will need both before the night concludes.

You are here because of the book you have written.

You know this, yet you cannot possibly comprehend it. You believe you have conceived your fiction within the framework of your own imagination and experience, and while that may have had some bearing on the outcome, I assure you, the story you wrote is not your own. This is how God works his will in the world, through his servants, willing or not. We assign certain things to coincidence or human choice, but the wise see the hand of God in play. Your book reveals certain secrets, divine mysteries that signal the arrival of the foretold end of times. One in particular, something you did not even intend to be significant, perhaps something you simply considered to be clever. And because I believe God was with you as those things emerged onto the page, I must also believe this is his holy intention, just as the Holy Bible itself was composed. Your book has become a catalyst, Gabriel, mobilizing forces on both sides of a very tall spiritual fence.

The politics of the bombing, be they spiritual or of this world, are beyond the scope of this message. But allow me to hit the high points, so that you will understand what you must do. The bomb was planted to kill a specific man and all those who enable him. At the time we believed that man to be none other than the Antichrist, the foretold Beast of Armageddon, as prophesized in the Book of Revelation. He is not the first pretender to that throne, and those who have come before him have by the grace of God been stopped. Just as this man would have been stopped just a few hours from now. I have been involved in this work all of my adult life. Those of us who serve God in this manner have done so with the faith that our efforts will be stopped when the true Antichrist, the one ordained by God to ascend to the dark throne, appears in our midst. It is important to acknowledge that the appearance of the true Antichrist in our world is to be at a time and place of *God's* choosing, not Satan's. By means too complex to explain here, we believe this has now happened."

Winger paused to take another swallow of water. Gabriel wished he could do the same, but he didn't dare try to pause the playback for fear of sabotaging the rest of the message.

"We were wrong about our target, Gabriel. God has intervened, and our hand must be stayed. The original target of the bombing is *not* the Antichrist. But in fact, the Beast stands next to him, and if the bomb goes off as planned, would be killed. This cannot be allowed. The Beast must survive this night in order to assume the throne, according to God's will.

"Because of this, the destruction of the Columbia Center must be stopped. Make no mistake, Gabriel, melodramatic as it may sound, the fate of mankind depends on your actions tonight. You alone possess the code that can disarm the bomb. You must be on the property when you make the call. Given the security that will be in place, this in itself may be a difficult challenge. If you go to the authorities, then your intentions will have been exposed, and a third party may manually detonate the device at any time prior to its preprogrammed detonation. And so, as you will soon understand, you are very much alone with these truths. And with a very difficult choice. One that, in the end, is solely yours."

Winger paused, though he didn't take his eyes off the camera. It was as if emotion had momentarily rendered him silent, the weight of his mission in conflict with his role in it. It was as if the man was aging right before Gabriel's eyes.

"Those who would stop you, who would do anything to ensure that the bomb goes off as planned, do so for political reasons. This, too, is how Satan manifests in our dimension.

They believe Armand Brenner must not be allowed to win the election, and they intend to kill him in order to achieve that goal. They know that the ensuing antiterrorist outrage as a result of the bombing will once again empower their precious president, much as it did in 2001. People need their leader most in the darkest of times. The incident will be credible, even provable, as a terrorist action, with a view toward an escalation of military intervention in known Middle Eastern countries that oppose our capitalistic, Christian ideology. It has happened before, and will happen again if this bomb goes off, only on a nuclear stage. It will be nothing short of a world war. But not the apocalyptic war that God will deliver."

Winger paused for effect.

"God has given each of us the capacity to deny him, to apply reason in place of faith. This is the human condition, the grand paradox of that faith. What is sin, if not the denial of that which we know in our hearts to be true? What is love of God, if not the sacrifice of self in service of a greater good? I believe God will grant you safe passage tonight, just as I believe it is his will that this bombing be stopped, so that the prophecy of the Book of Revelation shall come to pass."

Winger took a breath, visibly letting it out with a wheezing sound.

"There is more to tell, but it changes nothing. The voiding code was a safety mechanism. It goes live at two o'clock, and will remain active for a period of fifteen minutes. After that, at the sixteenth minute, if no voiding code has been entered, the bomb will detonate as scheduled. There is also a manual detonation code, but that, too, was merely a safety mechanism, and a suicidal one, at that. Do what you must, Gabriel, and at any cost required. I, too, must do the same."

Winger's eyes seemed to fog a moment, then he stood up, a piece of paper in his hand. He stepped toward the camera and held the paper close, like a cue card.

Room may be bugged. Check nightstand drawer.

He then went back to where he had been sitting.

"Godspeed to you, son."

He stared off into space, his expression oddly serene.

Then Simon Winger closed his eyes as he raised a gun to his temple and pulled the trigger.

GABRIEL SHRUNK BACK, slamming against the wall and causing a cheap landscape print to fall from its nail. The digital window on the laptop screen remained still for a moment—the gunshot had knocked Simon out of the frame at the moment of firing—then it went blank.

His eyes flashed between the laptop and the door, which he expected to burst open at any moment. There was no trace of blood on the floor where Simon would have fallen. It could have happened in another room, they would certainly look the same, but what of the water glass and the ruffled bedspread?

But someone *had* been in here, if only to leave the laptop for his viewing.

And what of Sarah? Where were the NSA and FBI? Maybe she *had* found Winger herself, but after listening to him decided to keep the feds out of it for fear of alerting the bad guys and thus triggering the bomb. Then again, what if Winger, for the same reasons he'd killed himself, decided to take her out first? Maybe his fear of intervention was greater than his fear of God's wrath. Maybe she was too close to The Brethren connection with her missing grad student. He'd said Gabriel was the only one who could stop it now, which could imply Sarah's involvement no longer pertained. What if Winger took this one-man-decides-the-fate-of-the-world crap too seriously?

Once again Gabriel wondered if Sarah was not who, or what, she seemed.

Perhaps, in a religious fervor bordering on fanaticism, Winger had just found and framed the triggerman they'd needed all along? Gabriel might waltz right into the Columbia Center lobby and dial what he believed to be a deactivation code, and in doing so blow them all to—and this little irony was not lost on him—kingdom come. He had no reason to believe Winger, and suddenly, plenty of reasons to doubt him.

Perhaps most frightening of all, what if Winger had been straight about everything he'd just said? That he'd exited the stage, to use his own words, in the belief that his work was over? Or worse, out of cowardice?

To do nothing was to choose—the bomb would go off. To take it to the feds was a choice—the bomb might go off anyway. To succeed at penetrating the perimeter of the hotel and dial in the code—the bomb just might go off then, too, if he was being played.

Then again, he just might be able to stop it. Everyone around him lately had been telling him to listen to his heart. Suddenly there was nowhere else to turn.

Except Sarah. Her mobile wasn't picking up, just a telling silence, one that was for Gabriel full of suppositions.

Perhaps for the first time in his life, Gabriel Stone finally understood what faith was all about. Suddenly it was all he had.

Gabriel lowered himself back onto the cushions and leaned forward, reaching for the computer. He positioned the cursor over the Play icon and tapped the mouse pad. He needed to hear it all again, without the filter of his fear and doubt.

Immediately he knew something was wrong. He could hear the drive spinning away, the screen suddenly blank. After a few seconds a smaller window appeared, with only the Microsoft logo and name at the top.

He pressed the *Escape* key, but nothing happened. He pressed Control-Alt-Delete, but nothing happened.

The whirring finally stopped. A few seconds later a message appeared in the graphic box. It read: *Disk Erased.*

Like Sarah, Simon Winger was gone.

HE REMAINED IN the room for a few more minutes, frozen on the couch as he tried to recount every word Winger had spoken. After a minute of contemplation he picked up the computer, checking to see if there was a way to unfasten the bottom panel and get at the components. Such a task required tools, which he did not have. He looked around the room for something solid, his eyes alighting on the bedpost. He picked up the laptop and smashed it across the square wooden peg. It took three tries, but the housing finally split and hung by wires, exposing the various boards and drives.

Gabriel was no computer geek, but he knew a hard drive when he saw one. Removal of one, however, required the use of tools. The only feasible prospect within reach was a wooden hanger, the edge of which he used to pry the drive from its berth, yanking away the wires with his hands.

He put the device into his jacket pocket and headed for the door. Keener minds than his knew how to extract data from disks that had seemingly been erased, and he hoped one of them could effect the resurrection of Simon Winger from this one.

Gabriel then took out his handkerchief and wiped the shredded computer clean of his fingerprints, as well as the bedpost and the hanger and anything else he'd touched.

He was at the door when he stopped dead in his tracks.

He went back into the room, sat on the bed, and opened the nightstand drawer.

A gun. Gabriel was no expert here either, but it looked like the weapon Winger had used to kill himself.

There was also a photograph. Gabriel recognized it immediately—it was a frame from the DVD he and Sarah had watched, showing the suit with Wayne Newton hair talking to a security guard in front of the capital reflecting pool. A ghostly image of the Washington Monument was visible on the surface of the water.

Taped to the photo was a square sticky-note, upon which was handwriting. It said: *Daniel Larsen, Senior Director, Central Intelligence Agency.*

Like the man he claimed to worship, Simon Winger had just delivered salvation.

GABRIEL WAS ALONE in the elevator. He stared at the gun that had been left for him in the nightstand drawer. It was fully loaded, minus one bullet. It smelled as if it had been recently fired.

He weighed the options. If it had been the suicide weapon, it might look like a murder weapon later on if found in his possession, a nail in Gabriel's coffin. Then again, Winger was sending him off to fight a war, and any field general knows enough to arm his men prior to battle. But if that were the case, a new question loomed—who put the gun into the nightstand drawer?

There were two possible answers: someone was helping Winger from off camera, perhaps even Sarah, or Winger wasn't dead at all.

GABRIEL ENTERED THE Hampton Inn lobby, looking around with an urgency that caught the attention of the desk clerk.

"Help you?" asked the man.

But Gabriel didn't answer. The bellman who had given him the keys earlier was outside the front door, sneaking a smoke.

Gabriel went to the glass and tapped.

He had to risk this. The kid didn't look like someone who'd been to Quantico.

"Did you see the people in the room you just sent me to?"

"Sure. Old guy, very hot woman." His bobbing eyebrows suggested something kinky.

"Did you see them leave?"

The kid shook his head, nervous now. "Listen, I see everything, I say nothing. I just park the cars, carry the bags."

Gabriel took out his wallet. He withdrew all the cash he had, about two hundred bucks, and a business card.

He held out the money. "Do something for me?"

He nodded eagerly, palming the cash as Gabriel handed him the hard drive, the photo printout, and the card.

"Send all this to the address on this card, FedEx. No matter what you hear on the news. We cool?"

The kid nodded as he took the items, his eyes huge.

"There's a computer up in the room, pretty trashed. Get it out of there, and hang on to it."

"This illegal?"

"Absolutely."

The bellman shot a quick look at the desk clerk, who was already bored watching them and had returned to his television.

"Your word, as an American citizen?"

The bellman looked impressed. This was the coolest thing that had happened to him since high school.

"Swear to God," he said, already discreetly tucking the items into the pocket of his own jacket. He then took the cash without looking down and stuffed that into his pants.

Gabriel peered through the thick glass wall into the lot, saw a taxi waiting at the end of the drive.

"Good," he said, "because that's exactly who'll be watching you."

He shook the kid's hand as he went through the sliding double doors into the night, heading for the cab.

- 63 -

GABRIEL BROKE INTO a trot in the parking lot. The taxi waited to the side, the silhouette of the driver visible behind the wheel. He could already tell it was not the driver who'd brought him here.

Suddenly a black SUV wheeled around a corner, coming to a quick stop right in front of him. Behind it the door to the taxi swung open, the driver sprinting straight at him. At the same moment the SUV's doors swung open, spilling two men who joined the pursuit.

Gabriel wheeled and bolted away, stumbling slightly over a curb before he got his legs under him. He was conscious of a flurry of activity in his peripheral vision, his pursuers gaining from behind.

His escape lasted twenty feet. One man dove for his upper legs, another applying a clothesline hit to his back. They tumbled to the pavement as a fused unit, and before they hit the ground the thug from the taxi had pinned Gabriel's arms behind his back and began binding them with plastic cuff restraints. Pain shot through his spine from the point where the gun tucked under his belt had impacted the ground.

He tried to kick out as they pulled him to his feet, which seemed to amuse the smallest of the attackers, who responded with a fist to the solar plexus. As he doubled over they dragged him to the SUV, which had moved closer during the struggle, stuffing him into the backseat, one of the men climbing in after him.

Another man waited inside the vehicle. As they placed Gabriel in the middle of the bench seat, the gun still prodding under his belt at the small of his back, he recognized him immediately. It was the suit from the DVD, the one who'd met with the assassin and later with Brock Carter.

Daniel Larsen, CIA.

"I'd shake hands, but . . ." Larsen said, leaving the comment hanging with an infuriating shrug and no shortage of smugness.

Gabriel was still trying to catch his breath from the sucker punch, but he managed to offer up his best defiant glance.

"Be nice," said the goon, sitting on the other side of him, who punctuated the instruction with a firm openhanded slap to the back of Gabriel's head. Gabriel responded by throwing a shoulder, defying all logic and a seventy-pound difference in weight. The thug dodged the move and quickly grabbed a fistful of Gabriel's hair, pulling it back to expose his throat. His other hand went there, his forefinger and thumb digging on either side of the windpipe, clamping for a moment to make his point.

"Don't do this," Larsen said. It wasn't clear which of the two he was speaking to.

The thug let go, reluctantly, actually taking a moment to smooth Gabriel's hair back into place. The SUV was moving now, heading behind the hotel on an access road with no lights. One of the takedown thugs sat in the front passenger seat, while the smallest one, the one who had sucker-punched him, was hurrying toward the door to the hotel. If he was looking for Simon Winger he'd be disappointed and confused. He just hoped two bills was the bellman's idea of patriotism.

"Comfortable?" asked Larsen, leaning close.

"Don't patronize me, asshole."

With a nod from his boss the goon produced a knife. He shoved Gabriel forward to gain access to his wrists and with a deft flick sliced through the plastic cuffs.

"Stranger than fiction, isn't it?" Larsen obviously had no intention of introducing himself. "To a man like you, an author, there must be a certain fascination with all this."

"Wait till you see the movie," said Gabriel, avoiding eye contact.

"Actually, I have the trailer right here."

He signaled the driver, who reached into the seat next to him and produced an iPad, the screen illuminated. He handed it back across the seat.

The scene was dimly lit, more shadow than substance. After a moment Gabriel realized he was looking at a woman lying on a bare cot in a dark room, her hands and ankles bound behind her with a length of rope that connected the two. She was gagged, struggling for each breath.

Sarah.

GABRIEL STARED AT the image of Sarah on the screen, his skin feeling as if it wanted to peel away. It was a live video feed, and with the jerky motion of low-end digital video he saw her squirming, the methodology of the constraints too crude for professionals like these. She was close. She had to be.

Gabriel passed the iPad back to his captor.

"You believe in God, don't you, Gabriel?"

"Everyone keeps asking me that."

"Just wondering," Larsen said. "I mean, given all this."

"I wonder if he'd forgive me if I tore your face off right about now?"

Larsen smiled as the goon again slapped the back of Gabriel's head, hard enough to bring a stab of pain to his neck.

"Maybe. But my friend here definitely would not."

Gabriel watched them share in the humor of the moment. Then Larsen returned his attention to his guest.

"We have no interest in your religious fantasies or your politics or even your book. If you do what I ask, you will get her back in one delectable piece. How does that sound?"

"Like horseshit," said Gabriel.

Larsen exchanged another glance with the man on the other side of Gabriel.

"Much of what I presume Simon Winger just told you is true. He is indeed the man of God he claims to be, and like so many men of God he has killed people in God's name. Whatever that means to you, I have no idea, but it meant enough to him to conceive and stage the most elaborate and sinister assassination plot in history."

Now it was Gabriel who laughed. "A government spook with a gun talking about God . . . aren't there laws about that? Wait, you're a Republican, I get it."

Larsen drew an impatient breath.

"What people like you don't understand," Larsen went on, "is that the law really doesn't matter. Take the ragheads. What matters is that their delusions drive them, cause them to perpetrate great evil in the world, in the name of what they call God. My job is to stop them and anyone with a similar agenda. Including Simon Winger."

Gabriel studied Larsen's face. He was normal in every way, a soft man with hard eyes.

"Way I hear it, you worked with Winger. Or should I say, *for* him."

"Whatever. The fact is, the man snapped. God supposedly sent word that our latest target must survive tonight's attempt on his life, that the bombing must be aborted. On that point, I agree with him."

Larsen held Gabriel's gaze for several seconds. Larsen sighed impatiently and continued.

"Armand Brenner is a madman, a megalomaniacal psychotic. There's one in every election, it seems. We have files full of things the public would never believe. Whether you buy into secret scrolls that say he's the bastard son of Satan doesn't matter, the man is a world war waiting to happen. He's fooled the entire country into believing he's a master strategist with a peaceful agenda coexisting with a zero tolerance for terror, when in fact he's totally driven by greed. And in case you didn't know, greed smells just like crude oil."

"So Brenner is the target," Gabriel offered, as if this file was just now being opened to him.

Larsen nodded. "*Was* the target. Winger spent millions creating the means by which Armand Brenner will die tonight. And then, because of some bullshit spiritual enlightenment, he and God have decided Brenner must live. With apologies to the Catholics, Simon might change his mind, but God doesn't."

"Sounds to me like you'd just as soon blow it all up."

Larsen closed his eyes, as if this was tiresome.

"Oh, don't get me wrong. Brenner must be stopped. But not like this. That bomb has to be deactivated. We'll deal with Brenner later."

Gabriel shrugged. "So go stop it yourself. I'll give you the code, on the house."

Larsen's eyes were fixed on something distant.

"It's not quite that simple."

"Sure it is. You walk in, pick up the house phone, done."

Gabriel held Larsen's gaze with intensity. Then he said, "You suck at poker, don't you."

Larsen was on the verge of losing it, which was precisely what Gabriel was after. It was harder to sell a lie when your nerves were throbbing at skin level.

"I'd love nothing more than to see Armand Brenner go down. But I'm an American, and believe it or not, a believer. There are innocent people in that hotel. I have a sworn duty, and a moral one."

"Don't we all."

Larsen leaned closer. *"You're* going in."

Gabriel made a show out of his confusion. "Me? That's crazy. Why don't you just do it yourself?"

Larsen sneered. "I don't owe you an explanation."

"No? If you're doing this for the right reasons, then you do. In poker that's called a *call.* Let's see what you got."

Larsen pursed his lips and closed his eyes.

Gabriel sneaked a glance at the thug on the other side of him, who was smiling, perhaps at Gabriel's ballsy attitude.

"That bomb seemed right for only one reason," Larsen said, his brow furrowed for emphasis. "It would change the course of the war on terror. So we watched, waited to see how it would play out. But times change, people change."

"Election forecasts change, too, don't they."

"I said it's simple, and it is. A senior official of the CIA on the trigger end of a hotel bomb isn't the best career move I can think of. It would embarrass the Agency."

"The Agency gets embarrassed all the time."

Larsen chewed at his lip and lowered his voice. "Jokes like that can be harmful to your health, Mr. Stone. A little professional courtesy would be appreciated."

Gabriel couldn't quite stifle a small laugh. "If the Agency claimed to have found the code," he said, "and if you arrive at the moment of truth and save the day, you get a gold star. That's a career move even you can appreciate."

Larsen looked like a man on the verge of a hemorrhage.

Gabriel smiled wider. "As I said, I think you're lying. You don't intend to get anywhere near that hotel, because you're not sending me in there to deactivate it, you're sending me in there to hit the trigger *for* you."

The car took a corner at high speed, enough to cause Larsen to look away momentarily. But he quickly turned back to Gabriel.

"What you think and don't think is no longer germane to this conversation. We have your girlfriend, and you'll do as I say or she dies. Straight up."

Now it was Gabriel who stared ahead, his own bluff called.

"You want your life back," Larsen said. "I was hoping you'd want to save American lives while you're at it. I was offering you a win-win deal. I thought that's who you were, a man of character. But you're just a cynic, a man who trusts nothing. You're a coward."

Gabriel leaned back and said, "As far as you're concerned, I'm just a guy with a target pasted on his ass."

The SUV took a hard corner, still navigating obscure back roads.

"Here's the deal," Larsen said, weary of the debate. "You go to that hotel and call in the code. Then you walk away. You never hear from us again. If we hear from *you* again, you have a new problem. Your call."

Gabriel feigned thinking it over. He was actually recalling Simon's words from the video: . . . *there is also a manual detonation code, but that, too, was merely a safety mechanism, and a suicidal one, at that . . .*

"I'm just supposed to show up and ask to use the house phone? On a high -security night before a big political bash? Yeah, that'll work."

Larsen frowned. "Leave that to me. Tell them you have business with the security director. Mention the name Mark Krager. Trust me, they'll let you in."

"How will I know Sarah is safe?"

Larsen held up the PDA. "You'll see for yourself. You do this, you both walk away. You get your book back, too. We open some doors for you, the thing gets published to great acclaim, which we can also make happen. Now you're rich. Famous, too. However, I'd suggest you make the bad guys talk with an accent. The country wants their villains in beards with diapers on their heads."

For a moment Gabriel allowed his eyes to burn into those of his host. Just to let the man see his resolve.

The truth was, he was visualizing an outcome of his own.

"Thanks," he said after a moment, "but I'll pass. On all of it."

LARSEN LOOKED MORE amused than alarmed.

"You're bluffing. You'll save the girl. You have no choice. If you don't, there's no place to hide where I can't find you. And when we do, guess who takes the fall? Your book is as good as a signed confession to *that,* my friend, because we'll have full documentation of an attempted bombing with your name all over it. We can paint a paper trail on anyone. You'll die in a shoot-out with the feds as they try to arrest you. Later we find a bomb hidden in the Columbia Center, just like you wrote in your book. It's a no-brainer. Regard-less of whether you believe me or not, there's really no choice here after all."

Larsen nodded slightly at the goon, who suddenly swung into action. With unyielding hands he gripped Gabriel's head, forcing it back. Larsen pitched in by pinning Gabriel's hands down. The goon's huge fingers clamped on either side of his jaw, causing it to gape open. Simultaneously he dropped some-thing into Gabriel's mouth and jammed the jaw shut again. Then he clamped his hand tightly over Gabriel's mouth and nostrils, forcing him to swallow.

Gabriel struggled for nearly a minute, gagging, until his body surren-dered by swallowing. Whatever they had put in his mouth went down easily, no bigger than a vitamin pill.

Satisfied, the assailant released his grip.

Gabriel brought his hands to his throat as he fought to regain air. The goon handed him a water bottle to help get it down, which he had no choice but to take.

"Transponder," said Larsen. "Ingenious little device, bonds to the stomach wall so it can't be digested. Takes about a week for the stomach acids to get to it, but that's all we need. Here, check this out."

Larsen had picked up the iPad and began tapping in a few keystrokes. Satisfied, he showed it to Gabriel. The screen displayed a rural street map, upon which was a blinking LCD. Below was specific location data, indicating that they were on an access road near the Hampton Inn at Dulles Airport.

"Binge and purge all you want," Larsen said, "but only a scalpel gets that out of you."

Gabriel could see the Hampton Inn straight ahead through the windshield. They had circled on airport service roads and were about to return to the hotel entrance.

"Be at the Columbia Center before two, or the woman dies. Don't be early, the code won't work and you'll be exposed. And you don't even want to think about being late. The first fifteen minutes after two o'clock is your window."

Gabriel nodded, as if he'd acquiesced.

They drove the rest of the way in silence. The van entered the property at a service gate and drew up to the front, where the taxi waited in a lot almost completely void of other cars. There was no driver this time—the car was for Gabriel.

The SUV stopped next to it.

"That's it?"

"That would be it," Larsen replied. With a glance he signaled the goon to get out to hold the door.

"Doesn't it strike you as odd," Larsen continued, "that you find yourself here?"

Gabriel smiled, "Right now the only thing that strikes me as odd is you."

"You trust your life to the widow of a man who tried to kill you, now you're distrusting me when I tell you that you can save dozens of lives? The lives of a presidential candidate and his wife, his entire staff? Food for thought as you drive into town."

Gabriel stared a moment before continuing.

"I mean, I'm just wondering why Joan McQuarrie gets the halo and I'm the guy with the Groucho Marx glasses. Why you look at me like I'm two beers short of a keg."

"Because I never lose at poker," said Gabriel.

Larsen shook his head. "Okay, smart guy, here's one for you—maybe the widow McQuarrie works for me. Maybe that's how you got here. Lots of options to kick around. Consider the possibility that you never had a choice in any of this. Just like you don't have a choice now. Maybe I've owned your ass since day one."

Gabriel stared as the smoked-glass window rose in his face. He managed a final comment before it closed completely.

"See you in hell, spy boy."

The SUV sped away.

Larsen was wrong about one thing. Gabriel indeed had a choice to make, and precious little time to make it.

- 66 -

GABRIEL DROVE TOWARD downtown Washington in a taxi that smelled like last week's vomit. And despite the urgency and the speed required to address it, he had enough time to second-guess everything.

Two men were telling him what to believe, and what to do in response to that belief. Both claimed to be servants of God, though the outcomes of their devotion were diametrically opposed. Both of them claimed to *know*.

This was Sunday school all over again: nuns brandishing rulers, preachers with dark secrets calling down the wrath of heaven, doctrines waging war for our souls. It was the same pitch, the same clichéd guilt trip wrapped in the same old brown paper paradox.

Suddenly he saw it clearly. Everything set before us, all experience and all knowledge, was a gift from and by God. Including his little ride in Larsen's SUV. In the vernacular of the divine, *gift* was often analogous with *test*. God—a sense of him, the rules of the universe, an understanding of love—was either there, setting up shop in the heart, or he wasn't.

And if he wasn't, then he was waiting for an invitation. He'd keep reminding you in ways you might not understand that the universe has rules. The details—which testament is divine, who baptizes who, who confesses what to whom, which scripture means what, all the commandments and dogma and doctrines and tradition and pageant and criteria—these things were not of God. They were of men, however schooled and well-intended, men with robes and pretensions.

And too often, men with agendas.

We are left to decide what is true on our own. And thus, the decision made, we write our names into the book of eternity.

Tonight, the pen had been placed in Gabriel's hand.

Driving toward his moment of truth at a hotel in downtown Washington, Gabriel Stone opened his heart and took inventory. His mother was there. Lauren was there. The little boy he once was still played there.

Sarah was there, too.

The only way to help her now was to show up at the Columbia Center on time.

He checked to see that the gun was still tucked beneath his belt behind his back. It was.

So be it. The answer had been given.

- 67 -

Auburn, California

ON THE TWELFTH floor of the Columbia Center Hotel, Armand Brenner turned off the television with heavy eyes. Lately his lead in the polls had dominated the news, making for the stuff of dreams as he slept. He had been surrounded all evening long by the usual suck-ups, pretending great insight into it all, but there was nothing new to add, and he was exhausted.

But sleep would not come easy tonight.

A cadre of forty-four people had accompanied him to Washington and were staying in the hotel tonight, for security reasons the only guests on the property. The senior among them occupied suites on this, the concierge floor, while others slept in rooms below. Secret Service and private security personnel patrolled the halls on this, the final night before the hotel's grand opening.

The Brethren had taken care of the rooms. Many doors were open to the Brenner camp here in Washington, but given that the election was weeks away, this was neutral territory. They were to be honored guests at the National Prayer Luncheon the next day, so a good night's sleep, free of political fallout, was in order for all.

Lying awake in the darkness, Armand Brenner heard the door to his room quietly open and close. A shadow sliced through the darkness, stopping next to the bed. He could hear the sound of clothes dropping to the floor, followed by the swishing of crisp sheets as they were pulled back, the visitor having successfully bid the staff good night while perpetrating the illusion of nocturnal solitude.

As he embraced his lover, Brenner's eyes went to the silhouette sitting across the room, offering a dark smile. The campaign chief pressed against Brenner's body, which responded to the first warm touch of flesh with instant arousal.

"The President has a sore throat," said Alex, his lips already brushing against the candidate's ear. "They've asked you to give the opening prayer."

Brenner laughed out loud. "God in heaven be praised."

"I thought you'd be amused." He, too, cast a smile toward the darkness.

Brenner snuggled closer, manipulating their bodies into his favorite conjoined posture. "Write me something," he said.

Alex's lips were busy at the candidate's neck. "Our father," he whispered, "who art in Washington, blasphemy be thy name . . ."

Brenner shut his eyes and sighed, waiting to be taken, running his fingers through his lover's hair.

"I like the next part best," cooed Alex, manipulating their posture to achieve their union at the precise moment.

"Tell me," whispered Brenner, anticipating it, allowing himself to be pressed down.

Alex looked to the side and smiled as he settled over him.

"Are you ready?"

Brenner nodded, his breath short. He closed his eyes.

Through a wicked smile, Alex thrust his hips and whispered, "Thy kingdom come . . ."

From a plush chair across the room, cloaked in darkness, Charlotte Brenner touched her fingertips together and smiled.

Book Seven

And when the seventh thunder sounded,
I saw the masses gathered in the name of the Lamb,
and the great inn was filled with the righteous.
And among them were those who used the name of God
but who in their hearts would do Satan's bidding.
And then there was fire and smoke enveloping them,
that old demon cloud which brings death,
and those who hold the secret book
put forth their sword and their wrath in His name,
and from the smoke emerged The Word.
Let it then begin, Lord.
Amen.

"WHISPER OF THE SEVENTH THUNDER"
by Gabriel Stone

GABRIEL WAS THANKFUL for the late hour and the absence of traffic. He followed the only route he knew, passing through Arlington into Georgetown, and from there to the Library of Congress, taking the route he and Sarah had walked from the Columbia Center Hotel.

He arrived fifteen minutes before the deactivation code, if that's what it was, would become active.

He parked two blocks away to avoid notice. When he rounded a corner and saw his destination, his body reacted with a jolt of adrenaline, fueling him for what had to be done.

At night the Columbia Center Hotel was even more mesmerizing in its use of architectural lighting. Huge panes of glass cast off a dual image, reflecting the city while exposing the luminescent interior.

He approached sliding glass doors to a magnificent lobby, only to find them locked. The hotel wouldn't officially open until the next day, and with dignitaries sleeping upstairs, security would be understandably tight.

But not tight enough to prevent someone from walking off the street, right up to the front door.

A barrel-chested man with a shaved head and an expensive suit approached from within. He was wearing an earpiece, the wire descending beneath a collar specially tailored for a twenty-one-inch neck. The man mouthed the words *We're closed,* but when Gabriel mouthed *I need to talk to someone,* he went to a black box affixed to the foyer wall next to the doors, pressing a speaker button.

"May I help you, sir? The hotel is closed."

"I need to talk to the head of security for the hotel."

He paused, then added, "I believe you know Mark Krager."

Alarm registered in the man's eyes. Gabriel noticed his hand moving reflexively to the lapel of his jacket, touching a button there.

"What's this in regard to?"

The guy was military all the way, no doubt an ex–SEAL or Green Beret, probably now with the Secret Service.

Gabriel knew he looked as nervous as he felt. The pace of his heart and the shallowness of his breathing made it hard to speak without an obvious edge.

"An evacuation of the hotel."

Gabriel looked the man hard in the eyes.

The guard released the intercom and turned back his upper lapel, behind which was a microphone. He spoke softly, no doubt summoning men with guns. Then he put a finger against his earphone, listening.

After a moment he turned back to face Gabriel.

"Would you step back from the door, please?"

"I need to talk to someone in authority. Now."

"Step back from the door. I'm afraid I must insist."

Gabriel not only stepped back, he retreated all the way to the valet station next to the driveway drop-off point, which at this hour, on this night, was abandoned.

As he waited he recited the six-digit code he had memorized, praying he would get the chance to use it. And praying, too, that it was the right one.

When he was done he muttered aloud, "Thy will be done."

- 69 -

DANIEL LARSEN HAD been on the property for ten minutes. They had taken another route into town, tracking Stone's progress on the iPad GPS app. He would have much preferred to be as far away as possible, but the plan required a backstop, and he was it.

There would be time to separate himself from the Columbia Center Hotel before it melted into a ceramic puddle.

He was walking one of the basement parking levels when he heard the call through his earpiece. He had no idea precisely where the bomb had been planted, but he knew it was down here somewhere, and he wanted to be sure someone with a locator device didn't suddenly show up with too many questions. Over the radio the door guard was calling in a yellow alert in response to a man requesting an audience with the head of security.

Larsen glanced at his watch. It was ten minutes until two. He'd left the iPad with one of his men, so he was surprised that Stone would reveal himself this early.

In the long run it really didn't matter what Stone believed, or even if he showed up or not. With the transponder in his stomach they'd know right where he was, and it would be a simple operation to nail him shortly after the explosion, which Larsen would arrange to occur after his own departure. In some ways that was an even better outcome, because it would make heroes out of the field agents who killed him.

Then again, if evidence of Stone's presence were to be found on the premises, that would seal the deal. His flesh and clothing would be vaporized, but there were other ways to retro-engineer certain forensics.

Larsen pressed the mike button on his own lapel device and said, "Alpha-one, describe the mark."

Alpha-One. Agency lingo really pissed the locals off.

A voice returned with: "Six three, dark hair, medium length, casual dress, square jaw."

"I'm on my way. Stall him. Don't let him leave the property."

"Roger that."

Daniel Larsen smiled as he headed for the elevator, where his bodyguard/ assistant waited with the iPad. If it was the head of security for the hotel Stone wanted, that's precisely who he would get.

NEAR THE REGISTRATION desk, a small crowd of Secret Service agents watched the arrival area where the suspicious man was waiting. He appeared nervous, hands pocketed as he shifted his weight from foot to foot.

Daniel Larsen and his beefy companion emerged from an elevator. Larsen was CIA, the Alpha-One guy, and they knew the pecking order in situations like these. The Secret Service actually had the hammer here, but the Agency always had the means to get even.

"Status?" barked Larsen as he arrived at Ed Krager's side. Krager, a portly man whom some described as jolly, was Secret Service, and no fan of Larsen's.

"Quo," said Krager. "He's waiting to talk to the head of hotel security about an evacuation."

"He said that? Evacuation?"

"Rhymes with ejaculation. You know him?"

"Maybe."

This comment might just come in useful later. The planting of seeds was half the battle in the interagency game.

"Guy's harmless. Let me take this one, okay, Eddie?"

Krager drew a deep breath, swallowing his instinctive response. He'd been doing that ever since Larsen showed up, unannounced and unwanted.

"Sure, *Danny*, whatever the Agency wants."

Larsen started toward the door, his guard a pace behind. Krager signaled one of his men to open the doors.

They slid open quietly, but the motion caught Gabriel's attention. His stomach kicked when he saw who was striding out to meet him.

Larsen and the guard stopped eight feet away. When he spoke, Larsen's voice was very quiet. This conversation was for their ears only.

"Does evacuation have one *c*, or two?" asked Larsen.

"Going down with the ship after all?" responded Gabriel.

"You're early. Unless, of course, you came for the evacuation, in which case, you just got your girlfriend killed."

Gabriel bit his lip as he drew an exasperated breath. "It was a *story*, okay? The door was locked, I need to get inside. What am I supposed to do, tell 'em I want a room? Hell, *you* said ask for the head of security, so I did."

They locked eyes, the excuse and the doubt colliding in the dead air between them. Larsen suddenly wondered if he was wrong, if Stone was actually playing this their way.

"You the head of hotel security?" asked Gabriel.

"I am now."

"Then you can just escort me inside for a little chat and a phone call. Actually, I'm glad you're here. I thought you might be. In fact, I was counting on it."

Larsen squinted. "What's your game, Stone?"

"It's called, Who's Got the Bomb. You said show up, I showed up. You said get inside, I'm almost there. You said call the code at two, it's not two yet. What's *your* game?"

Larsen nodded. "You must love her very much."

Gabriel hesitated, hearing the words very clearly, surprised at the wave of sudden emotion complicating his fear.

"What I love is my *life*."

"Really. I hear your life sucks."

"You said it," Gabriel said, allowing his anger to surface. "What choice is there, really?"

"So glad you appreciate the design."

"The Lord works in mysterious ways," said Gabriel sarcastically.

"Then you won't mind if she disappears." Gabriel's gaze became distant. Larsen had no way of knowing that Gabriel was saying another little prayer.

Larsen grinned as he put a hand behind his ear and said, "Hear that? That sound . . . it's forty pieces of silver falling into your pocket."

Now Gabriel smiled. He pulled open the front of his coat so Larsen could see the gun in his hand.

"See that?" Gabriel said, mimicking Larsen's tone. "That's the sound of your little plan going up in smoke."

Larsen jumped back. On reflex, his guard put his hand inside his own coat. But Larsen held out his arm, stopping him.

"Come to Jesus time," said Gabriel, fully intending the double entendre.

Larsen's eyes flashed a sudden fury.

"Chill," said Gabriel, glancing behind Larsen to make sure that the small security army at the door hadn't sensed a sour note. They hadn't, though they were watching carefully "I assume you or Buckwheat here have the iPad?"

Larsen thought it over a moment, then nodded.

"Okay," Gabriel said, "game on. I was going to go in there and dial the voiding code, take my chances. Like you said, it's the only choice. At least it was. But then you showed up. You inspire me. I have a better idea."

Larsen rolled his eyes. "You're wasting my time. All I have to do is raise my hand and this is over."

"Which in that case means you are the only one who can trigger the device. Not exactly how you wanted this to end."

Larsen shook his head. "I'll have five minutes to walk away. You, however, would be shot before you hit the street."

"Think so? That's what you *say*. But here's what I think. I think it's all bullshit. You want me to dial the code and go up with the building. Then it's easy to use the paper trail to set me up as the trigger. Hell, you as much as said so already."

He paused, watching Larsen's wheels turn. "You need me. None of this works without me."

Larsen's eyes darted about as he looked for a loophole.

"This changes nothing."

"Oh, I believe it does. Let's check the iPad, let me see her."

Larsen was motionless. After a moment, though, a flick of his eyes prompted the bodyguard to give it up.

Larsen took the tiny computer from the goon, held it up. The screen was dark.

"Get her back on," said Gabriel.

"If I don't?"

Father, forgive me. I need you now, as you knew I would.

Gabriel withdrew the gun from his belt, releasing the safety in one move. He held it in front of his face, then pressed the tip of the barrel against his own temple.

"Or you lose your trigger man."

EVERYONE IN THE lobby shifted, guns quickly drawn, bodies diving
for cover.

Larsen held up his hands, calling for calm.

"Let her go," said Gabriel. "I want to see it. I want her on a phone, I want
to hear her tell me she's free."

"Or what, you shoot yourself? That's some bluff."

"Yeah, it is. And guess who's calling yours? I do it, you have to trigger the
bomb yourself. There's no buffer and you know it. You're a company man all
the way, but you can't spell the word *martyr*, can you, Larsen."

Gabriel could see Larsen's face turning red, saw him grinding his fingers
into his palms. A step behind, the bodyguard had his weapon drawn, his posture crouched as he pointed it at Gabriel's head in an absurd redundancy of
his own threat.

"That's it? We free the girl and you call in the code?"

"That's it. I'm a dead man either way, and I don't give a goddamn about
your politics or Winger's religion. I just want Sarah set free. Then we'll see
who's bluffing who."

Larsen's eyes were slits. He raised the iPad to his mouth, pressing a button
that activated the voice link.

"Let her go."

A tinny electronic voice asked for clarification.

"Release the girl. Tell her to call Stone as soon as she's clear. Make sure she has a phone."

There was a pause, then the voice said, "Roger that."

Gabriel withdrew his iPhone from his pocket.

Larsen turned the iPad screen so Gabriel could see it. Nothing happened for a moment, then someone entered the frame, taking care to hide his face from the camera. He knelt next to the cot where Sarah lay bound, undoing the restraints. She sat up, rubbing her wrists, a confused look on her face. The agent handed over her purse, motioned toward the door. Her expression remained confused as she listened to the inaudible instructions of her captor. Suddenly, as comprehension dawned, she looked directly into the camera, her eyes moist.

The look was for Gabriel.

Then she stood up and hurried out of the frame. The agent remained behind, watching her for a moment before he, too, looked at the camera and nodded.

What followed was the longest sixty seconds of Gabriel's life. His eyes remained fixed on Larsen's, who held his gaze with a calculating intensity. Nothing moved, their universe eerily separate from the reality around them.

The phone in his hand rang. He clicked on and held it to his free ear. The other ear still kissed the gun.

"Gabriel?" came Sarah's shaky voice, her breath choppy.

"They didn't follow you?"

"No. I'm running like hell. What's happening?"

"Just keep running, Sarah. Don't stop."

Gabriel clicked off and put it back in his pocket.

Larsen looked at his watch.

"Two o'clock, Stone. Let's see your cards."

"My thoughts exactly. Tell meathead here to put the gun down and go inside. Tell him to bring me the real director of security. Tell him to do it or I'll end it now."

Larsen nodded without removing his eyes from Gabriel. The bodyguard lowered his gun, his attention fully on Larsen for direction. He was obviously confused by the standoff.

Without taking his eyes away from Gabriel's, Larsen flicked his hand toward the building for emphasis and said, "Do it."

The guard backed away, again raising his weapon toward the crazy man holding the gun to his own head.

"These people are innocents," said Larsen. "You can save them."

Gabriel nodded slowly. "I intend to do just that."

GABRIEL AND LARSEN watched in silence as the bodyguard backed into the hotel lobby, keeping his gun trained on Gabriel. When the massive glass doors slid closed behind him, it was Larsen who spoke first.

"You bastard! You just blew the only chance to save this hotel and all these people."

Gabriel shook his head. "No. I just blew your chance to set me up. Even if the deactivation code is real, I'll be shot dead before I finish dialing. They'll claim later I was inputting a detonation code. Then you split, taking a few witnesses with you, leaving some dumbass rookie behind to call in the detonation code. The bomb goes off, and you come forward to tell the world what happened. Why else would you even *be* here?"

"That's absurd."

Gabriel smiled. "You're a bad liar, Larsen."

"You're making a terrible mistake here, mister."

"Probably. I know, let's go inside, grab a house phone, and see what happens."

Gabriel grinned as he watched Larsen squirm. The man's teeth gnawed at his upper lip, his eyes wild.

"You're wasting your window. I can spin this any way I want. You know that. Your way or mine."

A crowd was gathering around the bodyguard inside the lobby as he breathlessly replayed what was happening in the loading zone outside.

"Only two possible outcomes now," said Larsen, not caring about the lobby. "You shoot yourself, which you won't do since you're bluffing and you're a coward. But let's be hypothetical. It'll be easy to buy that you'd already triggered the bomb on a timer, that you came here tonight to go out in your own warped sense of glory. Or, as you say, we shoot you in the act, which is the more likely conclusion. Boom—same thing happens. Gabriel Stone, recently widowed Islamic sympathizer, the psycho behind the bomb. And we got him."

Gabriel squinted, then smiled. "See, I knew you sucked at this."

Larsen's frustration was evident on his face. "All I have to do is blink in the right direction and you're a dead man."

Gabriel grinned. "In which case you have to trigger the bomb manually."

A faint trace of doubt show in Larsen's eyes.

"That's called an ace," added Gabriel.

Larsen's face was instantly red. But he didn't fold.

"Maybe I just have to get off the property by two fifteen. You see, you're not sure if the bomb is an auto-ignite at two fifteen, or if someone has to call in the detonation manually. Maybe you're just here to put a face with the name. And because you're not sure, you have no play."

Larsen's grin was the kind you wanted to kiss with a bat.

Gabriel slowly took the gun away from his own forehead and pointed it at the middle of Larsen's chest. As he did he shifted his position so that Larsen was directly between him and the door, making a shot from the lobby impossible without endangering Larsen's life.

"Maybe I just shoot you dead right here and find out."

"Not my first choice. Either way, you have twelve minutes before the bomb goes off. It's over. Put down the gun, I promise you we both walk out of here. From there you take your chances."

Inside the lobby, Mark Krager was going nose-to-nose with the bodyguard, his gaze alternating out to where Gabriel and Larsen were standing.

"How about we raise the stakes and see," said Gabriel. "I've got the computer disk with Winger's confession on video. And I've got your picture. They're already on their way to someone who can nail your ass to the front page. And there's Sarah to corroborate the whole thing. If my people don't hear from me by morning, guess who's the terrorist then?"

Larson shook his head. "We'll find her first. We'll find your so-called people. I'll kill everyone you care about."

"Not if you're dead in the next two minutes."

Larsen's smile withered. He stared, trying to discern a crack in Gabriel's resolve. He put his palm up toward the lobby, warding off any prospective shooters.

"You're still bluffing."

"Really? Then call me. But if you're wrong, everything you want out of this is gone. Then again, if tonight doesn't happen like you planned, you can still kill Brenner before the election, and take your best shot at pinning it on me. Might be tough with what I've got on *you*, so I'd advise another approach. I really don't give a shit about Brenner or you or even your politics. Which suck, by the way."

"What are you saying?"

"I'm making you an offer. Stand down on this, play it my way, we live to hunt another day. A win-win, we split the pot."

Gabriel paused, allowing Larsen to process. They locked gazes, the hatred between them palpable.

"What is *your* way?" said Larsen at last.

The doors slid open. Mark Krager was coming toward them, a cadre of security men with guns on either flank.

Gabriel smiled. "Lock your fingers on the top of your head and you'll find out."

IN A DARKENED suite on the twelfth floor, Armand Brenner stirred in his sleep. He had been dreaming, but as usual his dreams made no real sense, filled with confusing images that frightened him. The theme was always the same; he was in some form of cruel captivity, at the behest of creatures with fierce human faces and gargoyle-like bodies. They wanted something of him, but it was never clear as to what, and their impatience was threatening, the consequences dire. He would awaken with an audible gasp, the sheets soaked.

Tonight's dream was of particular intensity. He dreamed of fire, of being incinerated whole, as if the gates of hell had opened. It was at times like these that he was thankful he was not alone with his destiny. *That* was hell on earth, to navigate the landscape of ambition and power without a confidant, without a place to lay down the façade and succumb to the sweet liquor of dark, desperate desire.

He reached across the bed for his wife. She was the only person alive who understood the dreams and protected him from the weight of his mission on earth. Who would hold him in his fear? Of all the people in the broadening hemisphere of Brenner's existence, Charlotte was the only person who knew who Armand Brenner really was.

But Charlotte Brenner was gone.

- 73 -

MARK KRAGER WAS close to hyperventilating. The head of the security detail assigned to the hotel was being held at gunpoint, and the man
pointing the weapon wanted to talk to *him*. He knew this was a crossroads,
that he was facing choices that would dictate the course of his career, maybe
his life.

He approached, then stopped ten feet behind where Larsen stood with
his hands clasped on top of his head. He met Gabriel's eyes, surprised at the
lack of panic there. He had seen crazy men before, men with knives and guns
threatening violence if they didn't get what they want, and none of them
looked like this.

"Nobody fires!" yelled Larsen, barely turning. "This is a negotiation situation—do *not* fire until my command!"

A moment of quiet followed, everyone sizing up the scene.

"I'm Mark Krager, Secret Service."

"Mark," said Gabriel, "here's the deal. I don't care if you believe what I'm
about to say or not. But what you *must* believe is that you have ten minutes,
and ten minutes only, to evacuate your hotel and clear the area."

A siren was suddenly audible in the distance.

"And you are?"

Krager was pulling out the Negotiating 101 handbook, and this was definitely not the time.

"In a hurry," Gabriel said. "There's a bomb on the property, and it's going off in ten minutes, if not sooner. I've got Mr. Larsen here at gunpoint because he doesn't believe me and would not permit you to evacuate the hotel. I can't let that happen."

Krager's gaze shifted to Larsen. Gabriel watched carefully to see how Larsen was going to play it. He remained stoic, his eyes expressionless. But he did nod his head in the affirmative, not at all convincing.

"So now it's on you," said Gabriel. "I've put my life on the line to give the people in this building a chance. I'm asking you to not hesitate and order the evacuation now."

Krager thought a moment. "Where is the bomb?"

"I don't know."

"Then how do you know there *is* a bomb?"

Gabriel felt heat assaulting his cheeks. His response here might define the outcome. If it was too soft, Krager might place his bet elsewhere.

There was only one response that would seal the deal.

"Because I built it," said Gabriel.

"Then you'd know where it is," Krager snapped back.

"I said I built it. Someone else placed it."

His eyes shot to Larsen, who could refute the story. But perhaps not without posing questions he didn't want to answer.

Larsen shook his head, his eyes squinting to slits.

"Come on, Mark," said Gabriel, "what's the default response here? You have no right to take chances with these people's lives. Do your job."

"You don't look like a guy who builds bombs," said Krager, his gaze burning into Gabriel.

"You don't look like a guy who rolls the dice with people's lives. What's your gut saying here? I'd listen."

Krager was obviously conflicted. "I'm not in charge of this operation," he said, his eyes now on Larsen. "He is."

Everyone was looking at Daniel Larsen.

"Then ask him," said Gabriel, putting his last cards on the table. "Maybe *he* can tell you who planted the bomb."

Krager and Larsen, two men with a distinct distaste for each other, locked eyes. Larsen's chest was visibly heaving.

"He's crazy," said Larsen.

Krager now gave Larsen the same analytical glare.

"You only get one shot at this," said Gabriel, speaking to both men. "But you'll have eternity to live with it."

Larsen turned to Gabriel, a dark smile emerging. "Looks like a full house," he said quietly. Then he turned back to Krager.

"Shoot him."

The men quickly assumed a ready position, concurrent with Krager holding up his arms and yelling, "Wait! Stop!"

Everything froze.

"Shoot him!" yelled Larsen, his voice echoing off the neighboring buildings.

Krager still held his arms up, calling for calm. All of the men except Larsen's bodyguard worked for him, and none of them liked the CIA agent with the attitude and the bad hair.

"No!" barked Krager, stepping forward. He walked past Larsen to stand face-to-face with the gunman. Gabriel kept the gun fixed on Larsen, though his eyes now engaged Mark Krager.

"Talk to me, Mr. Stone."

"There's no time. Just evacuate. Please. Do it now."

"We have a presidential candidate upstairs."

Gabriel's eyes burned. "Precisely. And it's your job to protect him."

"Did you build this bomb?"

"You have less than ten minutes to get it done."

Krager's eyes were beginning to bulge.

"You asked me who I am," said Gabriel. "The real question here, in this moment, is who are *you*?"

Krager nodded. "Give me one reason to believe you instead of him. Just one, and I'll do it."

Gabriel closed his eyes. His choice, the only certain path, loomed before him, a dark doorway with no assurance of delivery. He had only the knowledge that no viable alternative remained.

Only faith.

His eyes popped open. "As you wish," he said softly.

Forgive me, Father, for I have sinned . . .

He leveled the gun and fired a bullet at Daniel Larsen's chest.

74

GABRIEL WAS ON the ground, swallowed by a wave of writhing humanity that clawed at him like famished beasts. A knee held his head to the ground while several hands gripped fistfuls of his hair to assist in keeping him pinned down. Someone pulled his arms up behind his back at an impossible angle, the pain causing him to scream out, which only added to his attackers' rage. Two men clamped his legs, while others applied their full weight to his motionless torso. Then an anonymous fist began thrusting into his face, again and again, until the blackness came, carrying him away on a scalding, screaming wind.

If not for Krager's intervention, they would have taken him out in a frenzy of suppression. Only Krager realized that the story behind this night was now a primary objective.

It took three minutes for the first police cruiser to arrive. Gabriel was dragged to one, where he was cuffed and stuffed unceremoniously into the backseat.

Daniel Larsen had seen the gun rise up as Stone's face grew tense, saw his wrist go firm. His training and his instincts prompted him to tuck and begin a tight roll.

The roll was too late to avoid the bullet, but the tuck saved his life. The bullet caught him in the shoulder, skimming the flesh of his left deltoid muscle but thankfully avoiding socket and bone. It hurt like hell and was bleeding, but he would live to spy another day.

Provided his next move worked.

THERE WERE NO guests on the first nine floors of the hotel. Krager assigned one team to the upper floors, another to comb the remaining floors for hotel staff. A third would clear the kitchen and banquet areas, where a night shift was making ready for the National Prayer Luncheon the next day.

Krager would remain in the lobby to supervise. Police were already arriving, fire and rescue units were en route. He wanted the place empty by the time they got there.

Daniel Larsen knew there was no time for waiting. After the shooting his bodyguard had dragged him inside to evaluate the wound, and to wait in safety for emergency assistance to arrive. But he had more urgent issues than his shoulder.

Larsen motioned for his bodyguard to lean down for a quiet conversation. A few yards away people were running back and forth and yelling into walkie-talkies, the chaos of evacuation in full motion.

"Listen to me," he said. "I'm bleeding to death. I have to get this looked at, and fast. An ambulance may have trouble getting close."

The guard was already starting to haul Larsen to his feet.

Larsen shook him off. He grabbed the guard by the lapel and held him steady, locking onto the younger man's eyes. "There is no two-fifteen auto-detonate. It was bullshit to get Stone to make a move. The bomb has to be set off manually."

There was no reaction, just the wide-eyed attentiveness of a subordinate trained not to ask questions.

"Wait three minutes, blend into the chaos, make sure no one notices I'm gone. Then find a house phone. Dial the code, then get the hell out of here. You'll have five minutes to get clear. Get as far away as you can."

His eyes burned. The young man nodded in return, having been called upon to serve.

"I need you to do this. Are you with me?"

The young agent nodded, his breath already quickening.

"Everything we've worked for is in your hands."

"What about you?" asked the subordinate.

Larsen shot a look through the glass, toward the escalating madness outside. "I'll get someone to drive me to the hospital. I need you here."

"Three minutes isn't enough," said the guard. "What if you can't find a ride?"

"It has to be. We can't crowd the two-fifteen cut-off. The bomb goes inactive after that. Just do it."

The guard nodded. "Give me the code."

Larsen spoke slowly, enunciating each number. "Six five five, three four four."

"Six five five, three four four," repeated the guard.

The number 666, squared, was the deactivate code. The reverse order of the numbers was the detonation code.

Larsen stood, steadied himself. As he took his first tentative steps toward the door, he said, "Three minutes. No more. Call me when you're clear."

The hulk nodded, hoping sacrifice would not be required.

"Good luck, sir."

Larsen shot a quick look back, his expression complex. Then he pushed through the door.

The bodyguard turned toward the lobby, scanning for a house phone, alone with his solemn duty.

Outside, Larsen gave a last look back, saw that his bodyguard had blended into the interior madness.

Once he reached the loading area, and despite the pain, Daniel Larsen began to run.

75

ON THE TWELFTH floor, Armand Brenner heard a frantic pounding on his door. He grabbed a robe as he stumbled toward the door. His ancient football legs required more notice than this to function well, and he moved slowly. The knocking continued, even louder than before. Someone, not Charlotte, not Alex, was calling his name in an urgent tone.

He opened the door to find a trusted campaign executive accompanied by two security guards.

"We have to go, sir," said his employee. "Bomb threat, and it's serious."

Brenner nodded. They'd had drills for this. On any given day there was at least one death threat on the table.

"I'll get my clothes."

"No," snapped the man, visibly upset. "The robe is fine. Let's move."

"Where's Charlotte?"

"Already out, sir."

One of the guards took him by the elbow and began escorting him down the hall, his feet bare, his body naked under the robe. They were hurrying, much too fast for his aching legs.

He wondered where Charlotte had gone. But not for long.

All hell had broken loose in the lobby. People in robes and pajamas were emerging from elevators, escorted by security staff. Ed Krager was directing the chaotic flow, a Bluetooth unit at his ear, barking instructions and pointing. Police escorted people to the street, urging them to move quickly away.

The young CIA bodyguard observed it all from his position near a waterfall, his hand resting on a wall-mounted house phone.

He checked his watch. In a few seconds it would be three minutes since Larsen had left.

He raised the receiver and began punching in the six numbers. Another part of his mind wondered how far he might get in five minutes, already planning his route of escape.

He smiled as he listened to the ringing.

76

GABRIEL CAME TO in the back of a police car parked at the curb in front of the Columbia Center Hotel, his hands bound behind him. Men in suits were conferring urgently with men in uniforms just outside the car.

Other police cars were parked nearby, one arriving alongside him in the street, its lights casting a red-to-blue-to-red flash against the sides of the neighboring buildings. He heard high-pitched voices, everyone suddenly in charge of everything.

People were emerging from the front entrance, many of them wearing robes, a few men only their underwear.

These were the saved.

One problem remained, and it was huge. There was still a bomb hidden inside the building. And if the same instincts that had driven his actions this evening had been right, it would go off at any moment.

A news helicopter happened to be airborne covering a fire in Arlington when they'd picked up radio chatter about an evacuation at the Columbia Center. They had quickly banked and headed across the Potomac, their camera already trained on the target.

They were less than a mile out when night became day.

THE PILOTS WOULD describe it as something like a massive flashbulb from hell, a blindingly intense fissure in the fabric of the universe, exposing its very core. The flash was gone almost as soon as it appeared, leaving the pilots momentarily blinded, replaced by a glowing, smoldering pyre where the building used to be, a billowing cloud of smoke masking the true dimensions of the inferno.

There were few witnesses, since those standing on the sidewalk had been propelled across the street, flung against the buckling walls of adjoining buildings at a speed in excess of three hundred miles an hour. Several witnesses, who had seen the fireball from a distance, would say they saw a face in the flames. Some claimed that it looked like that of a demon, and that it was screaming.

Others claimed it looked more like laughter.

77

DANIEL LARSEN WAS in a hurry. He needed to be home when the call came through, tucked in bed next to his wife, who would back whatever alibi was required. He had begun the process of crafting a credible story earlier in the day, laying a paper trail, talking to a few "witnesses" who owed him favors. If it came down to it, he'd ask his wife to lie, and with her comfortable lifestyle at stake, she'd do it.

The wound on his shoulder would remain their little secret. No one who hadn't been there would think to ask, and anyone who had would be dead.

He drove through his neighborhood slowly, with the lights off. With any luck the neighbors were asleep.

Thankfully his wife was asleep, too. He disrobed quickly, throwing his suit across the back of a chair in the closet. Then he went into the bathroom and washed the blood off his flesh. Three Band-Aids and some rubbing alcohol did the trick. It would heal in two weeks, and no one would be the wiser.

He slipped under the covers without switching on a light. When he turned to face his wife, he noticed that she was lying on her back, which almost never happened.

And that her eyes were open.

It was then he felt the sticky wetness of the sheets. He rolled back to the edge of the bed, feeling for the nightstand light. When it came on he froze, the sight before him piercing his heart.

His wife was dead. Her eyes were indeed open wide, as was her mouth, as if her last breath came with desperation. A black hole punctuated the center of her brow. A yellow pillow soaked with brain tissue remained under her head.

Larsen froze. With his eyes riveted on his wife's dead face, he began to fumble at the nightstand drawer. He got it open, his hand searching for the barrel of the handgun he kept there, when he heard a voice.

"Stop."

The gun was gone.

A woman stepped out from the closet doorway. She was dressed all in black, including a baseball hat with a Navy SEAL logo. Her gloved hand pointed a gun directly at him.

"Who are you?" he asked. The woman was still shrouded in shadow, but he was sure he recognized the voice.

"The tragic widow," she said. "Carrying out her husband's last wish."

"Larsen squinted into the shadows. "Mrs. McQuarrie."

"I'll take that as a confession," she said.

Larsen's stomach turned. "You didn't have to do this." He flicked his eyes toward his wife's body.

"What, you were expecting some sort of professional courtesy? Spare me the drama."

A moment passed while he considered what this might mean.

"This isn't McQuarrie's style. He was a professional."

"A dead professional. And you're right. There's a reason for everything."

He just stared ahead, straight out of a POW manual he had once memorized.

"This is your gun," she said. "My husband knew right where to find it."

Larsen was nodding now. "Of course. With my prints. Am I leaving a note?"

"No. Just a dead wife."

Larsen exhaled, his cheeks puffing out. Then he hung his head in resignation. In spite of his fear, there was a very real sense of anticipation, the answers he'd sought for a lifetime only a heartbeat away.

"Then do it now," he said.

Joan McQuarrie stepped forward, raising the gun. She stopped a few feet away, far enough from his reach to get a shot off should he make a move. The gun pointed at the top of Larsen's head, which had sagged toward the floor.

Shot twice in one night. It was almost funny.

"Look at me," she said.

He did. For the first time in thirty years, his eyes were filled with tears. They locked on to hers and waited.

She smiled, allowing the moment to last longer than it needed to.

The gun went off.

The answers were not at all what he expected.

78

AT FIRST IT was believed only one person within the perimeter of the Columbia Center property had survived. A woman was found in the rubble the next morning, her clothes burned from her body, her face mangled beyond recognition, and her skull partially crushed. She had been fully conscious, her fingernail tapping a piece of metal pipe to call attention. Somehow she breathed, her heart continued to beat, though in the ambulance she lapsed into unconsciousness. She was expected to die within the hour.

That assumption would prove to be wrong.

During the same hour, one other survivor was discovered.

THE POLICE CAR in which Gabriel had been sitting when the bomb detonated was rendered airborne, hurled like a discarded stick down New York Avenue, coming to rest nearly five hundred feet away. The car had spun like a top in the air, landing on the roof of a panel truck full of fresh produce.

Gabriel Stone was found just after dawn, his back broken, skull cracked, left femur shattered. His blood pressure upon arrival at an overburdened George Washington University Hospital trauma center was eighty over forty and fading, and the attending doctor had actually moved on to more hopeful prospects in the belief the man would be dead by the time he returned.

Those who bothered to look closely at his chart would recall his survival that night as something of a miracle. The second one in a night in which miracles, however earnestly prayed for, were scarce.

But the true miracle was the fact that Gabriel Stone's memory would remain completely intact. Which meant he was, for many months to come, the most sought-after man in the world.

79

I saw one of his heads as if it had been slain, and his fatal wound was healed. And the whole earth was amazed and followed after the beast.

—REVELATION 13:3

ONLY TWENTY-EIGHT SOULS lost their lives at the Columbia Center Hotel. Nineteen bodies were recovered, the rest unaccounted for. Emergency personnel would comment that the site recalled Ground Zero in Manhattan, only smaller, a pile of rubble framed by grotesque freestanding structural supports somehow remaining erect. The landscape was Cathedral-like, a science fiction tableau of the macabre still belching smoke and emitting radiation, the effects of which were yet to be determined, or at least publicized. Nearby buildings were imploded by the blast, one of them collapsing an hour later. Another seemed to have melted, literally, its vertical beams resembling massive spent candles. The entire site was dotted with smooth ceramic pools that once were windows and walls.

The explosion was determined to be thermonuclear in nature, though to a calculatedly small degree. Analysts would confirm that temperatures at the site had, for an instant, reached 1800 degrees Celsius, hot enough to boil lead. The amount of weapons-grade plutonium required for a blast of this scale was less than two ounces, about the size of a small meatball. Human flesh and bone on the lower floors had been instantly vaporized. Others, less fortunate, were killed by some combination of slow roasting and their participation in a hellish twelve-story descent.

The press was never told about the nuclear nature of the bomb. There was speculation, but it was never confirmed.

The majority of the guests and hotel staff made it out alive. Mark Krager, the Secret Service agent in charge of the site, had perished in the blast. He was credited with saving dozens of lives through his quick decision to evacuate, and his courageous manner in the face of death.

Anyone in the passenger loading area outside the hotel was killed instantly, including several who had been successfully evacuated but hadn't yet moved far enough way. Four policemen arriving moments before the blast were among the dead.

Rumors quickly spread about a suspect on the scene who had issued a threat, and that a man had been found in a police car with his wrists bound behind him with police-issue plastic cuffs. But the FBI made no comment on either story.

Islamic extremists were quickly blamed. CIA intelligence networks were reporting an eerie silence across the global grid, the implications of which were dark. Known terrorist leaders, including some still at large from 9-11 and various other Middle East atrocities, hailed the bombing as yet another example of God's justice, smiting the proliferation of American evil in the very heart of the beast itself. The first major break in the case corroborated these early reports. An Al-Qaeda operative captured in Germany, under unofficial CIA interrogation tactics, told of funding an American who was sympathetic to their cause. Authorities admitted they had followed such a money trail into foreign banks with which a specific person of interest had reported ties, neither confirming nor denying it was the man found at the scene. They assured the media they were pursuing this lead aggressively.

Religious leaders on every continent condemned the bombing as a work of despicable evil perpetrated by those whose hatred of goodness and freedom threatened all of civilization.

Some went so far as to say they suspected the current reign of terrorism to be part of biblical prophecy, that the end of times was forthcoming, and that salvation was still available to any who would humble themselves before God. Islamic leaders continued to insist that Islam was a religion based on love, and that the jihad claimed by those in their midst represented only a fringe element, and not the nation of Islam itself. Nonetheless, as had been the case for decades, these same leaders refused to provide any names of those who would continue to perpetrate a wrath of terror on the United States.

The President wept on national television. He had been scheduled to attend a function at that very hotel the next day. His anger channeled into a renewed commitment to the American people to put an end to terrorism in our lifetime, and to exact justice on behalf of all who had died. This promise was made on the graves of the dead, and backed with the fullest extent of military force available to this, the most powerful nation on the planet.

Armand Brenner was dead, as was his senior staff. Many of those bodies had been found, though few were identifiable without DNA tagging. Brenner's body had been one of the more intact, and a shot of his corpse had made its way onto the Internet, creating an informal icon around which all who favored a harsh and immediate reprisal would rally. The President praised Brenner as a man with the courage of his convictions and the best interests of the American people at heart, and at the nationally televised memorial held in his name, he again wept openly.

Brenner's wife, Charlotte, was among the missing and presumed dead.

The nation was once again at war.

Within the week the President's approval rating went through the roof. The election continued as planned, Congress committing to a stance that no one could compromise the forward movement of democracy in our nation. The opposing party quickly named a new nominee, Brenner's vanilla running mate, but it was a gratuitous gesture without a prayer of success. The President, who had trailed Brenner in the major polls by eight percentage points, would win by the widest margin of any incumbent in history.

It had worked exactly as Daniel Larsen hoped.

IN THE MIDDLE of the fifth week the woman who had survived the Columbia Center bombing suddenly woke up. After thirty-nine days on an IV without opening her eyes, her face still hidden beneath bandages, she suddenly touched the arm of an attending nurse one morning and, with a sweet smile, asked for a glass of water and the TV remote.

The press went crazy. Some called it a miracle, a sign from God.

The woman's name was Charlotte Brenner.

ARMAND BRENNER'S WIFE, a former congresswoman herself, maintained that she had not been able to sleep on the night of the bombing, and with her husband's campaign manager at her side she'd gone for a stroll around the hotel to talk strategy, as was her habit. The truth was she had been on a kitchen-area patio sneaking a cigarette with a few hotel employees, but this was hardly the image she wished to put forth to a public suddenly calling for her to take up her husband's great cause. Brenner's campaign manager, Alex Goldman, who was with her, had been killed instantly, as had the kitchen workers. This reinforced a commonly held and quickly spreading belief that it was only by the grace of God that Charlotte had survived.

All the world now knew that Charlotte Brenner was alive and recovering with remarkable speed. She assured the press that she was looking forward to carrying on the work to which she and her husband had devoted their public lives. She called upon the citizens of the world to pray for an end to hatred.

She pleaded for space and privacy while she healed. She needed to grieve the loss of her beloved Armand.

Their private life was never brought to light. Anyone and everyone who knew the specific nature of it was dead.

Seven Months Later
Location: Unknown

ANYONE WHO KNEW the name of Gabriel Stone assumed he had left the country, or that he was dead. Not from the explosion at the Columbia Center Hotel in Washington—no one outside of the intelligence community had the slightest reason to think he had been there that night—but from a deftly planted series of clues and implications perpetrated by the Central Intelligence Agency. His bank and brokerage accounts had been closed, his car sold for cash, his passport renewed, all hallmarks of a man planning on leaving the country. For now they'd let the scenario continue, and it was no coincidence that these very clues could be applied to good use as a backstory for a man who had planted a bomb at the behest of terrorists.

It could go either way. It was, they said, entirely up to him.

His lawyer in Auburn was dead. He'd been killed in a freak boating accident two weeks after the Columbia Center blast. The accident occurred one day after he'd contacted the local FBI, claiming to have information about the case.

At least, this was what they told Gabriel.

His room was quite comfortable, the master suite at a rural estate located in what he guessed to be Vermont or Montana or perhaps the Pacific Northwest. There was no television, no newspapers, and certainly no one willing to tell him precisely where he was. From the window he could see a huge manicured yard surrounded by trees, with magnificent mountains beyond. It would be the perfect place for a wedding reception, or perhaps a game of touch football. An access road emerged from the tree line, heading around to a side of the house he'd never seen, and daily there were at least fifteen arrivals and departures, almost all vans and SUVs. His room had all the accoutrements of a modern ICU ward, and his nurses were pleasant yet robotic in the execution of their duties.

His doctor was a woman with the bedside manner of a tax auditor, but she was thorough and seemed genuinely interested in his comfort and full recovery. They fed him generously, with an eye on his preferences, and as a reward for his cooperation they'd recently brought in a DVD player hard-wired to a TV monitor, just in case he knew how to jury-rig an antenna.

This was torture by seclusion, Middle America style. They were trying to bore him to death.

Until they believed him, until they were certain he had told them everything he knew, he would remain here, either officially or unofficially dead, whichever suited their purpose.

He was a person of interest, and that was all.

They met with him daily, concurrent with a regimen of physical and occupational therapy. Two surgeries had restored the functionality of his vertebra and spinal column, and his burns and fractures and the massive concussion that should have killed him had all healed nicely, leaving a full and complete recollection of that night and all that had preceded it. No one mentioned the removal of a silicon chip from his intestinal tract, and when Gabriel asked the question was met with a referral to someone else. That referral never materialized.

He spoke the truth, the whole truth, even when they spun it back at him with an incriminating spin.

He was interviewed by nineteen different investigators, thirteen men, five women, and one who could have gone either way, a total of seventy-seven times. They always wanted to hear it from square one, trying to catch a seam in the narrative.

But his memory was seamless. The truth was always the easiest story to tell.

They had many questions, and to the extent his answers were vague or nonexistent, they went away curious. Why was a piece of paper found in your pocket containing a six-digit code? Where did you get the unregistered gun? Why didn't you contact the police or FBI the moment you were able to do so? Why does the bellman at the Hampton Inn deny helping you? What were your intentions in going to the hotel that night? Where was Sarah Meyers now, and why hadn't she come forward to corroborate your story? Where was Simon Winger or his body? Why can't we find the hard drive and the photograph you supposedly sent to your lawyer? When your wife died, isn't it true that you disavowed God? Have you ever met Armand Brenner? How about his wife? How is it that we have been able to link you to certain elements of radical Islamic movements in four different countries?

And so it went, for the last six of the seven months he'd been here.

He had his own questions, too.

Was anyone checking his version of the story? Had the leadership of The Brethren been questioned? Was there a search under way for Simon Winger? Was there a missing NSA agent once named Matthew Pascarella? Was there a female ex–Denver police officer named Sarah Meyers? Were there any female ex–officers who shot and killed a fifteen-year-old within the last decade or so, one with a degree in religious history? One now on staff at NYU who moonlights as an NSA agent? What does Special Agent Daniel Larsen of the CIA have to say about this, and is he being investigated? Is there a missing CIA contract killer with ties to Larsen? Are they aware of Brock Carter, special counsel to the President, having a meeting with such an agent in the Capital Mall? Is Carter connected in any way to The Brethren? Don't they find it odd that his lawyer in California, the one man who can corroborate the front end of his story, turns up conveniently dead?

They wrote every question down, every time he asked, as if they truly cared. But an answer never came. Just a promise to see what they could do.

He complained about his civil rights, but they told him that despite recent hiccups in the system, terrorism suspects have few civil rights, part of the Patriot Act legislation forged in the aftermath of 9-11. They told him if he cooperated and if his story eventually panned out, he'd be given a chance to sign a confidentiality agreement and become an American hero—which, if he could resurrect some semblance of his book, could have lucrative implications. If his story tanked or if he refused to sign, he would suffer consequences for which there would be no paper trail.

Until then, he had no choice. There were technologies they could employ if he got feisty or restless, but this approach was better for everyone. They were making progress, they assured him, but no other encouragement was offered.

His room was always under guard, and with a luxurious granite-countered bathroom in his suite and his food arriving on the appointed hour, he had no reason to test the perimeter. They had taken him for walks around the grounds, while men wearing suits and sunglasses lurked nearby. He tried chumming up to his therapists, asking questions about the world and the status of the investigation, but all he got were game scores, league standings and movie reviews, and an occasional sympathetic smile.

They wouldn't even tell him who had won the election.

81

THE MAN WHO arrived with Gabriel's lunch wore a baseball cap, the house staff blouse, khakis, and tennis shoes. There was no hiding his age, something far north of fifty, his hair gray at the temple, his hands veined with age.

"New blood," offered Gabriel, his voice upbeat. He'd never met this guy and wanted to win him over. He was wearing sweatpants and an FBI sweatshirt the staff thought was hilarious.

The man put the tray on the desk, then turned and stared at Gabriel, as if expecting a tip.

He took off the hat, a sheepish smile already in place.

Gabriel, who had been lying on the bed recovering from a particularly rigorous session of therapy, experienced a sensation of déjà vu. Then, with a rush of blood to his head, with a stab of ice to his heart, Gabriel realized who it was. His mouth fell open, unable to inhale.

As if he were looking at a ghost.

Simon Winger stood before him, nodding smugly.

"Hello, Gabriel."

Winger still had that gentle grace, a sense of knowing muted within an aura of patience. He hadn't aged; in fact, he looked as if he'd just returned from a sunny vacation.

"Don't be frightened."

"Easy for you to say. You're dead."

This widened his smile. "What do your eyes tell you?"

"Maybe I'm dead, too."

"Illusion is relative. If you prefer to think of me as dead, a messenger from the great beyond, be my guest. Perhaps it will allow you to hear me more clearly."

The two men stared at each other in silence.

After a moment Winger asked, "May I sit down?" already having positioned the desk chair to face the bed.

"Are you a federal agent?"

Winger shook his head, a father sadly answering his son's inevitable questions about Santa Claus.

"Then how'd you get in here?" Gabriel pressed.

"The pulling of strings has always been my long suit."

"I liked you better when you were alive."

Winger smirked. "You've been through hell."

Gabriel just nodded, involuntarily averting his eyes. There was no escaping the fact that he hadn't disarmed the bomb.

"You were tested, Gabriel. I believe that everything that has occurred was ordained. Like each of God's milestones, it is the will of men that dictates history."

Gabriel was impatient. "Why are you here?"

"To help you understand."

"They think I planted that bomb."

"I know much more than you do about what they think."

A tiny explosion detonated in Gabriel's stomach. "Everything you told me in that tape was true, wasn't it."

Winger didn't move, other than a sad softening of eyes.

Gabriel sat up on the edge of the bed, strangely energized. "Start at the beginning," he said.

Winger shot a look at the door, the only indication that his presence was perhaps unscheduled.

"The Seven Thunders of Revelation were not the only signs shown to John. Nor were they the only ones he was ordered to keep hidden. John beheld other visions of specific people who would live through the centuries, and in describing them in a different set of scrolls he created a sort of psychic fingerprint, a means by which men of faith might identify them, to be used for centuries to come."

Gabriel was nodding slightly as he processed this.

"Satan's pretenders to the throne of the Antichrist."

Winger nodded in return. "Precisely. When he was released from Patmos John traveled to Ephesus, the first of the Anatolian churches to whom Revelation is addressed. It was there he delivered the secret scrolls to trusted allies, and thus began a succession of disciples devoted to them over the centuries."

Gabriel's eyes were wide. "And you were one of them."

"There was no more important work. From the beginning the disciples of the scrolls were kept separate from the Church, which was fraught with secret societies and vigils of its own, some divine, some not so. I was recruited by a brilliant man in Israel. The heritage of the scrolls knows no boundaries of race or religion or creed. Those who are chosen are selected not only for their capabilities and their faith, but by the scrolls themselves."

Gabriel's eyes bulged. "*Your* name appeared?"

Simon nodded, suddenly emotional. He drew a deep, tired breath. "Many have died by my hand. We labored in the faith that a sign would come when the time of the true Antichrist had arrived, an indication that our work was finished."

"Tell me who it is," said Gabriel. "After all this, I deserve to know."

"You already know," said Winger, closing his eyes to gather his thoughts. "The fact of the matter is, it was you who first properly identified the Antichrist, in your book."

82

WINGER POURED HIMSELF a glass of water and took a long series of gulps. Gabriel waited patiently, his body more alive than at any time since the explosion. He wondered if the room was bugged, certain that it was. Hopefully they were listening now.

"The name of the Antichrist was always there, in the Book of Revelation," said Winger. "But it was encoded, and in an ingenious way that only God could comprehend."

"Bible codes," said Gabriel. "I've heard of them."

"Fascinating science. So fascinating that my associate in Israel built a massive computer devoted to that single application. By delving deeper into the code, we discovered clues and directions for further decoding, eventually leading us to the name we had been waiting for, for the last two thousand years."

"The Antichrist."

Winger nodded, his eyes heavy.

Gabriel felt a cold breeze envelop his flesh.

"*Here is wisdom,*" quoted Winger. "*Let him who has understanding calculate the number of the beast, for the number is that of a man. His number is six six six.*"

The cold breeze now became an icy touch, penetrating Gabriel's spine and radiating throughout his limbs.

"There are translation issues to consider," said Winger.

"Often with translation comes a loss of proper context, and here is where anyone who reads and teaches Revelation must take great care. Out of context, one could argue a difference between a *mark* and a *number*. Or a *man* and a *woman*. There are translations, mostly discounted by the old Church, that assign no difference in either from the original Aramaic."

Winger let his eyes burn into Gabriel's.

"The number of a man," he continued, somewhat wistfully. "Meaning, perhaps, that the number could be *used* by a man to unlock the code."

"That man was you," said Gabriel, almost under his breath.

Winger nodded, the emotion in his eyes obvious.

"We found your name in the code—Gabriel Stone. Even in Hebrew it translated perfectly. That's how I knew you were destined to be a part of this."

Gabriel felt a sudden wave of emotion. A memory crystallized, seemingly out of nowhere.

"My mother used to tell me God had a special purpose for me," he said, his voice suddenly weak. "I never believed her."

"I don't pretend to know what everything in Revelation means," said Winger, "but I can tell you this—I've seen with my own eyes what the coded messages are. One of them led us to a passage in Exodus, chapter twenty-eight, verse sixteen: *It shall be square and folded double, a span in length and a span in width.* At first I had no idea what this could mean."

"But you prayed on it," interjected Gabriel.

Winger smiled. "I did. And that's when, and *why*, it hit me. We were programming the code in a three-dimensional array for the first time, and we were finding coded messages that put everything we thought we knew about prophecy in a whole new light. But we had to go deeper to find the prize."

"The name of the Antichrist."

Winger's eyes were now alive with energy.

"Imagine taking all the letters of Revelation, written in original text, and arranging them in a perfect square. Now make that square a perfect cube, so that no matter the direction from which you approached it, you were looking at the entire book. A massive cubic grid, turned into an even more massive matrix."

"And that's when you found the name."

"No. Not even close. It hit me—what if such a cube wasn't big enough? What if the message was hidden deeper than that? I suggested to our programmer that we take the cube and expand it, use it as a brick, so to speak, in a larger structure. So we *stacked* each cubic array of the entire book of the original text of Revelation upon itself, by a factor of six hundred and sixty-six times."

"The number of a man," said Gabriel reverently.

"Six hundred sixty-six cubic units high," said Winger, "six hundred sixty-six cubic units wide, six hundred sixty-six cubes deep. What you get is a universal matrix encompassing 443,556 units, each brick consisting of the entire book itself."

Something about the number struck Gabriel as familiar. A new stab of ice skewed his heart—four four three, five five six. It was the deactivation code he never got to call in to the house phone at the Columbia Center.

Winger put his finger over his lips, calling for silence. Some things required no debate, no analysis. Then he nodded.

They both smiled at once.

"We not only found the name," said Winger. "We found the verification that it was the one we'd been waiting for."

"Armand Brenner."

Winger stared a moment, his own emotion evident.

"No. Another name. Which is why we had to try and stop his death. Brenner was *not* the Antichrist. His name was in the secret scrolls of St. John as a pretender to that throne, making him our initial target. But Satan was playing hardball now. He had the real thing waiting in plain sight all along."

"Tell me," he said.

Winger withdrew some folded papers from his pocket, handed them over to Gabriel.

When he started to open it, Winger put his hand on Gabriel's and said, "Wait until I leave. This is between you and God."

83

WINGER STOOD, READY to leave Gabriel alone with what he had brought him and whatever thoughts and prayers it might inspire.

"Wait," said Gabriel, sliding the papers under his pillow. "Tell me about Sarah."

"They never found her," said Winger, his eyes distant.

Gabriel felt a stab of pain in his heart.

"Some claim Christ had a daughter by Mary Magdalene," said Winger, seemingly apropos of nothing. "Her name was Sarah, too."

"I read that book a few years ago. *Everybody* read that book a few years ago."

Winger's eyes snapped back to Gabriel. "No trace of her existence could be found, no legend corroborated."

Gabriel was about to ask which Sarah he was referring to, but stopped. The answer was the same either way.

Winger broke the moment with a smile. "They do check everything you say, you know. They went to the Denver police, to NYU . . . nothing."

"Who *was* she, then?"

"Good question, that. One I've been asking myself. She saved my life, too, you know. And in many ways, *touched* it."

"She had that effect on people."

"For a while I thought she might have been working the inside, maneuvering you into position for Larsen to play."

"Fair enough. She pretended not to know who you were where I'm concerned. What was that about?"

Winger's smile was paternal. "The Lord often manifests through his servants. Perhaps you needed to be guided rather than shown. It is not our place to question Providence."

Gabriel nodded. Somehow, in light of what he now understood about the ways of Providence, such things made sense.

"Larsen is dead?" asked Gabriel, snapping back to the present.

Winger nodded solemnly. "The official line is suicide."

"I hear that's going around." Gabriel was referring to the video in which Simon appeared to shoot himself. The fact that Gabriel had not actually seen the wound inflicted would haunt him from this day forward.

Winger returned a sheepish little shrug.

"And now you're a spirit, out there doing God's work."

"I believe the term is ghosting," offered Winger, his eyes twinkling. "There is a season to all things. I am but God's humble servant. I go where and how I am called."

Winger went on to brief Gabriel on the state of a world that had changed dramatically in the seven months he had been locked away. The Middle East had exploded with even more violent conflict, Syria becoming the centerpiece of Islamic resistance to Israel and the United States. Syria had welcomed Al-Qaeda's power players as they were run out of Iraq, shrugging an indifferent ignorance all the while.

It was these newly minted Syrians who had bombed the university in Haifa in an effort to seed an Israeli-Palestinian showdown, killing Professor Gerson in the process. Some factions of the global intelligence community, unendorsed and unrecognized by U.S. officials, claim to have proven an alliance between a vast Middle Eastern coalition of nations and North Korea, the centerpiece of which was the sharing of nuclear resources. It had long been known that Al-Qaeda had been actively seeking a nuclear device long before September 11, and according to these same sources, they were lining up as the coalition's means of covert delivery of a nuclear bomb to U.S. soil.

It was never confirmed that the Columbia Center bomb had been nuclear in nature. The same people who had employed Daniel Larsen told the President that to let that particular cat out of the bag, basically admitting to the citizens of the country that all concerned had failed to protect them, was in no one's best interests.

Nonetheless, in the months that followed the Washington explosion, the President had mounted an unprecedented offensive against known and suspected pockets of Islamic radicalism, leaving many civilian deaths in its wake.

The entire Middle East was a killing field.

The terrorists were cockroaches, they crawled out from under rocks where no one else would live, they just wouldn't seem to die. Isolated incidences of violence were occurring at regular intervals in locations around the world, seemingly with a different Islamic splinter group claiming credit each time. U.S. citizens were divided on the issue, and the incumbent party was in a state of chaos it hadn't seen since the Nixon era.

A fully healed Charlotte Brenner had emerged as the voice of reason, preaching a message of moderation and diplomacy that appealed to a growing percentage of the masses. Her plan for peace was radical but practical, with an economic fringe benefit: she offered a blueprint to create an environmentally safe technical infrastructure for the reemergence of nuclear energy within six years. She promised to also eliminate our reliance on Saudi oil within ten, using newly discovered polar oil reserves and the practical evolution of fuel-efficient hybrid vehicles.

The plan was to simply back out of the Middle Eastern desert, leaving Israel alone to wage their holy wars without our money or the lives of our sons.

The press reported that leaders of the major Islamic terrorist networks claimed they would cease their hostilities against the United States if such measures were ever to be implemented.

She also vowed to reinstate the distance between church and state that the Republicans had eroded over the course of two campaigns. A population grown weary of them flocked to her support.

Charlotte Brenner not only had the attention of the powers that be, she had the ear of a nation desperate for a charismatic savior.

84

THE TWO MEN shook hands at the door. Winger offered no further explanation for his presence or his destination, and Gabriel didn't ask.

As soon as the door closed, Gabriel returned to his bed to retrieve the papers Simon had left for him.

He spread them out on the bed. There were four items, all from different sources. Three he recognized, one he did not.

But he would remember each until his dying day.

The first was a page from his own manuscript. He read what he had written so many months ago—a flashback to the island of Patmos in the year A.D. 86, where a political prisoner named John was on his knees, staring into the black depth of a cave, his hands outstretched, his eyes wide and pleading.

Then the perspective changed, and the reader was suddenly inside of John's mind, seeing what he saw, things no man of his era had a way of comprehending, but things the reader certainly would. A nuclear bomb being tested on a remote island, then dropped on two cities of innocents to make a terrible point. A country born in blood in 1947, the child of a holy war. A president shot down, his brother and then his son falling after him. Man setting foot on the moon. A terrible epidemic emerging out of Africa, threatening the world. Airplanes flying into office towers like missiles.

And a hotel blown into the early-morning sky, its dust settling over the great city like heavenly tears.

But it didn't end there. At least, in the scripture according to Gabriel Stone.

He had gone on to reveal what *else* John the Divine did not write down. Because to John, in that day and age, what he saw made no sense whatsoever. It was either of no consequence, or it was the most heretical vision of all, depending on the century in which the reader lived.

In his vision John had seen a woman emerging from a wall of fire, striding into the night, naked and darkly beautiful. Ravens descended carrying a cloak for her shoulders and placing a crown with ten points on her head, which was bleeding.

In Gabriel's version of John's visions, the Antichrist had been a woman. John could not write it down, because never in the history of the world had it been possible for a woman to assume the political power required to mount that throne and spin the world into a final confrontation with destiny.

That is, until now.

THE SECOND PAPER on the bed was a newspaper article, neatly clipped, dated several months earlier. It was the story of Charlotte Brenner's survival, how she remained in a coma for five weeks, on the very brink of death, her face hidden beneath bandages, her skull shattered beyond all hope. How she had emerged from the precipice of eternity with a smile, and a determination to assume her dead husband's political mantle.

Now, seven months after the explosion, she was mobile and working with trusted counsel on the resurrection of her husband's political platform. She had another year of therapy ahead of her, claimed the doctors, but her recovery was expected to be full and complete. And in her case, meaningful. Because she was fully qualified to do what she said she intended to do.

In three years Charlotte Brenner would become the next President of the United States.

The third piece of paper was a xeroxed page from a Bible. It came from the Book of Revelation, with one passage circled in red ink. Chapter thirteen, verse three:

"I saw one of his heads as if it had been slain, and his fatal wound was healed. And the whole earth was amazed and followed after the beast."

Another chill assaulted Gabriel's spine. He remembered a discussion he'd had with Sarah, in which she used her perspective as a religious scholar to discuss the use of gender in scripture. The scribes of the day wrote their passages in the context of the times, times that barely recognized the existence of women in society, especially politics and religion. An entire subculture had recently developed around this issue, the so-called "divine feminine," which had been subverted and hidden in religious texts for two thousand years, effectively erasing it from the pages of history.

John may have been a political prisoner on Patmos, but perhaps he was a *political* animal, as well. The last thing he would have wanted was his writings to be discredited by an unacceptable use of gender, in a manner that would turn the heads and hearts of the very constituency he was trying to reach.

God was without gender, and yet scripture constantly referred to the Creator in the male person. The same might be argued about other divine players on the apocalyptic stage.

It is indisputable that those who wrote the books of the Bible, not to mention those who translated and compiled it two hundred years later, were subject to the political climate of the time.

Perhaps, as Winger had hinted, Gabriel had gotten the gender right, even if John hadn't.

THE FOURTH PIECE of paper was in many ways the most disturbing. It was a business card, with a printed telephone number under the name *Sarah Meyers.* She had given it to him at the deli that day in New York after approaching him in the Cathedral of St. John the Divine. This now seemed both poetic and prophetic.

The card had been in his wallet, which he hadn't seen in seven months. He had no idea how Simon Winger had come into its possession.

He stared long and hard at the phone number. Suddenly he took out some scratch paper, did some calculations. Staring at his math, his heart skipped a beat.

This was a Denver area code, for her mobile line, she'd said, the account for which was still out of Colorado. Which made perfect sense, in a way, since she said she'd worked there before the NSA. But clearly that wasn't the point.

The phone number was well beyond coincidence.

Simon Winger had mentioned a passage of scripture from Exodus, which was referenced in a coded message hidden in the Book of Revelation.

A passage had led him to the idea of cubing the matrix they used to search for further codes, ultimately leading them to the name of the one true Antichrist.

Which he now knew was Charlotte Brenner.

He ran the numbers in his head.

The number of the beast was 666. That number cubed was 295,408,296. The telephone number on Sarah's business card was 295-408-2960.

Staring at the number, numbed with the realization, the card suddenly slipped from his fingers and fluttered to the floor like a liberated leaf. It landed with the printed side down.

Staring at it, Gabriel's heart now froze. Handwritten on the back of the card were several words. Words he'd not noticed when Sarah had handed him the card that day in New York, not noticed when he'd taken it out on several occasions to contemplate calling her.

They sent me back for you.

A chill shot up his spine. As it did on that day thirteen years before when he'd first met Lauren in the cave known as The Grotto of the Revelation.

These were the precise words she'd said to him then, too.

85

THERE WAS THE ritual knocking at his door, followed by the entrance of an entourage of suits led by a man he did not know.

Gabriel was thankful he had flushed the four pieces of paper down the toilet, as Simon had suggested.

The man approached him with his hand extended—this wasn't de rigueur among the other investigators who had visited him over the months—and a smile straight off a campaign trail.

"Mitchell Hayes," he said, "Deputy Director of the Central Intelligence Agency."

Two other agents the size of outbuildings stood by the door, with no intention of introducing themselves.

"You look happy," said Gabriel. "Should *I* be happy, too?"

The man shot a look to his younger associates. "We've broken a lead in your case. An anonymous tip."

Gabriel wanted to respond with something acerbic, but his throat was suddenly tight.

"You're free to go home," the man continued.

Several thoughts battled for supremacy—the absence of a home to go to, a guess as to what they'd found, a lacerating *it's-about-freaking-time* bon mot. Instead he just stared.

"Information has surfaced that substantiates your version of events. I wouldn't quite say you are *exonerated*, but that will get an official stamp soon."

"Simon Winger came forward," Gabriel said, taking a shot.

"Actually, we believe Simon Winger to be deceased."

"Really? I hear there are ways around that. They call it ghosting. A friend of yours told me all about it."

The agent's contrived expression was supposed to convey surprise, which made Gabriel grin.

"We've made some arrangements, in light of your situation."

"Send the bill to my health insurance carrier. Thank God for Obamacare."

Now Mitchell Hayes grinned. "Don't you want to know?"

"Yeah, actually I do."

"We found a copy of the the video you described, the one with Agent Larsen speaking with a known covert operative. An informant recently identified that same individual as the broker in the sale of a small quantity of black market plutonium out of Russia fifteen months ago."

"Let us not forget the one-on-one with the White House chump."

Hayes's smile vanished instantly. "We have no official comment on that."

Of course not.

"Where'd you find the DVD?"

"It was a thumb drive, actually. In Simon Winger's home. His lawyer released a letter stating that in the case of his disappearance, which Winger had apparently anticipated, his assets were to be distributed according to his wishes. One of those wishes was that we conduct a sweep of his home, which turned up the video. It actually had a note on it addressed to the director of the CIA."

Gabriel just nodded. Sarah, he was guessing, had a hand in this.

"You don't look surprised," said Hayes. "I'd think you'd be beside yourself."

"Oh, I am, I'm right here next to me."

"We expect you to continue to cooperate in the investigation, which is far from over. In fact, it's a condition of your release today. First and foremost, you *cannot* speak to the press. You cannot write a book, go on a talk show, or anything remotely close."

Gabriel grinned, this time for their benefit. "Let me guess, you'll want me to take it from the top, one more time."

"Something like that. For now there's a car waiting, and then an airplane. We've set something up for you in Washington, if that's okay."

"Where the hell are we, anyhow?"

"Oregon.

"Go Ducks," he said.

"Rain should have given it away."

He smiled, casting his eyes to the window that had been his only friend for months.

Gabriel Stone was free.

- 86 -

Auburn, California

THERE WAS INDEED a car waiting, and what a car it was—a black H2 Hummer urban assault vehicle, perfect transportation for a guest of the Central Intelligence Agency. A young man *not* wearing a suit was holding the rear door for him, while one of the Agency suits carried a small bag of his belongings, clothes and toiletries that the good taxpaying citizens of the land had purchased for him during his stay.

He thought of the day Simon Winger had shown up at the hospital in California to whisk him to relative safety. And, as before, an older man was waiting for him in the backseat. This guy even had Winger's taste in clothes—country club pro shop all the way.

The man shook his hand without offering a name.

"You look well for someone with a broken back."

"Thanks. Appreciate the ride. Who are you?" Suddenly it was easy to go straight at moments like this.

"My name is Franklin Moss."

A familiar sensation assaulted Gabriel's nervous system. He knew the name well, if nothing else than from the research he had done prior to the world caving in around them. This was the man who had run The Brethren for the last thirty years, friend of presidents and dictators, humble servant of Jesus Christ.

"I am aware of your work," Gabriel said.

The man regarded him with fatherly wisdom. "And I of yours, as well."

"I was expecting a federal escort. Someone in a bad suit."

"We've been known to work closely with the federal government from time to time. But we prefer our own tailors."

Gabriel drew a deep breath as the Hummer pulled away. He turned to see where he'd been living for the months since his transfer from the hospital, a massive Tudor estate that could have housed that pro shop where Moss did his shopping.

"Why are you here?" Gabriel asked, watching the structure recede into the distance.

"Simply to offer assistance. You need a place to stay, you need resources to help you rebuild your life. And to represent your legal interests, which are significant."

"Mind if I ask why?"

Moss nodded slightly, as if the question had more layers to it than Gabriel could possibly comprehend.

"Because we can, and because we should. And because we're aware of what you have done with your life. Brother Simon left a sizable bequest in your name, with no strings. But we're hoping you see fit to continue our association."

For the moment Gabriel had no response. He was conscious of his facial expression, as stoic as he could muster. But inside he was fielding emotions at a rapid pace. He could feel Moss's eyes on him, an uncomfortable dynamic.

"We seek to associate with men who have experienced life as you have. You have seen the face of God, if you will allow me, and lived to tell the tale. There is no hiding from the truth once one has traveled that road."

"My guess is you have enough friends."

Moss smiled, perhaps running his own inner dialogue.

"We're not looking for friends, Mr. Stone," he said. "We're looking for soldiers. Warriors for God, men of courage and vision. Men who *know*."

"You're asking me to join The Brethren?"

"That's just a name. There is nothing to 'join,' as you put it. There is simply work to be done, important work. You come highly recommended, sir. And in case you're still in doubt, you need to know we had nothing at all to do with Simon Winger's agenda, specifically the bombing at the Columbia Center. No foreknowledge, no complicity, not even moral support. I hope you believe me. We are men of honor, synonymous with men of God."

Gabriel tried not to show the emotion he was experiencing.

"I would thank Simon for the referral. If he was alive, of course."

Moss smiled again. He knew the truth, perhaps even more clearly than did Gabriel.

"Oh, it's not Brother Simon that you should thank. In fact, you owe no one your gratitude. You've earned this. We want to give you every chance to expose yourself to our work so that you might see fit to become one of us."

Gabriel rode in silence, his eyes straight ahead.

"You've been chosen. From the moment you sat down to write that book, you have been watched. Since then you've been severely tested, and with the courage of your response you've shown God the man you are. You don't think any of this happened to you by chance, do you? That *anything* in this life is chance?"

Gabriel opened his mouth to answer, but realized he didn't know how to respond. There was a time, not so long ago, when the tests and the seeming coincidence of his life were accepted as simple fortune, good and bad. Life sucks, then you die. But if he'd learned anything from his little wrestling match with the dark side, it was that the tests keep coming, the challenges repeat themselves until you *get* it.

After that, there were new choices to make. One of which was just proposed by the man sitting next to him.

"I'm tired," he said. "Let me sleep on it, if that's okay."

He feigned sleep for the remainder of the ride. He had nothing else to say, and he was done asking questions.

GABRIEL FELT A hand on his knee. He opened his eyes to see that they had arrived at a rural airport, not unlike the one he'd departed in California as he left Sarah to go meet Simon Winger. It was night, the air crisp and clean under a partly cloudy sky. A sleek private jet waited beyond a short fence, hatch open, engines already running.

The driver had gone around to open his door. Moss was outside, waiting for Gabriel to get out of the vehicle and join them on the tarmac.

"That's our plane," said Franklin Moss, his smile huge and knowing.

Gabriel grabbed the bag. In his pocket was two hundred dollars, the precise amount he'd had in his wallet on the night of the bombing, before he gave it to the bellman with no memory.

He got out, stretched his arms, inhaled the crisp air. It was good to be back in the real world.

Then he extended a hand toward Franklin Moss.

"Thanks for everything," he said. Moss shook the hand, obviously confused. "Good luck with your war."

Then Gabriel turned and started walking toward the small airport office a hundred yards behind them. The lights were on, which meant there was a phone. And coffee. He had a sudden desire for coffee. A taxi was a phone call away, and from there he had any number of choices, all of them good.

"Where are you going?" Moss yelled after him.

"California," he said. "I'm going home."

"The Lord has called your name, Gabriel. You can't hide from that. He *needs* you. He needs *us*."

Gabriel smiled. "No, *you* called my name. Besides, something tells me everything is going just the way God planned. He'll be fine. And so will you and I."

Moss was obviously not a man accustomed to rejection.

"What will you do?"

Now Gabriel laughed. It was raining slightly, and he turned his face toward the sky to greet it.

"I'm going to fall in love again. Maybe raise a kid, play catch in the yard. And I was thinking about writing a book. Under a pseudonym, of course."

Suddenly he turned back to face the man, backpedaling as he continued toward the office. Moss was standing next to the big Hummer, his hand on the open door, his expression dumbfounded.

"Matter of fact," said Gabriel, "I have a killer story. About a bunch of rich guys trying to save the world. But they can't because they're too late, it's out of their hands. It always was. Needs work, I know, but that's my hook. Like it?"

Moss shook his head and slammed the Hummer's door, then walked toward the airplane that would take him back to Jesus.

"God bless you, sir!" yelled Gabriel, but he received no response.

Gabriel turned and strolled toward the office. He was suddenly filled with an unexpected lightness, in defiance of all that he knew lay ahead. The age of darkness was at hand. Charlotte Brenner would be elected, and the long-prophesied apocalyptic fuse would ignite.

But he was alive, and even in the dark days to come it was a gift to savor.

No one knew how many sunsets remained. He would do what he could, if and when his name was called, if nothing else to honor those who had died in the wake of what he had written. Especially his lawyer, who was guilty of nothing other than friendship. And for Sarah, whoever—and whatever—she really was.

And, of course, for Lauren. He had a feeling she was watching.

Gabriel didn't need to get on that airplane with Franklin Moss to find God. He didn't need a war to find purpose, or a membership card to discover truth.

Jesus was already here, waiting by that office door, a cup of hot coffee in his hands and a gentle smile of understanding on his face.

Epilogue

WE ARE WATCHING YOU.

As it has been since your innocence was eternally withdrawn, we are at your side.

We are not flesh, though when summoned we may assume your transient form, and it is then we are reminded of your blessings, the gifts of sensation and perception. Our substance transcends thought, though more often than you know your inner voice is the quiet echo of our prayers. Nor are we simply the stuff of dreams, though in dreams we show you truth in mirrors of what you already know.

We are essence, born of physics beyond your comprehension, purer and swifter than light in the vacuum of space.

We move among you. We are the soft edge of shadow at the periphery of sight, though as you turn we are already gone. On occasion you hear our footfalls, masked within the rattling of your own disbelief. When you sense in your heart that you are not alone, rest assured you are not. Know that the occasional random notion or unprompted memory is neither random nor unprompted. We are the architects of what you assign to coincidence. You will come to understand there is no such thing.

We witness the consequence of your desire, and sometimes we must weep. We know your suffering and exalt your joys as if they are our own, as indeed they are. We know your destiny but not your fate—one was written in sand at the dawn of time, the other is yours to etch onto the tablet of your own will. The two embrace, and the dance is life itself.

We are bit players in the drama of your days.

Know this, and take caution: others dwell in shadow, denied the Light. They know your yearning, and would use it to mark your soul. And thus the battle is waged.

You call us angels or ghosts or other names which are neither right nor wrong, yet despite this veiled awareness your scholars write us off as lore or imagination. But like much of what has been written, they are misled. We are real, as tangible as the unseen air that sustains you.

We are witness and scribe to all that you do. We are with you always.

And upon occasion, we are obliged to intervene.

CPSIA information can be obtained at www.ICGtesting.com
Printed in the USA
BVOW04s1656031214

377752BV00002B/2/P